Riddle 11.

D0513661

# JADE GATE

Dr Robert Gunn, the physician turned merchant in the Far East, has a rare gift for instantly recognizing an opportunity, however obscure it may seem, and then moulding it to his own advantage. . . . It is the mid-19th century, and such an opportunity presents itself when warships and merchant vessels of all nations are about to go over to steam propulsion after centuries of sail. But steam engines need fuel, and for vessels operating in Eastern seas this means sending out coal from Britain or India at great expense, plus the ever-present risk of fire at sea. Thus the man who can discover coal in the East can also command the whole area—commercially and strategically—for himself and for his country. . . . Dr Gunn is determined to be that man. He believes that Jade Gate Island, off Borneo, contains coal deposits. Others also share that belief and seek the wealth and power that this discovery will bring. But in that age and hemisphere human life is held cheap, and these ambitions inevitably bring danger of death.

# JADE GATE

*

## JAMES LEASOR

THE
COMPANION BOOK CLUB
LONDON AND SYDNEY

## THE COMPANION BOOK CLUB

The Club is not a library; all books are the
property of members. There is no entrance
fee or any payment beyond the low Club
price of each book. Details of membership
will gladly be sent on request.

Write to:
The Companion Book Club,
Odhams Books, Rushden, Northants.

Or, in Australia, write to:
The Companion Book Club,
C/- Hamlyn House Books, P.O. Box 252,
Dee Why, N.S.W. 2099

*Made and printed in Great Britain
for the Companion Book Club
by Chapel River Press, Andover, Hants*
600872254
3.78/325

# CHAPTER ONE

## *In which a proposition is accepted*

THE WANING AFTERNOON SUN stretched long, inquisitive fingers through the faded green shutters and caressed the sleeping figures on the bed.

The American moved first, putting up one hand instinctively to shield his face. And then, as the movement drove sleep away, he opened his eyes and lay for a moment, thinking. He had gone to bed with the English woman after lunch; and the time must now be nearly five. He knew this because he could hear the cries of sweetmeat sellers outside, and then a series of sharp cracks and explosions and the beating of many gongs. A Chinese funeral was passing the house, and they never took place in the early afternoon.

He raised himself on one elbow, half intending to get up and look out of the window, and then he saw, as though for the first time, the woman by his side, still asleep, with that curiously innocent expression on her face that graces all sleeping women; even when they are as devious and cunning as Patricia Bankhausen.

She opened her eyes under his gaze, smiled, and ran long, expert fingers through the matted black hair on his chest.

'There is something I wanted to tell you, Hiram,' she said slowly, as though she had been pondering it even while asleep. 'A proposition I would like to make to you.'

'I am at your service, ma'am,' the American replied, wondering what this might be. He was strong and young, and while this woman was demanding, he would be the master still.

'My time is completely my own. At least, for the next few weeks.'

'How few young men can say as much! And you have another advantage over your contemporaries. Your profession of a newspaper correspondent enables you to gather information and to ask questions which from others would appear insolent or even personal. Also, you can readily introduce yourself to people whose lives might not otherwise cross your own. Am I correct in these assumptions?'

'Perfectly correct, ma'am.'

Hiram C. Jerome looked at her in silence, wondering how old she really was, who she really was. She had been married, he knew, but that was all; her husband no longer lived with her. Her breasts and her body were firm, but already the years had etched faint lines of discontent, narrow as single strands of stretched hair, about her mouth. Soon, they would deepen. She was beautiful but she was hard, and deep down inside him, despite his youth and self-assurance, he feared her. And this was a rare feeling for a travelling correspondent for the *New York News*, who had landed here in Singapore only a month before, from the clipper *Samuel Russell*, one of the fastest vessels in the fleet of the Low Brothers

6

who ran regular services from Salem and New York to Canton and Macao.

Jerome had been unexpectedly offered a passage at a discounted price to enable him to gather material for a series of articles on American influence in the East. The Lows were strong patriots, and very much aware of the enormous potentialities for American trade in Malaya and China. But many American bankers and merchants were too occupied with problems of their own country—opening up the Far West, building railroads, taming a vast continent—to have time or inclination to concern themselves with Eastern opportunities. It was altogether different for small countries like England and Portugal and Holland; they were intent on opening up the East for their own benefit, because they had exhausted possibilities for expansion within their own frontiers, because they needed new markets for wares from their manufactories.

Indeed, in that May of 1843, Hiram Jerome had met only one American in Singapore, a missionary from an obscure monastic order, going home to die, his frame racked with fever, deep-set, disillusioned eyes burning like live coals in his head.

"I have followed the path of Our Lord, labouring in the vineyard as He advised us to do,' the old man explained sadly. 'But as the good book truly says, while the harvest is plentiful, the labourers are few. My son, this corner of the world is sunk in degradation, poisoned by the greed of white men, nominally Christians, who should set an example to their less fortunate coloured and heathen brethren.

'Were I to tell you of the huge fortunes made here

7

within years or even months, of murders deliberately committed in the name of trade or national honour, you would not believe the half of it, and neither would your readers.'

'Are there no Americans working here honourably in business or other honest enterprises, about whose experiences our countrymen would wish to be informed, so that they might feel proud of their enterprise and achievement? Have we no vessels in the area bringing trade and prosperity, apart from those of the Low family?'

'We have indeed, but nothing when compared to the efforts of the European countries. The East is but an extension of European influence, but without the restraint of European law. I give you my blessing, my son, for I can give you no more.'

And the old man had gone on his way wearily, leaving Jerome musing on what he had said. If so much wealth could be made so quickly, might he not be able to involve himself personally with some trading endeavour, instead of simply seeking to describe in print the success of others who had done so? Why live by proxy when he might enjoy wealth at first hand?

The woman spoke again in her quiet English voice. It conjured up for him a vision of taking tea on a manicured English lawn, perhaps under a white silk parasol to shield her fair skin from the afternoon sun, while a housemaid wearing black bombasine, with white apron and cap, waited discreetly beneath the shadowy elms. He had seen lawns like that when he had visited England before coming East; the sense of peace and grace and effortless superiority had impressed him more

8

than anything else he had encountered so far on his travels. That atmosphere could only be bought by money; not the little a man might earn by the work of his hands, but the fortune some could make by harnessing their dreams. All the difference in the world lay between money earned and money made.

'Let me tell you my proposition,' the woman said, still stroking his chest gently. 'There is an Englishman in Singapore, who is already one of the three most powerful Europeans in the East. His name is Robert Gunn. He is only a few years older than you, but of the same build, and, shall I say, thrusting temperament.'

Jerome allowed himself a small smile.

'May I ask if he has thrust at you, ma'am?'

'That is a personal matter,' replied Patricia Bankhausen coldly.

'Forgive me, ma'am. It is but a Yankee jest.'

'We may speak the same tongue,' Patricia allowed, 'but sometimes you are, shall I say, a little cruder than one would wish in more temperate climes?'

'We are what we are, and who we are, ma'am, because God has made us that way. Pray proceed.'

'This man Gunn,' she went on,' is a doctor of medicine. He sailed east to Canton in a British second-class Indiaman about nine years ago. He went ashore and was almost immediately kidnapped from a chop house by emissaries of a rich Parsee. Under threat of death, Gunn was ordered to get the Parsee's daughter with child. I would point out to you that among some Parsees it is a matter of honour to maintain their family's fair skin. They do not favour a dark complexion. Gunn was offered a large sum for his task.'

9

'Many men would wish that others might make such offers,' interrupted Jerome, smiling. 'They are content, nay honoured, to give these services without thought of financial reward.'

What an incredible tale! Did she really imagine he would believe it? Then he remembered the sad face of the American priest, and his despair at the wickedness of the East. Patricia Bankhausen could be speaking the truth after all. And if he listened, he might learn something he could put to his own use.

'Listen, you young ignoramus,' she retorted sharply. 'You laugh at things you do not understand, because they have not happened to you. Because, as a scribbler, you live at second-hand, content to chronicle the deeds of other men.

'The Parsee had no intention of paying Gunn the fee he promised of 3,000 guineas. Instead, he gave him a cheque on his bank and then marooned Gunn on the Chinese mainland, believing that the Chinese, hating and fearing all Red-Bristled Barbarians from the West, would speedily murder him as an uninvited and alien intruder. The Parsee would thus keep his secret—and his money.

'Gunn, however, eluded his Chinese pursuers and fled inland, and met a renegade Scot, one MacPherson, the only survivor of a British ship that had been seized by pirates, some time earlier. The Chinese had tolerated MacPherson among them because he spoke their dialects well and could translate honestly the prices quoted by European opium traders for their products—what we out here call, mud.'

'It is golden mud, ma'am, if what you say is true.'

'It is gold indeed. Men who entered what they dignify by the name of the Coast Trade with barely a shirt to their backs, have in a few years made millions of pounds sterling out of its trade, and bought estates in England and seats in Parliament.'

'Is Gunn one of these?'

'He is among the most successful of these traffickers, perhaps the richest pedlar of dreams in the East.'

'But how did he achieve this desirable state of affairs?'

'By panache and courage and the gift for intuitively realizing which out of several options would be the most profitable for him to take. But you interrupt my story. With MacPherson's help, Gunn seized one of the Parsee's own vessels when she called along the coast, sailed her back to Macao and turned her guns on the Parsee's house and so, literally under threat of bombardment, forced him to make over a trading company to him.*

'Bully for him, ma'am. Gunn sounds a real man.'

'He is. And I hate him more than anyone else in the world,' said Patricia bitterly. 'He has built up this modest company he seized into the vast trading empire known as Mandarin-Gold. Its name is symptomatic of Gunn's whole attitude. He chose it because a mandarin in the East means a ruler, and gold is what all men seek here, even above the heavenly riches of eternal life.'

'I can see what he means, ma'am. But how can I align myself with him—or against him, if that is your wish?'

'I will tell you, but first allow me to explain my own interest in Robert Gunn. I knew him in London. Indeed, he is disposed to give me a small pension—as well he might. My husband, Sir Richard Bankhausen, from

* For details of this adventure, see *Mandarin-Gold*.

11

whom I am now separated, is a distinguished physician there. Gunn sought his advice about a rare and mortal disease of the blood, from which he believed—quite erroneously—he was suffering.

'Gunn overstepped himself, we became lovers, and my husband—a much older man and consequently jealous—was informed of our relationship. He drove me from his house.

'Gunn had already left London to return to the East to die. I followed him to explain what had happened to me as a result of his attentions. I had obtained a letter he had written and copied his signature on to a document I instructed a lawyer to prepare. This document made over the majority shareholding of his company to me, should he die.

'But Gunn did not die. He was introduced to Chinese physicians and their ancient treatment of acupuncture, which, absurdly to our Western ideas, involves sticking fine gold needles into his body. Would that they had been nails, for then, instead of a pittance, I might have inherited a fortune from him! And so he recovered and now enjoys splendid health—while I enjoy his tiny pension.

'I forged his name, Hiram, and he discovered what I had done—and how nearly I had succeeded in my plan. And instead of hounding me or putting me on trial, he awarded me this pension. No doubt he felt guilty at having put me in the position of needing money so desperately. He had me at his mercy—and he was merciful to me. And I hate him for that.'

She paused. Jerome said nothing. He was sufficiently experienced an interviewer never to interrupt a speaker when he guessed they still had more to say. That way, they invariably revealed more than they had initially intended.

He had first met Patricia Bankhausen at a dinner party given by a Scottish jute merchant, and they had speedily formed a liaison, for she was pleasant and amusing and both were alone. But was that all? Could it be that she had also been testing him for this task?

'I want you to meet Dr Gunn, to become his friend, to discover his weaknesses, and then we can move against him—both of us. And just as he, in the beginning, seized a trading company from another, so we can seize a part of Mandarin-Gold for ourselves. Then, Hiram, you would not have to wait upon the instructions and preferences of an editor 10,000 miles away. You would not be like a boy in the schoolroom, still writing essays for a master to approve. You could buy the newspaper. You could be your own editor. You could live anywhere in the world, where you pleased, how you pleased.'

She paused, and ran a fingernail gently down his back, scoring the flesh.

'With whom you pleased. Tell me, have you any dependants? Any family?'

'None, ma'am. I am an orphan. I grew up outside New York. I was good at the English language in high school, for I liked words and their sound. I also wished to travel. I was fortunate in being able to find employment with a printer, who later founded a local newspaper. This prospered, and so he acquired another, and then a third. When he bought the majority shareholding in the *New York News* very cheaply, because it was in the receiver's hands, he asked me to travel abroad in

13

search of news. I enjoy the life and my hours are my own.'

'That is a fair answer for a young man,' agreed Patricia, 'but when you grow older, would you still wish to be sent at another man's whim, to be dependent on his opinion—or even his successor's opinion? Is not such a person like a horse in a livery stable, to be ridden by any who can pay its owner's price?'

'Perhaps that is why old writers are often called hacks, because they do what is asked of them?'

'I am offering you an opportunity to escape from that prospect. Will you accept my offer?'

'I will certainly accept an invitation to meet Dr Gunn.'

'You will receive no such invitation. Dr Gunn is not much given to social intercourse; he is too concerned with his business. He maintains a huge house here, in addition to offices and godowns. All those ships in the harbour flying the red and gold flag marked "M.G." belong to him. He maintains even larger premises on Hong Kong Island, and I am told, one of the greatest houses in all the East in Macao. I hear that he is presently planning to expand his interests to India, and even along the east coast of Africa. If you take my offer, you must act swiftly, for soon his company will be too large to infiltrate with ease. Others will be involved, whereas now only Gunn and the drunken Scot, Mac-Pherson, are the principals.

'There have been attempts in the past—I have told you how I tried myself—to gain a share of his wealth, but he outwitted us all. Possibly this was because the attempts were made by his own countrymen. He knows how we think and react. But he does not know Americans. Few of us do. Agreed, we speak the same language, and so we assume you are the same as we are. But this is not so. Your outlook as an American is different from ours. So are your ways.'

'Even our ways of making love, ma'am?'

'That is another subject,' admitted Patricia, smiling. 'Why do you keep returning to it?'

'Because you are lying so close to me,' said Hiram hoarsely. 'Because you make it as impossible to keep my mind from such thoughts as it is to keep my body from yours.'

He rolled against her, reaching out for her breasts.

'Wait,' she said, stiffening. 'Will you do this for me, on the understanding that if you are successful, we shall share what we make?'

'I appreciate your kindness, but I cannot see how I can succeed, ma'am. I am not a man of business.'

'Now is the chance to become one. You like money, do you not?'

'I have never possessed a great deal of money. But I like what it can buy, I must admit.'

'You have not yet tasted its fruits, Hiram. You have only sipped their juice. I am offering you a fortune. And myself.'

'I accept both your offers,' said Hiram, and moved against her, into her.

\*　　　\*　　　\*

Robert Gunn sat in a cane chair beneath the freshly scrubbed awning on the afterdeck of *Hesperides*, the ship he had seized from the Parsee years before, and which was now the flagship of his fleet. He lifted his glass and focused it on the shore. The new white buildings along the dockside blazed like chalk cliffs in the sun behind a forest of varnished masts. On Flagstaff Hill the Union Jack stood square in the wind, and over to the east, near the barracks of British and Indian troops, huge defence mortars pointed black gaping mouths insolently out to sea.

Gulls and kitehawks dived and swooped around the vessels. Over the side, Gunn could see the reflection of *Hesperides*'s black hull and the intricate chequerboard pattern beneath the deck. All brightwork glistered; ropes were pipeclayed, wooden tackle polished, copper rivet-heads burnished like newly minted coins.

Captain Fernandes, the Goanese skipper of *Hesperides*, approached him.

'Will you be staying in Singapore long, sir?' he inquired.

'Possibly for a week. Why do you ask?'

'I understand that a gentleman from Scotland, from the ship-building company of Campbells in Glasgow, urgently seeks a meeting with you.'

'Have you any idea what he wishes to discuss?'

Fernandes took a visiting card from his jacket pocket and read: 'Mr Emmanuel Bridges, Engineer.'

'We have no engines, save in our mills,' said Gunn. 'What could be so important to Mr Bridges that he sails all the way from Glasgow to Singapore to discuss it with me? Could he not have sent a letter?'

'Possibly,' agreed Fernandes, 'but I think he has come in his own steam vessel.'

'Then he must be a very successful engineer?'

'I think he is a sound man, sir. My information is

that he is travelling throughout the East in this vessel, *Thor*, demonstrating its virtues to merchants in the hope that they will order similar craft for themselves and their companies, or at least cause their existing ships to be adapted to accept his steam engines. His vessel has come all the way from England in 87 days under steam. *Thor* is equipped with sails, of course, but I have the captain's word, which I fully accept, that not once has any sail been unfurled.'

'That is an impressive voyage to make in the time,' said Gunn slowly. His own clippers, even when carrying such an enormous spread of sail that they ran the risk of capsizing in their quest for speed, took five days longer to cover the same distance. Speed in his business was another word for profit, for the first ships to reach English ports carrying the first of the season's tea from the East, commanded the highest price for their cargoes. He had therefore bought and built ships based on the designs of American privateers, which enabled him to overhaul the slower vessels of other more conservative companies.

This meant that Gunn could buy the second crop of tea, always cheaper than the first, and then, by cramming on all sail and paying huge bonuses to captains and crews to risk their lives, would still beat his rivals into British ports, and so make double their profit.

With swifter steam-powered vessels, independent of winds, he might be able to buy the third tea crop, which would be cheaper than the second, and still overhaul the sailing clippers of his rivals. But surely these steamships were expensive and complex to run—and what about their fuel?

17

'Do they have to carry coal?'

'Of course. Just as the new steam railway locomotives in England draw tenders full of coal.'

'But to cover any distance at sea against wind or tide, steamships must surely carry an enormous tonnage of coal, with a consequent reduction in their cargo space?'

'I am not a technical man, doctor,' said Fernandes. 'I am a man of sail, and I would like to remain such until I am convinced there is a better method of propulsion than the free winds of heaven.'

'This may be that better method. When I was studying at St Andrews University to gain my medical degree, I would work every night by candle or oil lamp. But when I was in England on my last visit, many of the houses were lit by gas, unheard of only a few years ago.'

'So I have heard,' agreed Fernandes. 'And that must be a great convenience. No bowls to refill with oil, just turn on a tap in a pipe of gas and strike a match.'

'And I have also heard it said that this scientist, Michael Faraday, is conducting further experiments with electricity, and has announced plans for lighting houses and maybe even cities, by current from a spinning dynamo. So then you would only need to press a switch and the room would be bathed in light.'

'I will believe that when I see it,' said Fernandes drily. 'In the meantime, I think you should see this engineer.'

'Have you met him?'

'Aye. Once. With his captain, when they were here last.'

'Why did he not seek an interview with me then?' asked Gunn.

'Because he was engaged with Dr Jardine and Mr Matheson.'

'Was he now,' said Gunn softly. 'Then we shall certainly have to see him, and speedily.'

Jardine, Matheson & Company were the premier British trading company in the East. Like Gunn, Jardine was a doctor who had forsaken medicine to become a merchant. With Matheson, the son of a Scottish landowner, he had built up an extremely successful company from similar small beginnings of running opium along the Chinese coast. Other European trading companies in Macao and Hong Kong were also rivals to Mandarin-Gold, but none were so important as Jardine, Matheson. If they went over to steam, Gunn would be forced to follow or risk being squeezed out of business altogether.

'How do I get in touch with this gentleman?'

'He will present himself to you, sir. As a matter of fact, he has asked if you would join him for dinner aboard his vessel tomorrow evening.'

'I will not join him there, captain, for I feel more at home with my own decks beneath my feet. Pray be so good as to ask if he will be my guest here aboard *Hesperides* at the same hour.'

Gunn preferred to meet strangers in his own ships, in his own houses, at his own offices, for, as a man who lived alone, he was constantly reassured by the sight and sound of familiar things. This was, he admitted, an animal feeling. But then trading in the East was treading a far more terrible jungle than ever any wild animal knew.

\*　　　\*　　　\*

Patricia Bankhausen turned against Hiram Jerome's bare body in the heat of the evening. His chest shone with sweat after his exertions.

'I hate to see you go,' she said drowsily, 'but you must leave now. Gunn's ship lies at anchor, and I am told he is entertaining a guest—some engineer from Scotland. They will undoubtedly eat on deck in this weather. If you take a doolie to the quay you will be able to see what sort of man Gunn is, and that creature, Mac-Pherson.'

'I will come back tonight to see you.'

'I will wait for you,' said Patricia. 'But go now. For me.'

She kissed him, and watched his tall body as he dressed.

Jerome tiptoed out of the room.

\*       \*       \*

Emmanuel Bridges stood stripped to the waist in his sea-cabin, legs braced against the slight dip and roll of the anchored vessel, *S.S. Thor*. He was shaving and hummed a song from the *Barber of Seville* which he had seen when he was last in London, six months ago. He was a stocky man, black-moustached, slightly bald on top, with long, greying sideburns. A few more weeks in this heat, he told himself, grimacing distastefully as he knocked the shaving brush handle on his chin, and he would be able to return to his little terraced house overlooking the Clyde, to his plump wife and their two small children. More, he would surely return to promotion, for he had secured five firm orders for new steam vessels, and one commission to convert two Jardine, Matheson sailing clippers to paddles, when they were next in British ports.

This would keep the shipyard busy for at least a year, and more important, whenever they sailed, these steam vessels would be an abiding advertisement for Scottish workmanship and Scottish enterprise. It was good at forty to know that so many people depended on your skills, on your persuasiveness; and they did not look to Emmanuel Bridges in vain. He wiped lather and greying dots of hair from the edge of the razor with his face towel, and folded the blade carefully in its ebony case. Then he ducked his head in the cold water of the basin and towelled his hair vigorously.

He relished the thought of meeting Gunn, and he wanted to be as fresh as he could, for Gunn by all accounts was a hard man. That was the challenge. An easy sale lacked the savour of turning a potential customer's prejudice to Bridges' advantage. I might have been a missionary, he thought, and, in a sense, I am. I convert people not to a new religion, but to my own way of thinking. The power of steam in place of the power of the Lord, as exemplified in the proud free winds of heaven.

A steward knocked gently on his door.

'The doolie is waiting, sir.'

'Aye. Thank you, Jock,' he said. 'Would you be so good as to ask the captain to come to my cabin?'

Captain Kennedy was a tall thin man with a red beard and watery blue eyes, and a habit of nervously wiping his lips with the back of his hand, as though fearful he had left crumbs on them.

'You wish to see me, Mr Bridges?'

'I do indeed. I have an interview tonight with Dr Gunn, who runs Mandarin-Gold. I have a feeling we may make a sale of at least one vessel to him—if only because Jardine, Matheson are going over to steam, and Gunn cannot afford to be left behind. I want to put on the most convincing demonstration against all opposition tomorrow, or whenever I can persuade him to see it. What would you suggest?'

'The glass is set fair,' replied the captain. 'I would propose we take Dr Gunn and any of his officers out to sea for 10 miles in *Thor*, put the ship about, turn her hard to port and starboard, full steam astern, a short burst ahead with full pressure on the boiler, and then answer all questions he and his colleagues may put to us.'

'Not dramatic enough,' said Bridges, pushing studs into the front of his shirt. 'I want something that will prove beyond all doubt that steam is the answer to every merchant ship. And not only steam, but steam in *our* boilers, pushing *our* pistons, powering *our* paddles, turning *our* screw propellers.

'Why not throw a couple of lines to one of Gunn's own ships, bid him cram on all sail, even give him a start into the wind, towing us, and then you open your steam cocks and we pull *him* astern?'

'We would only do that, sir, if the winds were not too strong.'

'Well, damn it, you say it's set fair. You cannot have it better than that, can you?'

'I would not wish to mount a demonstration in which Gunn's vessel pulled us.'

Bridges grunted. He hated reasons for not doing something on which he had set his heart; and he had heard so much about Gunn's character that he was certain he must convince him in a spectacular way.

'What's the maximum pressure you can take in the boilers?'

'You're the engineer, Mr Bridges. You helped to design them. We've had them up to 180 pounds to every square inch.'

'They'll take 200,' said Bridges shortly. 'With that, we can pull a bloody house down.'

'We could also burst them. That will be your responsibility, sir.'

'I will take it,' said Bridges confidently. 'But have your engineers check over the engines thoroughly and order the stokers to sift the coal so only the best sea-coal goes into the furnaces. None of that rubbish these Chinese swine have tried to shift on us. Have the men work on it tonight.'

'They were going ashore tonight, sir.'

'Well, stop them going ashore. If any have left the vessel, send a runner after them to bring them back. They will be found easily enough in a whorehouse or in the eating house that a former crew member of *Hesperides*, a Welshman, Huw Jenkins, has opened. Tell them how important it is for us to make a successful demonstration.'

'They have been promised this leave ashore for days, sir.'

'Promise it to them after the demonstration. Say we shall double their leave if we make a sale.'

'Very good, sir.'

The captain withdrew. Bridges put on his tail coat, polished the glossy side of his top hat with his sleeve, and went up on deck. Humidity hung strong as a steam bath; his shirt was already sticking to his body, and his hair felt damp as though he had stepped from under a shower when he climbed into the doolie. He removed his hat and moped his brow and listened to the jingling bells on the coolies' backs as they jog-trotted along the quay towards *Hesperides*.

Gunn greeted Bridges as he came aboard. He was wearing light check trousers, a deep blue dinner jacket, a silk shirt with a maroon bow.

'I thought, Mr Bridges, that we would dine on deck as it is rather cooler than in my day cabin?'

'I am delighted, sir,' said Bridges, glancing about him appreciatively. 'What a magnificent vessel this is.'

'You are right, sir,' agreed Gunn, pleased by his obvious admiration. 'She is a tribute to British design and craftsmanship.'

'Where was she built, sir? The Clyde?'

'No. In Dartmouth.'

'I dare say we could not have done better on the Clyde.'

'I take it then from your accent and your pride in your native land, that you are Scottish?'

'You take it correctly, sir.'

'Then I must tell you that you are among your own people, Mr Bridges. My mother was Scottish, and so is my colleague here, Mr MacPherson.'

'It is a long time since I saw the banks and braes,' MacPherson admitted, standing up, holding half a glass of neat Glen Grant in his hand. 'Which increases my pleasure in meeting one who has but lately come from them.'

MacPherson was a strong, thick-set man with a red beard and long red hair. Fine blue veins criss-crossed his nose and his cheeks, live rivers on a schoolboy's coloured atlas. It was true what Bridges had heard about him. Obviously, MacPherson did drink heavily, but his eyes were still clear and light blue. He was no fool, Bridges thought; not a man to be easily dismissed. I must get him on my side; Bridges bowed deeply and shook hands.

'Will you take a Geneva drink?' asked Gunn. 'I have some De Kuypers with fresh lime juice.'

'A pleasure,' said Bridges. 'Our vessel is rather more abstemious.'

'Sailing ships give a man a thirst,' remarked Mac-Pherson philosophically, pouring out five fingers of whisky.

'So does steam, gentlemen. If you could see our stokers stripped to the waist, shovelling coal into the roaring furnace like demons, you would admire their strength and their stamina. But no steamship captain could allow them to imbibe alcohol in the heat of the boiler room.'

'A noble and inspiring sight they make, no doubt,' agreed Gunn. 'But to my mind it takes a lot to beat men going up aloft to furl the top gallants, when you are running before a Force 10.'

'As a spectacle, I agree, sir, but as a matter of commercial wisdom, let me ask one question. What happens should your Force 10 blow *against* you? I know you can tack into the wind, but with steam propulsion the captain does not greatly care whether the sea is rough or smooth, whether a storm is blowing in his ship's direction or against her.'

'But what about the complications of all that mechanism?' asked Gunn. 'How can one train sailors who have spent their lives in sail to deal with the tantrums of an iron engine?'

'The Royal Navy has been using steam engines for the last 20 years. A number of sailors with long experience in steam are therefore now time-expired, and ready to demonstrate their skills in merchant vessels. Others can be readily bought out of service, and we at Campbells operate a scheme for teaching the ways of steam to those who have lived with sail. We find they learn very quickly.'

'You are a convincing advocate,' said Gunn, 'but like Doubting Thomas in the Bible, I must be convinced by the evidence of my own eyes. Boilers can burst, can they not? And vessels can run out of coal, or even fresh water for their boilers. Engines can also break down from a dozen different reasons—from a loose nut to a leaking steam-pipe. But with sails, so long as your ship has a stout mast and canvas and spars and a hull able to bear them, you can follow your course.'

Bridges nodded gravely, saying nothing. He sipped his drink.

There was no point in arguing too soon; he would let a demonstration prove his point. To see was to believe, and to believe was to be converted.

They sat down to dinner. A steward in a starched white monkey-jacket, wearing white gloves, set dishes of paw-paw in front of them on bowls of crushed ice. Another steward poured claret into their glasses and then placed a full carafe by each place. Outside the huge brass-rimmed portholes, the sky dimmed to indigo.

Lights flared along the docks; the wind carried music from the bazaar, strange, haunting, and melancholy.

On the quayside, strollers on foot and Europeans in fancily painted carriages paused to admire the great vessel ablaze with oil lamps as though for a fleet display. What a magnificent sight she made! What better symbol of success and British power and prestige than this graceful vessel, able to carry her owner to England faster than a mail clipper!

One of these watchers was the American, Hiram Jerome. He stood in the shadows, his back pressed against the high whitewashed wall of one of Gunn's godowns, where no one was likely to see him. The wall had soaked up the sun's heat throughout the day, and its rough surface felt warm as oven bricks through the thin stuff of his shirt.

He took an opera glass from his pocket and turned it on to Gunn's face.

The man has the face of power, he thought admiringly. Possibly he is morose and sometimes even taciturn. A different kind of face to this newcomer, the engineer, who sat nodding almost obsequiously, turning his hands out, palms upwards, to prove an argument, then busily wiping his mouth with a starched napkin, and eating again. He was clearly dedicated to his theme, presumably trying to persuade Gunn to buy an engine.

The third man must be MacPherson, from his description. He sat well back in his wicker chair, and drank one glass of wine after another, and finally, when the carafe was empty, he beat crudely on the side of his wine glass with a spoon until the wine steward materialized with a replacement. His was also an interesting face, flushed now with alcohol and food, but still bearing lines of courage and character. But Jerome kept turning his glass back to Gunn, the man he must meet and then know, and in knowing, discover some weakness in his character, his outlook, his armour.

Every man had such a flaw, for perfection was not a human quality. He must find it and then use the power of his discovery as the termites he had watched in his room use tenacity to eat a hole in a bamboo screen. This knowledge would make him rich. He might never have such a chance again; he would not let it slip from his grasp now.

Jerome turned and walked along the quay, stepping carefully over mooring ropes, tangy with tar in the soft night wind. He had gone for several hundred yards before he realized he was walking in the wrong direction. He had promised Patricia Bankhausen he would go to her, and instead he was walking away. In the excitement of seeing Gunn, even from a distance, he had completely forgotten the woman who had set him on this road to fortune.

\*    \*    \*

MacPherson sat back in his chair. The lights aboard the clipper were dimmed now, and the quay was all but empty. The masts of the moored vessels moved together on the gentle swell of the harbour. Here and there along the dock front, Indian coolies, lacking any homes, had wrapped themselves in white cloths like winding sheets, and lay sprawled on doorsteps, thankful for the shelter of doorways and the walls of buildings. Cats and stray dogs prowled restlessly for scraps of food between bollards and huge coils of rope, under the tall and silent derricks. Bridges had gone back to his hotel. Now Gunn and MacPherson sat alone, holding balloon glasses of brandy.

'What do you make of that fellow?' asked Gunn at last.

'I like him,' replied MacPherson at once. 'He is Scottish, which helps, of course. He is also proud of his job and what he has to sell, which is more important. And I believe what he says. We *are* at a time of change, doctor, and as we have already proved to our own satisfaction and the discomfiture of our rivals, we do best when we make decisions before our competitors. But I would suggest that we make sure Mr Bridges' demonstration is convincing, not a half-hearted affair which could leave any doubts in our minds—either way.'

'I already have,' Gunn replied. 'When I saw Bridges to his doolie, we arranged to put out into the bay at seven o'clock in the morning, the day after tomorrow. His vessel will follow us and then, out of sight of land, we will have a trial of strength between our vessels— the winds of heaven against steam from Bridges' boilers.'

'Why not tomorrow?'

'Because first I wish to ask Lieutenant Blackman, who commands Her Majesty's Ship *Aeneas*, what his views are on steam. He is an experienced officer, and I would value his opinion, which will not be biased to either side.'

'And why not stage this demonstration in the harbour?'

'Because it is possible that steam may win. Bridges is convinced of it, and even Captain Fernandes has an open mind on the matter. I would not wish for any Mandarin-Gold vessel to be pulled backwards in front of native eyes.'

'You are a great one for loss of face,' remarked Mac-Pherson, pouring himself another Martell.

'Part of our success,' Gunn pointed out, almost speaking to himself now, 'is that, so far, Mandarin-Gold has *never* lost face. We have had some very narrow shaves, agreed, but somehow we have always come out on top. It would be intensely damaging to our reputation should anyone begin to think, however wrongly, that we could ever be beaten or, worse, humiliated.

'And damaging not only to us, but to the whole of the British Empire. We must *always* win, MacPherson. The day we compromise, the day we lose a decisive struggle, whether on land, at sea or in our commercial undertakings here, that is the day when the white races will also begin to surrender all they are so steadily building up in the East.'

\*       \*       \*

Lieutenant Richard Blackman, RN, commanding HMS *Aeneas*, a 22-gun frigate of the line, now on her way home to refit at Chatham after three years' continuous service in the East, leaned over the rail of his bridge, a Havana cigar in his hand, and regarded with detached amusement the antics of ten Indian coolies on the quay.

The new godowns—there seemed to be more built every time he came into harbour, such was the astonishing prosperity and growth of Singapore as a trading port between East and West—cast short shadows over the shining cobbles, where the coolies were manhandling a grand piano. First, they had crawled beneath its base, then they had raised it carefully on their heads, and now they were jog-trotting along beneath the vast unwieldy burden that resembled a swollen crab with a hard lacquered shell shining in the sun.

Blackman wished that he could sketch the scene, for otherwise he would soon forget it, and he would like to recall it for the entertainment of his wife and son when he reached England within the next three months. Perhaps he could find one of his officers with sufficient artistic talent to record the oddities of life in the East, which appeared commonplace there but utterly bizarre, sometimes almost unbelievable, when translated to England?

Blackman was a saturnine-faced man of thirty-five, without private means or influence. He had resigned himself to his life of obscurity, being regularly passed over for promotion because he could not afford the extra expenditure a higher rank would bring. All his pay—pathetically little when viewed by the wealth of even obscure Eastern merchants—was already bespoken before he received it. His young son Erasmus had been ill for years, and was backward in mind and sluggish in body. Blackman had readily spent his free money on doctors' fees and consultations with specialists, but without any positive result. The boy was as he had always been, and his father's life was darkened by the knowledge that apparently he would never be cured; for how could any physician cure a complaint which he could not even diagnose?

None of the medical men the Blackmans had visited seemed capable of helping them. Then by chance—or, looking back, would it not be more gracious to say, the mercy of the Almighty?—Blackman had met someone who had helped him: Dr Gunn.

How strange, he thought, that meeting a man in the wide spaces of an empty ocean had totally changed his life and outlook and given him new hope. Gunn had been desperately seeking the support of a Royal Navy vessel to help him subdue an uprising of insurgents, organized by Dutch mercenaries with Malay pirates, in a coastal province of Borneo.

He had commandeered a native canoe to row across the sea lanes in the hope of meeting *Aeneas*, and had made his request for help.

Blackman was reluctant to involve one of Her Majesty's ships in such a dubious mission, but Gunn had gently reminded him that under an Act of King George IV, every pirate killed on the high seas meant prize money of £5 in specie to the captain of the vessel who could prove the death.

Not only this, but when Gunn heard of the captain's concern for his son, he had immediately offered his assistance. He had many medical friends in London, and he had written a personal letter to a friend at the Royal College of Physicians, so that Blackman's son should have the best treatment and every medical amenity he desired, and that all fees, whatever they might amount to, should be sent to Gunn's bank in St James's for immediate payment.

All this was nearly a year behind Blackman now; the boy had been examined by a more eminent physician than he had reached on his own, and a diagnosis had been made and confirmed by a second physician of equal renown. The treatment they had prescribed was now producing excellent results.

Blackman had also been gratified by the change in the letters his wife wrote to him about the matter. From scepticism and doubt—first, that Gunn would honour his promise, and then that the doctors could effect a cure—she had been delighted with the results. Every bill presented to Gunn's bank had been paid on sight; and the doctors had satisfied her that, in time, they could cure her son completely. Indeed, the evidence was there for all to see; the boy was showing an obvious improvement. From being listless and sluggish, he was now playing games, and making steady progress with his lessons.

Blackman hoped he would meet Gunn on this trip, so that he could thank him personally for his generosity and explain what wonderful results it had brought. His visit was due to last for a week for he had to revictual the vessel, and some timbers beneath the bows needed caulking before they faced the next leg of their voyage to Colombo in Ceylon, and then north to Bombay.

Blackman's first officer came up on the bridge, and handed him two sealed envelopes. Blackman ripped open the first. He was delighted to discover that it contained a note from Gunn welcoming Blackman to Singapore, and saying how he hoped he would have the pleasure of seeing him as speedily as possible since he had some unexpected matters to discuss with him, and on which he sought his advice.

'Pray take a letter,' Blackman told his officer. 'Address it personally to Dr Gunn. Assure him of my great pleasure at receiving his communication—indeed, I was thinking of despatching a letter to him this evening —and then invite him to dine with me here aboard *Aeneas* at eight o'clock tomorrow evening, if that is convenient to him. Should he wish to discuss any matter with me beforehand, I am, of course, at his service. Have that sent to his office immediately.'

'Very good, sir. And the other letter?'

Blackman opened the envelope and skimmed through this letter without interest. It was addressed from one of the new hotels on the outskirts of the city, and had been written by an American newspaper correspondent, Mr Hiram C. Jerome.

'Sir,' Blackman read aloud, 'I write to present my compliments and those of the editor of the *New York News*, which organ I have the honour to represent in this hemisphere.

'I am preparing a series of articles about various aspects of the East and the policy of the North American Government thereon. In this connection, I have been favoured with interviews by many important members of the European commercial community in Singapore, but I have not yet had the pleasure of meeting a Royal Navy captain who has served with distinction in these waters.

'I pray your indulgence so that I can explain to you what I have in mind, for I trust and hope most earnestly that the articles I write will not only be of interest to our readers, but will also further cement the warm feelings of cordial regard between your country and mine.

'I am at your disposal, sir, at any time or place that may be convenient during your stay in this city.

Believe me,

Yours respectfully,
Hiram C. Jerome.'


'What do you make of that?' asked Blackman.

'I do not know, sir,' replied the officer truthfully. He had never met a newspaper correspondent or even an American before, but this did not mean he held no views on them.

'No doubt he is one of these "doff-hats", these "penny-a-liners" who scribble about anything, obsequious to all, but owing loyalty to none,' said Blackman distastefully, handing him the letter.

'That may well be, sir. On the other hand, it has been noted that certain correspondents who have published accounts in the past, on naval and military, as well as civil matters, have brought dignity and even honour to those whose deeds they describe.'

'I have yet to read anything in the popular Press that brought dignity or honour to any officer in Her Majesty's Navy. But still, I suppose I *could* meet the fellow. Yes, I will. Nothing is ever gained by incivility. Take a letter to him. Tell him that I reciprocate his complimentary remarks, and look forward to meeting him at some time during my stay.'

'But you will not extend to him a definite invitation?'

'No. I am not seeking the man's company. But neither will I shirk meeting him. No doubt he will pursue the matter. I have heard that these scribbler fellows have skins thick as a rhino's hide.'

'Very good, sir.'

The first officer saluted and left Blackman on his own.

The coolies had disappeared with their piano; now others were laboriously manhandling a huge wooden crate, like ants struggling beneath some impossible burden. And when that had been disposed of, some other task would claim them. Their actions are an allegory of life, Blackman thought ponderously. As soon as one task is completed, another demands to be begun. He sighed, and went down to his cabin. It was time for a glass of claret.

*     *     *

Patricia Bankhausen faced the American.

'So you have not yet met Dr Gunn?' she began accusingly. They were in her sitting room, overlooking a small garden in which *malis*, Indian gardeners, had hacked a space free of jungle creeper, which seemed to flourish overnight, while flowering plants faded and withered in the harsh humid heat.

'Not so far, but I have made my plans.'

'And what are they, pray?'

'To avoid appearing before him almost as a mendicant or a supplicant, I have made inquiries as to his friends in the hope that one may introduce me, so that I shall meet Gunn on a social level—and then seemingly by chance.'

'You have been engaged on this scheme of yours for two weeks now, and what progress have you to report? Gunn will not stay in Singapore for ever. He will take ship to Macao or Hong Kong, or even to Calcutta. He is a restless man, not given to staying anywhere for long. Time is ever on his side, not on ours.'

'I have approached the captain of the British frigate *Aeneas*, which docked two days ago, asking for an interview. He has sent me a non-committal reply, so I am going down to the quayside today. I will go aboard the vessel, and present my compliments.'

'And if he is not there?'

'Then I will leave my card and ask him to dine with me tonight. And if that is inconvenient, tomorrow night, or the night after.'

'I wish you success,' said Patricia, but she felt disappointed. How odd that a man who appeared so handsome, who was such an accomplished lover, should lack those other qualities that Gunn possessed: energy, ingenuity, resource. Gunn would never wait for fourteen days to make his first appointment if business—or even pleasure—were involved. But then there was an abiding difference between the two men, despite outward similarities of physique. Gunn was a man of action; Jerome only wrote about men of action.

\*　　　\*　　　\*

Gunn sat in a cane chair in his docks office, built above the godown, overlooking Singapore quay. The room was plainly furnished, with a few rush mats scattered on the tiled floor; the walls were distempered in pale green. A couple of paintings of Chinese scenes hung behind his desk. He had bought them from George Chinnery, an English artist who moved between Canton and Macao, painting local people and places, and selling his prints for the price of a week's lodging.

It was seven o'clock in the evening, and the sun was sliding steadily down the sky, turning orange, then red. Soon, it would be dark, and the air chill, leaving only warmth stored in cornerstones and buildings as a remembrance of the fierceness of its power. The sun, he thought, is like a man, coming up slowly into prominence, enjoying a brief bright success—on some days even happiness—then sinking gently but just as inexorably into oblivion. And then—what?

MacPherson poured out two more whiskies; the sound of bottle on glass broke Gunn's reverie.

'When you are dining with Blackman tonight,' MacPherson told him, 'be so good as to give him my regards. Tell him I hope he will find time to dine with me in my house before he sails. I will keep free the next seven evenings in the expectation that he will join me on one of them.'

'I will carry your regards and invitation with pleasure. But in the meantime, have you any questions you feel I should ask about these new engines?'

'They're a wonderful invention,' said MacPherson slowly, proud that a Scotsman had designed them. 'Wonderful. And no doubt they will still be greatly improved. But I feel that they must always have the one weakness you have already remarked upon—fuel. I suppose the Navy is establishing depots for coal at various ports on their sailing routes, much as cab horses and drays have watering troughs all round London? We have had one coal dump here since last spring.'

'I know,' said Gunn, wrinkling his nose in distaste. A pyramid of black shining coal for the new P. & O. steamships had disfigured the quayside for months.

Sometimes it fumed with suppressed heat; on other days, the wind blew dust from it like a black cloud of locusts. This dust settled everywhere, making canopies filthy and flecking scrubbed decks with tiny glittering specks of coal.

'There *must* be a better and more efficient way of refuelling than to rely on these dumps. They will only encourage pilfering, and so require special guards. This may be easy for the Royal Navy to organize, but it is more difficult for those of us who have to show a commercial profit.'

'There is only one thing I would suggest, then,' said MacPherson, finishing his glass of The Glenlivet, and pouring another. 'Find your own coal mine out here. Time spent in searching would be time well invested. As it is, this coal mostly comes out from Wales and Newcastle in the holds of sailing vessels, and at great physical risk to their captains and crews, for there have already been instances of coal catching fire in the heat. It is like travelling in a ship in ballast with explosive.

'And if you load coal supplies aboard cargo ships, then you cut down by a proportionate weight the amount of cargo they can carry. It is no good to us beating the sailing clippers back home, if all we can carry is coal to propel our vessels.'

'I agree. Our hope must be that we will find some indigenous source of coal out here. Then no doubt we could come to some arrangement with the Royal Navy so that their ships could benefit from our discovery— possibly if we shared their fuel stores along other shipping lanes.'

'I hear that the Navy has been conducting its own

search for coal, in Borneo and Labuan and Jade Gate Island. But without success so far, although Labuan seems a likely place.'

'That does not necessarily mean others would also be unsuccessful,' Gunn pointed out. 'Maybe they searched in the wrong areas, or they employed the wrong people. After all, many of our employees in Mandarin-Gold, working as clerks and coolies, were similarly employed when the Parsee owned our company. They had a far better chance of success than we had, marooned on the China coast with the whole population against us. But we managed to overcome our difficulties, and turned them to our advantage— while these same clerks are still pushing their pens and these coolies still humping loads! All that has changed is that now they labour for us, and not for their earlier master.'

'You have a sound point there, doctor. No one could argue against it. So let us now drink to our success in this new venture.'

'We'll do more than drink to it,' Gunn replied shortly, draining his glass. 'We'll achieve it.'

# CHAPTER TWO

## *In which Mr Bridges' engine does not fail him*

CAPTAIN KENNEDY faced his officers in his small sea-cabin in the steamship *Thor*. Although the hour was early, the sun had already burnished the sky; now it winked on polished brass fitments and copper steam pipes. A tall frond of smoke spiralled into the bright still air from the high thin funnel.

'Gentlemen,' began Kennedy, fingering his beard as he spoke, 'Mr Bridges tells me that this morning will see our final demonstration, and so shortly thereafter we will sail for home. On our way, we will call for coal at Colombo and Bombay, then at Aden and Cape Town. We should make the Clyde within three months from today's date.

'He stresses that this last demonstration can be the most crucial of all we have undertaken, because if it is successful an extremely important order for engines and possibly new vessels as well, should flow from it. I need hardly add that I expect everyone to do their utmost to ensure its complete success. Have you any questions?'

'One, sir,' said the ship's engineer. 'You are satisfied that our engine *can* pull Dr Gunn's clipper astern if she is under full sail?'

'I am optimistic,' Kennedy replied, stroking his lips nervously. 'Mr Bridges is eager for such a dramatic manifestation of the power of steam because he feels that this will tip the scales of doubt in our favour. Provided the wind does not rise, and the glass holds steady, we should manage it.'

'I hope we are able to do so, sir, but I must report that we have a persistently leaking gland in one of the main steam pipes. It is impossible to repack this gland without damping down the furnace, and we should require at least a day thereafter to raise steam.'

'We all have our problems,' replied Captain Kennedy evasively. 'I have no doubt that you will overcome this by some ingenious means.'

The engineer grunted. It was one thing to be bland and confident in the captain's cabin, but altogether another when you were down below decks with the engines. There was nothing of the silence and grace of sail about them. Their huge connecting rods, moving to and fro, the great oiled cranks turning steadily in all weathers, the whole sensation of enormous power waiting, nay, eager, to be set free, sometimes frightened him. This was a different world from any that seamen had experienced before, and time and again he had wondered whether he was seeing the end or the beginning of an age. The crew were called sailors because sails propelled their ships. Would they require a new name when steam became their propelling power?

The feeling at the heart of the vessel, locked in an iron shell beneath the level of the sea, with enough power to devastate a city, was something he could not describe, but he felt it. So did the stokers, feeding endless shovels of coal to their insatiable furnace that roared like a burning beast.

If *Thor* failed to beat Gunn's vessel, their company would possibly lose a contract. But if that boiler burst in their efforts to force more pressure into the cylinders then, down below, they would certainly lose their lives. The steam would simply scald the flesh from their bones. So the engineer grunted and said nothing. The captain was quite right; this was his problem. But if he and his team overcame it, theirs would not be the glory. All they could expect would be a gruff word of praise from Captain Kennedy—and the opportunity to risk their lives at a later date on another demonstration.

The officers bowed respectfully to the captain and left the cabin. The engineer immediately went below decks, to the familiar compounded aroma of hot oil and scorched paint and damp, condensing steam. A Lascar seaman had brewed a tin pail of tea by withdrawing some water from the boiler. He handed a full enamel mug to the engineer; he drank it, savouring the sugary warmth, feeling sweat immediately start from his pores, and at the roots of his hair.

The stokers were coming in, big bearded men with bodies curiously pale, like miners', wearing leather trousers, and wide, brass-buckled belts. Each man picked up his own shovel, spat on the palms of his hands, and without a word, went to work heaving coal into the gaping, roaring, shimmering mouth of the furnace.

Coal dust thickened the air into a black, lampwick fog. Sweat trickled in shiny rivulets down their suddenly darkened bodies, hanging like tears on tufts of under-arm hair, making thick beards shine like ebony wire.

The ship's telegraph clanged for half steam ahead. The engineer picked up a piece of wadding rag, wound it around the handle of a polished brass lever, and pulled. Black-tipped needles leaped and trembled against white pressure-gauge dials. Steam bellowed briefly at a safety valve, then the huge connecting rods began sluggishly to move. Measured drips of amber oil dropped regularly from lubricating nozzles on to polished bearings. The smell of warm oil, and the dry hot breath of the furnace grew stronger until it completely filled the engine room.

On either side of the vessel, the big blades of the paddles thrust through the sea, slowly at first and then, as they gathered strength, threshing the muddy harbour water like captive mill wheels. The *Thor* shuddered from bow to stern under the impulse of their hammering blades. Then she began to move slowly forward without the benefit of wind or oars, driven by this thundering, throbbing mechanism.

The engineer thought, as he often thought when the engine was running well, that he and the stokers and the other engineer-seamen were like acolytes or high priests administering to a strange and powerful god. This was undoubtedly the future, while sails represented the past. But could the power generated in this boiler and transmitted to two cylinders, successfully challenge the power of four tall masts crammed high with sail? That was a question which another hour would answer.

\*　　　\*　　　\*

Captain Fernandes tapped on the door of Gunn's sea-cabin.

'We are now eight miles offshore, sir. The steam vessel, *Thor*, is approaching. She is to leeward, so the smoke from the funnels will not soot our sails. Her captain has signalled for your permission to begin the tests.'

'Whenever he likes,' replied Gunn briefly, and came out on deck.

The early morning air was clear, with a salty tang from the long slow swell of the sea. A few gulls dived and swooped hopefully around the sterns of both vessels. Signal flags fluttered from the mast head, and aboard *Thor*'s main deck he saw Mr Bridges wave to him, and then gouts of black smoke and glowing sparks belched from the funnel behind her bridge.

White feathers of steam played at the exhaust which discharged near the top of the main mast. *Thor*'s two paddles thrashed the water into foam, as she began to reverse. As the ship drew within five yards of the *Hesperides*'s elegant gilded stern, his crew threw thin ropes aboard the steam vessel. Three sailors tied them to huge hawsers, thick as a man's wrist, which they pulled across to *Hesperides* and made them fast around mooring stanchions.

'We are putting three hawsers aboard,' Fernandes explained. 'They are sufficient to hold *Hesperides* against an ebbing tide, so they should be able to take the strain.'

'I leave the details to you, captain,' Gunn replied. 'You are in command at sea. I command on land.'

'Aye, aye, sir.'

Fernandes turned to the mate and began to issue his orders. Men were already swarming like monkeys up rope-ladders, swinging from one to another, and then out along the high varnished spars, with complete unconcern for height and the sway of the vessel. Sails that Gunn had never seen in use before, now flapped loosely, and then suddenly rounded with wind as skilled hands on blocks and tackle tightened them. The slack of the three hawsers came dripping out of the sea, and their entwined strands trembled with the strain, squeezing out drops of water in a fine spray. Slowly, *Hesperides* moved out to sea, towing behind her the vast iron bulk of the paddle steamer.

'Lucky I am not a betting man,' said MacPherson slowly. 'I'd be hard put to it to know on which side to place my money, because the wind's freshening, and Fernandes has clapped half a square mile of canvas on the masts. They'll need a mighty powerful engine to beat us now.'

Slowly, but with gradually increasing speed, *Hesperides* bowed before the wind. Fernandes stood in the wheelhouse, looking anxiously from his straining, creaking masts back to the steamship, and then up at his sails again. Only he knew the very real risk of bringing down a mast by the enormous pressure of the huge area of sails he was using. Pray God that did not happen; *Hesperides* could be in dock for weeks as a result of such a catastrophe.

Mr Bridges, aboard *Thor*, raised a megaphone and shouted: 'Your permission, captain, to take the strain?'

'Whenever you wish, Mr Bridges,' Fernandes called back, and braced himself against the varnished rail, already warm in the sun. His crew watched expectantly, keeping away from the stern lest one of the hawsers should break and whip back.

A clang of telegraph bells aboard *Thor*, and then a thudding, like a great hammer beating somewhere in the heart of the ship, the hammer of the god from which the vessel took her name. Huge mushroom-shaped puffs of black smoke blew out of the funnel's scalloped rim. White steam played at the exhaust; the whole vessel trembled and shook as though gripped by a palsy. Then the paddles were churning the sea on either side of *Thor* into a white salty foam.

Faster and faster the paddles turned. Soon it was no longer possible to distinguish their separate blades; they were simply two spinning blurs. All around *Thor*, the sea was white. Shock waves ran out from the centre, making *Hesperides* roll and dip and rise again uneasily. The noise of the steam engine was now a continuous rumbling thunder of pistons, and the crash of the flails against the water increased to a roar like a giant water-fall.

Slowly, as the paddles bit, the speed of *Hesperides* decreased. Masts bent forward dangerously. Ropes stood tight and taut as strips of steel, humming in the breeze like giant violin strings. Gradually *Hesperides* stopped all forward movement; and then imperceptibly, almost unbelievably, she began to be pulled back against her will.

The crew of *Thor* cheered wildly, waving their hands, throwing up sweaty, oil-stained caps into the air. Their whole vessel was now covered by a pall of smoke like black fog; only vague outlines of the deck could be seen, at the centre of a widening circle of foam, and now and then the tip of the mast or the rim of the funnel.

Then, above the clatter of the engine and the crash-

47

ing thunder of her paddles, Gunn heard the tiny tinkling of a telegraph bell. The paddles slowed and then
ceased and the throb of the engines died. Smoke blew
away gently, a low alien cloud drifting lazily on the
wind, away from the sea, towards the shore. Gunn
thought that it seemed somehow symbolic of sailing
ships admitting defeat in face of the future. The pendu-
lum of history was swinging from one extreme to
another, and he had been present as it moved. The
proud ships with their great sails and high masts and
gilded figureheads were now a part of the past, like the
coracles of the ancient Britons or the war canoes of
Borneo.

The engine ceased entirely. Captain Fernandes gave
the order to run down the sails, and they flapped against
the masts angrily, wearily, in defeat, until the crew
could run aloft and furl them.

'Permission to come aboard, sir,' called the engineer.

'Whenever you please,' shouted back Captain Fernandes. A small boat was lowered with six oarsmen. Mr
Bridges climbed up *Hesperides*'s scrubbed white gangway.

'Well, sir, that was our demonstration,' he said to
Gunn, trying hard to keep excitement from his voice.
He was shining with sweat and triumph, his white
uniform dusted with black smuts of soot. He looked as
though he had stepped from a burning building, but
was clearly unaware of his bizarre appearance.

'Come below and have a claret,' invited Gunn.
Together, they went into his day cabin. Glasses and
two decanters of claret stood on a side table. Gunn
poured out the wine in silence.

48

'Let us drink to tomorrow,' he said. 'To the time when Mandarin-Gold's fleet—her steam fleet, I must now add—cover the world. Let us drink to a time when distance is diminished and ignorance about other countries and those who live therein will decrease with it. Let us drink to the future and the friendship of all nations, soon to be linked, as distance between them shrinks to weeks, and perhaps to days, instead of needing months of voyaging, as now. To the time when East and West are one.'

'You mean you were impressed, sir?' asked the engineer hopefully, as he lowered his glass.

'Very,' said Gunn. 'I must say, I was also impressed by the way in which my wooden ship took the strain. Your engine pulled with such vigour that I feared *Thor* would tear the stern right out of her—which could have resulted in an unpleasant claim against your company!'

'You will have your little joke, sir,' said Mr Bridges, laughing half dutifully, half doubtfully. Looking from one to the other, he suddenly caught sight of himself in a wall mirror.

'I must apologize for my appearance, gentlemen. But I went down into the engine room myself to make sure that the pressures were kept up.'

He turned to Gunn.

'Am I correct in expecting, sir, that you will now place an order for one of these engines, or would I make too bold to hope we could sell you several, or perhaps the entire steam fleet to which we have just drunk, constructed to your design, to suit your particular needs?'

'I would that I might agree at once, for there is no

49

doubt in my mind now that steam is the power of the future. I have travelled in steam trains in England, and covered distances there in hours which only a few years ago would have taken days by the stage. Now I have witnessed its power over the winds of heaven. Only one thing gives me cause to doubt—and then only, I trust, for the moment.'

'And what is that, sir?'

Surely the man must place an order now? What more could he do to convince him? Bridges' anxiety showed on his homely red face.

'This, Mr Bridges. How can we be assured of stocks of coal for the steam vessels which I would like to buy from you? There is now no question that a steamship can overhaul any sailing ship—but only so long as she has sufficient fuel. Without coal, she becomes just a scientific anachronism of floating iron fashioned in the shape of a ship.'

'We carry sails as well, sir, so as to be prepared for any such eventuality.'

'But surely that is like a tailor selling a man a pair of belted trousers—and then throwing in braces, in case the buckle breaks? Let us put our faith wholly in sail or in steam, not half-heartedly in both. But if I filled the hold of one of your steam vessels with tea, or any other commodity for the successful sale of which speed is essential, what would happen if our coal ran out?'

'The Royal Navy, sir, is making its own arrangements against any such contingency. They already have one coaling station here in Singapore, another in Bombay, and others in Colombo and at the Cape.'

'What about the East, for this is where our treasure

lies? What has the Navy got here that could be of benefit to us?'

'I must admit, sir, that I have not sailed farther East than Singapore, but I can assure you that my friends in the Royal Navy tell me they are energetically examining the problem.'

'Does that mean that some luckless clerk in the Admiralty is looking at maps and reports, and hoping that by some miracle of good fortune or friendly Providence, coal may somehow become available?'

'I am assured their plans are rather farther ahead than that picture would suggest, sir.'

'If I could be assured of enough coal,' replied Gunn, 'I would give you an order now to fit my vessels with engines, and to lay down the keels of one and possibly two new iron steamships. If you can give me that assurance, Mr Bridges, then I will give you the order.'

'Would that I *could* give you that guarantee, sir. But unfortunately, it is entirely beyond my power to do so. I can only introduce you to captains in the Navy who will, I know, bear out what I say.'

'There is no need, Mr Bridges. I have already arranged to meet one of my own acquaintance to discuss this matter. In the meantime, Mr Bridges, please accept my congratulations on a splendid performance. And my word that if fuel is forthcoming, I will place an order as I promise.'

\*　　　\*　　　\*

Two Royal Navy stewards in white tropical uniforms swiftly set out a decanter of port and a box of Havana cigars, a silver piercer and a silver jar of lucifers.

After bowing to Lieutenant Blackman they left the cabin.

Gunn lit a cigar and stretched out to his full length in his cane chair, enjoying Blackman's company, and pleased to hear that his host's son was showing such a marked improvement.

'Apart from renewing our friendship, I wanted to ask your personal views on a matter that could be of great importance to my company,' he said. 'I thought it politic to wait until we had finished dinner and were on our own.'

'If I can help, I will be honoured to do so,' replied Blackman. 'Please be assured that no one can overhear our conversation.'

'I seek your opinion on the steam engines which the energetic salesman, Mr Bridges, is endeavouring to persuade me to buy for my fleet. What is your personal estimation of them—as opposed to sail? Do their mechanical complications outweigh their advantages?'

'I cannot answer, for I have no personal experience with steam engines, doctor. I was brought up in sail. But I must tell you that *Aeneas* is being fitted with a two-cylinder reciprocating engine by Campbells of Glasgow as soon as we pay off in Chatham. That shows the faith which their Lordships at the Admiralty put in Mr Bridges' company and their products.

'I can only add that reports I receive from captains of steam warships are that the benefits are little short of amazing, so far as ships of the line are concerned.

'I do not know whether you are acquainted with naval strategy, doctor, but when a fleet depends upon the winds, as all fleets have done until quite recently, it is essential that they position themselves to windward if they plan to engage an enemy. In sailing ship tactics, this line of battle is formed by arranging ships in line ahead at six points from the wind, either on the port or the starboard tack. The Navy calls this sailing in close-hauled lines.

'The advantages of this are very great. The fleet in this position sails before the wind, and so commands the enemy, who can only either retreat or tack in the opposite direction, because they also are dependent on the wind. The commander of the windward fleet can thus force the enemy to close action, or compel him to edge away, bear up, and finally retreat altogether.

'At Trafalgar, Nelson had it in his power to penetrate the line of the combined Spanish and French navies because he kept the wind in his sails and not in theirs. In the simplest terms, the fleet able to place itself in position first can simply sail in line abreast down the line of their enemy, firing as they go. If the wind drops or changes, or if there is no wind at all, then the whole situation can change dramatically—and, believe me, it often does.

'With steam power, ships are independent of all winds. They can sail in any direction, and converge on any point with speed and precision. In an engagement with sailing ships, their superiority thus needs no amplification from me. I would assume, doctor, that even greater benefits could accrue to merchant vessels equipped with the screw propeller or the paddle.'

'But what are the difficulties?' persisted Gunn.

'In a naval sense, there are two, possibly of almost equal importance. First, the paddle is a cumbersome contraption that can be shot away, or jammed by broken spars or rigging. Similarly, the screw propeller, which the Admiralty favours because it gives greater speed and economy, with less vulnerability, can be fouled by fallen rigging. This has happened in engagements already to such an extent that Her Majesty's ships are now being provided with a "trunk", a square aperture in the stern through which the screw can be hoisted up or a diver in a bell lowered to free it.

'Our orders in sailing vessels, if we have to engage any steamship, are first to fire at the rigging in the hope that the ropes *will* fall and foul the screw propeller. I need not dwell on the unhappy situation in which a captain in a steamship would find himself with his propeller locked. He is in command of a floating iron coffin, unable to move forwards or astern, or turn to port or starboard unless the tides take him: a target for the guns. But such problems would not affect merchant ships.'

'You believe then, Blackman, that the advantages of steam entirely overcome the advantages of sail?'

'Without any doubt whatever. There have been some mechanical troubles, of course, because steam engines are still in their infancy, and improvements will obviously be many. But in this connection, I would recall to you, sir, the words of the American politician and scientist, Benjamin Franklin, when he saw an ascent in a hot-air balloon, and a spectator asked him condescendingly, "What use is *that*?" Benjamin Franklin at once replied: "What use is a baby?"'

'There is one drawback, surely, Blackman, that you have overlooked—the huge amount of coal each vessel must carry? The furnaces must burn endlessly while the ship is at sea, and all day and night they must be fed. I know that the Admiralty is building coaling depots in several important Empire ports. But coal still has to be brought out to them from England at enormous cost and complication. Has not the Royal Navy examined the prospects of extracting coal from Labuan and Jade Gate Island?'

'Yes. Our surveyor, Mr Partridge, returned in my ship and he is still in Singapore. In Labuan, he reported traces of coal, and we are hoping to examine that island further, but in Jade Gate he could find nothing at all.

'If I may be frank, doctor, Mr Partridge is a man of nervous disposition, and I think rather he was overcome by the knowledge that the island contains head-hunters and kindred Chinese ruffians who dislike uninvited visitors. They have been known to castrate men who landed unannounced and send them as eunuchs to the Court in Peking, where the humiliation of Red-Bristled Barbarians meets with great favour from their Emperor. Our surveyor, Mr Partridge, thus feared to lose one or other of his physical extremities, his head or his manhood!'

Blackman chuckled at the recollection. Because he was going home, such fears and dangers would soon be far away behind him, simply stories to tell around the fireside to relations who might listen politely enough, but only half believing what he said, for such happenings were totally beyond the narrow safe spectrum of their own routine lives.

'You do not appear to be greatly impressed by Mr Partridge's thoroughness on Jade Gate Island? Do you believe that coal deposits exist there?'

'I could hazard no professional opinion, but I went ashore on two occasions, so I can tell you what I learned myself. One of our galley hands spoke the lingo, and he told me that farther inland the locals burn a black hard substance that they scratch out of the soil. From his description of its qualities, I would assume this to be a kind of coal. But whether it has the quality the Royal Navy demands, would be another matter altogether.'

'Did you tell Partridge of this?'

'I did. He expressed no interest whatever. I think he felt that the risks he might run to his person in advancing inland to verify the story outweighed all other considerations. He was eager to be elsewhere.'

'So his cowardice may have denied the Royal Navy the use of coal from Jade Gate Island?'

'I would not disagree with that, doctor. As I say, the quality is unknown. But I think coal is there.'

'Viewing this problem dispassionately, Blackman, if one could discover coal in quantity on Labuan or Jade Gate, and secure the rights for its extraction, even if its quality was not the highest, you would view this as a valuable commercial proposition?'

'Probably as profitable as when you were running opium, doctor, and without any of the social stigma that now attaches in liberal minds to the Coast Trade. Steam is still a novelty in ships, as gas-lights are in London. But I wager that within a decade, at the most, steam will propel every vessel of consequence. The great sailing ships will then become as much creatures of the past as the monsters that roamed the earth before history was written.'

'I am also of that opinion, Blackman. And whoever

commands a source of coal in the East can command trade in the East and the China Seas, and hence, by inference, all the East itself. I am much indebted to you for your views on this matter. I intend to engage a surveyor and prove to my own satisfaction whether you are correct, or whether the timid Mr Partridge was right, after all. I will sail as soon as I can make my preparations, and if I do not discover coal—or at least sufficient for my purpose—then I will prospect for it in Borneo. Within a very short time, coal will be as essential out here for business survival as water is to keep the human body alive.

'Now I have one more question to ask you, Blackman. If I do discover coal, I would be honoured if you would join my company as a director. Will you accept?'

'I am touched and flattered by your invitation, doctor. I am, however, not a man of commerce, but a professional naval officer.'

'And what does your profession hold for you? Promotion to captain, perhaps, and maybe—with luck and influence—to vice-admiral. Then retirement to a cottage home in a fishing village somewhere along the south coast of England, watching ships in the Channel through a telescope you have purloined from Admiralty stores!'

'Come, come, sir! That is a gloomy prognostication, and not a picture of the retirement of an officer in Her Majesty's Navy.'

'Truth is often gloomy,' smiled Gunn, pouring himself out more port and passing on the decanter. 'You could make it less so by resigning from the Navy and bringing your wife and son out here, to start a whole new career as a director of our enterprise. Your knowledge of this area and your experience as a naval captain would be of the highest value to us.'

'But I know nothing of commerce.'

'Nor did I until I began to trade. One sadness of our age is that, like dray-horses, too many people stay in the same familiar safe routine all their lives. Yet it was not ever thus. Leonardo da Vinci was a great painter. But he also claimed to discover gunpowder *and* built a flying machine. In our present time, Dr Jardine abandoned the teachings of Hippocrates and Galen to become a rich merchant. I also followed his example.

'MacPherson was a sailor, like you. Then he saw what rewards commerce could offer to those with strong arms and sharp swords and iron nerve.

'This is the time, Blackman, to be in the East, while the maps are still being drawn, while whole countries remain unknown, with mountains no white man has climbed and treasure-houses no one from the West has yet imagined.

'It was too early fifty years ago. And fifty years from now it will all be too late. Now is the hour for action. And I would be honoured to have you by my side as we labour to increase our enterprise, moving into India and then along the coast of that dark continent, Africa.'

'Perhaps we may discuss this further at a later date, doctor?' said Blackman, drawing on his cigar. 'I am deeply honoured and flattered that you should think of me so highly, and am much moved by your eloquence. After I have discussed the matter with my wife—for, as you know, we live in her mother's house—I will write to you of our decision.'

'Were I married,' replied Gunn with a wry smile, 'the thought of living in the house of my wife's mother, and in England's damp and foggy climate, where the sun rarely shines, would be sufficient spur to send me over the seas to a land of warmth and wealth. Think on these things as you sail home. And then, my friend, write to me that you will join me.'

# CHAPTER THREE

### *In which two North Americans agree on a course of action*

MR BRIDGES paid off his doolie, adjusted his top hat carefully, smoothed down the frock-coat that felt hot as astrakhan in the afternoon heat, and walked up the scrubbed gangplank into *Hesperides*. He moved slowly because of the warmth, and because by so doing he could better conceal the nervousness he felt at Gunn's unexpected summons. A sailor waiting on deck saluted him smartly and led him down to Gunn's day cabin.

'Divest yourself, sir, of your coat. It is far too formal for this climate,' Gunn said as he poured two measures of De Kuypers Geneva gin with fresh lime juice.

'You are very kind, sir,' said Bridges thankfully, and removed the heavy coat. Sweat stuck his white silk shirt to his chest like a pale, transparent skin.

'I have asked you here,' Gunn went on, as soon as his guest was seated, 'because I believe that I am on the track of a new source of coal. I am not sure yet that my search will be successful, but if it is not, then I will look elsewhere, until I find what I seek. For I am determined to discover a supply somewhere in this hemisphere.

'I understand that you are leaving shortly for Scotland.

so I have invited you aboard today so that we can draw up an agreement for Mandarin-Gold to purchase eight of your steam engines.'

'I am delighted, Dr Gunn,' said Bridges, beaming.

'As each of my company's eight clippers reaches East India Docks, I will give their captains orders to discharge all cargo and then proceed north to your shipyard. Your company, I am sure, will advise me wisely as to the size and type of engine best suited to each vessel, having regard to their carrying capacity, and so on.

'I need hardly remind you that if these conversions prove successful, this will be but the beginning of a long association—and I trust a profitable one—between your company and mine. If these engines are reliable, then I intend to commission your company to lay down keels of a new fleet of iron merchantmen propelled by steam.'

'You appear convinced, then, that you will discover coal?'

'Totally,' replied Gunn quietly.

*        *        *

Mr Bonnarjee, the Parsee's son, was a plump, soft-fleshed man in early middle life, with light brown skin, well-oiled black hair, and a lot of gold in his front teeth. The gold gleamed, not only when he smiled, which was seldom, but when he talked, which was often; and most of all when he gave orders, which was nearly all the time, for he and his father were among the twelve richest and most powerful Parsees in the East.

Mr Bonnarjee had the Indian habit of jigging slightly up and down as he sat in his leather chair behind his desk, sandals pushed off his bare feet, mind bent to some new problem or concern. He was shaking now in this curious, tireless, unrealized rhythm, while above him the tapestried punkah creaked to and fro gently with a movement that matched his own. Beyond the window, he could see the new Commercial Road and the fine offices of his rival merchants. The hour was eleven in the morning, and the air was filled with the hoarse entreaties of sweetmeat vendors and paw-paw sellers, of coolies shouting breathlessly for space to trot through the crowds beneath enormous bales of cloth or other vast amorphous burdens.

Above these human sounds came a constant metallic clatter from the open-fronted banks. This was caused by clerks biting coins between their teeth to test for forgeries, as they counted them. Years of practice had given them the gift of instantly telling a counterfeit.

Mr Bonnarjee's office was large, with a red-tiled floor. On the whitewashed walls he had hung prints of Persian temples, including a monastery at Ahwaz in Southern Persia, where, according to the Christian Bible, the prophet Daniel had been imprisoned in the lions' den, and the Lord had made the lions merciful, so that Daniel survived his experience, while those who had imprisoned him were later rent to pieces by the ravenous beasts.

The thought crossed Bonnarjee's mind as he sat, biting his lower lip, that he knew only one man in all the world for whom he would willingly reserve such a fate, and then on the strict condition that the lions had been kept from food for days beforehand, so that they would rend his flesh with the most terrible mauls. He could imagine their razor teeth gouging his delicate parts, and the thought gave him as much pleasure as his victim would suffer excruciating pain. This man, whom he hated now with total obsession, was the English physician-turned-merchant, Robert Gunn.

Bonnarjee knew, of course, how Gunn had got his wife with child, how the boy who would inherit his fortune was not of his own seed. Others within the family also knew, but they kept the knowledge secret; every family had incidents in their history of which they were not proud. But now the doctor's personal Chinese clerk, Lin Yang, stood, hands folded and his head down, on the other side of Bonnarjee's vast inlaid desk, and he brought news that caused Bonnarjee great concern.

Lin Yang was very thin. His shoulder-blades protruded like folded wings through the cheap cotton of his shirt.

The contrast between the two men was total: they represented Eastern privilege and Eastern poverty. This creature, thin, ill-clad, hollow-faced, brought Bonnarjee what titbits of news he might glean about the inner workings of Mandarin-Gold. Usually, for his fee of one English guinea each week, he had little to impart; indeed, any stroller along the quay could see what cargoes were being loaded and unloaded, and other of Bonnarjee's informers in local banks would gladly supply details of loans, debts and mortgages. But on this occasion Lin Yang had brought him items of news that were both dangerous and valuable.

First, one of Gunn's stewards aboard *Hesperides* had told Lin Yang that Gunn was the father of the boy who bore Bonnarjee's name. Lin Yang had been reluctant to pass on this information, but did so in the belief that

64

Bonnarjee would be pleased to scotch the lie. Only when he saw Bonnarjee's face cloud and his eyes narrow did Lin Yang realize too late that it was no lie, but the truth.

The other item of news he brought was that Dr Gunn was provisioning his flagship for an unexpected voyage; he wished to prospect for coal. There were only three sites he had mentioned, and of these the likeliest—because it was nearest to Singapore—was Jade Gate Island. In this connection, Lin Yang had been able to recommend a surveyor, lately in the employ of James Brooke in Sarawak, one Josiah Castle.

Mr Bonnarjee wrote down the name; he always found difficulty in spelling English names, and had several times been surprised to learn that Europeans faced the same problem with Eastern surnames. Gunn was clearly hoping to secure coal to make him independent of any other supply. This must mean he was seriously considering the advantages of fitting steam engines to his clippers.

Now if he could thwart him here, if he could somehow deny him coal. . . . Bonnarjee's mind was already forging ahead to possible deals and counterdeals, to bribes and persuasions, so that he could find coal first and then hold to ransom all the European merchants, such as Jardine Matheson, Mandarin-Gold, Dent, and the rest.

Bonnarjee picked up an engraved brass bell and rang it impatiently. An Indian clerk came into the room and bowed.

'Give Mr Lin Yang specie from our treasury to the extent of five golden guineas,' Bonnarjee told him.

The man withdrew.

'You are more generous, my master,' said Lin Yang, 'than your humble servant deserves.'

'Go in peace,' Bonnarjee told him. As soon as he was alone, he rang the bell again four separate times.

Now another man entered, a dark-skinned Madrassi, strong shouldered, with muscles that rippled beneath his white silk dhoti.

'A Chinese informer has just left my office,' Bonnarjee told him briskly. 'He will be collecting five golden guineas. Follow him and have him made away with, using discretion. But I wish his body to be left where it will be found eventually, as a warning to others of his kind who speak loudly and think not at all.

'One important point,' added Bonnarjee. 'Keep his five golden guineas for yourself. But if he has any other money in his purse, do not interfere with that. I believe he will leave a widow and children who may have need of it.'

'My master's generosity is warm as the sun at noon.'

'It is always so,' agreed Bonnarjee, slightly mollified; the Madrassi left his office, his bare feet making no sound on the smooth tiles. Bonnarjee sat alone, digesting what he had heard. When a hireling clerk knew such a secret and spoke of it, then honour demanded silence, and silence now meant death.

The man who had told Lin Yang this secret would zealously preserve his own silence in order to preserve his life. He would guess why Lin Yang had died, and who had killed him. And he would know this was no casual robber, for Lin Yang's purse would not be opened.

Bonnarjee felt sweat dampen his back, and rage

hammer in his blood like the pistons of the new steam engines that the Scottish engineer, Mr Bridges, had been trying to sell him on the previous day. He was feeding Gunn's son, not his own; his energies and enterprise would bring wealth to another man's heir, not his. Every time he looked at the boy, he saw Gunn looking back. Every time he looked at his wife he would wonder, in fevered imaginings, how often she had lain with Gunn; worse, whether she still did.

There was only one way to escape completely from this impossible nightmare; he must take his revenge on Gunn. Somehow, Bonnarjee would deny Gunn his coal; he was not quite sure how yet, but ways and means would be forthcoming. Then he would break Gunn's firm and then Gunn himself. He would torment him, as he had been tormented; and then he would kill him, slowly, very slowly, enjoying each convulsion of his death.

And out of another man's anguish, Bonnarjee would draw some sweetening modicum of comfort in his own, as a man bitten by a deadly snake may still live—if he can only suck the poison from the throbbing mortal wound before it totally consumes him.

*     *     *

For the second time that evening, Hiram Jerome faced a stranger whose support he desperately needed, and endeavoured to bend that man's mind and will into a direction of his choosing.

The first time had been beneath the scrubbed canvas awning that Lieutenant Blackman had ordered to be rigged over *Aeneas*' afterdeck, and which stretched tight as a drumskin above their heads in the evening offshore wind.

Blackman lay back in a cane chair, cigar in one hand, balloon glass of Martell in the other, his white uniform immaculate, a man at ease. Jerome sat opposite him, in a slightly smaller cane chair, wearing a crumpled suit, his top hat on the deck by his feet, holding down some papers. He scribbled assiduously in a slanting hand, pausing every now and then to dip his pen carefully into his special travelling ink-well which also stood on the deck, its screwtop open.

'And then, sir? After this engagement with the pirates, you returned to your normal duties?'

'To my *usual* duties,' corrected Blackman gently, savouring his position. God alone knew what this Yankee fellow would write, but even if it were highly coloured, it could scarcely all be unfavourable. In due time, their lordships at the Admiralty would doubtless receive a copy of the newspaper from the British Ambassador in North America. Doubtless they would approve of the manner in which Lieutenant Blackman had helped Dr Gunn to restore to its rightful ruler a province friendly to Britain in the teeth of insurrection organized by pirates under the jurisdiction of Dutch mercenaries. As a naval officer, of course, Blackman could not speak directly about his own capabilities or achievements, but if this very civil American chose to make what he called 'a good story' out of his experiences, then who was he to prevent him?

And Jerome appeared so genuinely interested in everything Blackman could tell him, and so patently eager to foster American friendship after the lamentable events of former years, that Blackman would have felt churlish not to furnish him with as much information as he decently could. In so doing, their conversation had ranged far beyond events in Borneo.

They had talked about the strange Chinese medical treatment of acupuncture, which had cured Gunn, when, according to Western medical opinion, he was mortally ill. They had discussed the changing face of the seas, as more ships abandoned sail for steam. This in turn had brought them to the subject of coal aboard such vessels, and the hazards mariners faced should they exhaust their supply in mid-voyage. Then Blackman enlarged on the danger of spontaneous combustion of large quantities of coal in a ship's hold, and how much safer it would be if coaling stations could be supplied with indigenous coal, dug by native miners instead of being transported at great risk and cost from mines in Britain, thousands of miles away.

Jerome appeared to know about the negative results that naval surveys had shown in Jade Gate Island; or maybe Blackman had told him. After his fourth brandy, he was not quite sure, and anyway, what did that matter? Jerome seemed to share his doubts as to whether Mr Partridge had conducted his search with sufficient vigour, and he was especially attentive when Blackman said how a merchant like Gunn, interested in making a commercial profit, would have tackled the problem with infinitely more energy and diligence.

Did the lieutenant know Gunn well? Of course. And he believed that Gunn was planning his own survey for coal on Jade Gate, in spite of the earlier negative report? Yes, indeed. And if he found coal, then Blackman could claim some credit, for he had told Gunn that he believed coal was there, just waiting to be dug up.

Jerome appeared extremely impressed. He seemed, in fact, a most agreeable visitor, pleasingly deferential but not subservient; and on his own lower plane of social life, he must lead an interesting existence. Usually, of course, a person of Jerome's calling would not be admitted to a gentleman's table, but nowadays the pen was apparently a key that could unlock all kinds of privileged and unlikely doors.

At last Jerome stopped writing, bent forward, screwed on the cap of his silver ink-well, opened a small leather box and placed it inside. Then he carefully laid his pen in its special, velvet-lined ebony case, gathered his papers together, and stood up.

'I fear, sir, lest I have overstayed my welcome,' he said, 'but I found your hospitality so engaging and your conversation so entertaining that I trust you will forgive me for taking up so much of your time.'

Blackman stood up now; it was his turn to be generous and charming.

'My dear fellow,' he began, rather thickly, for he had been drinking much more brandy than Jerome; the rich fumes of his Havana cigar wreathed his sweating face. 'My dear fellow, the pleasure is all mine. It is always interesting to meet men of endeavour like yourself, and to offer such hospitality as we can aboard one of Her Majesty's ships of the line.'

A steward stood, awaiting his instructions.

'Show this gentleman ashore,' ordered Blackman.

'There is no need,' Jerome assured them both, 'but I mightily appreciate your civility.'

He followed the steward along the deck, the metal heels of his shoes echoing on the scrubbed boards. Masts tall as stripped trees towered above his head. Brasswork and glass portholes gleamed and glittered in the lamplight. Male scents of salt and tar, of oil and warm resin, filled his nostrils; the smell of the seas. Jerome went down the rope-treaded stairs to the quay, and the frigate soared like a black wooden tower above him, timbers creaking sleepily in the gentle harbour swell.

The steward saluted. Jerome waved back to him and watched until the man was out of sight. Then Jerome took off his hat and wiped sweat from his forehead. What a pompous English fool that captain was! How could Jerome possibly entertain newspaper readers in New York with an account of a renegade English doctor and a drunken Scot killing natives on an unknown Eastern island? Blackman had told him something of infinitely greater value than a few facts for an article to be read and then discarded, matter only for a day. He now knew Gunn's next move; and he must translate this knowledge into power. Jerome climbed into his waiting doolie, and told the patient coolies brusquely: 'Grand Hotel'.

The hotel's name did more than justice to the white-clapboard building that stood wedged between the house of a Parsee money-lender and a shop selling paper scrolls and fireworks for mourners at Chinese funerals. But then, Jerome thought, his calling sometimes took him to strange places, to interview even stranger people. Now his visit had a special urgency because the man he wished to meet, could, like Lieutenant Blackman, help him on his way to wealth.

To look at, Abner Jones did not appear influential, but Jerome consoled himself with the thought that the rulers of some countries did not look the part when seen out of their fancy uniforms or swallow-tail coats. Jones was a stocky, thick-necked man of forty-five, a former mate from the United States ship *Bulwark*, swarthy faced, black-browed and with a strong Welsh accent. His old father still lived in Glamorgan, although he had not seen him for twenty years.

Jerome nodded with an interest he did not feel as Jones regurgitated stories of his youth. He had jumped a British freighter in Halifax and crossed the Canadian border to join the newly growing American Navy. Many of their non-commissioned officers were similar deserters, drawn by the prospect of better conditions and more pay.

Jones had immediately felt at home and had risen swiftly through the ranks to first mate. Then, when his ship docked in Macao, he had been put ashore with fever, secured his discharge and somehow had never been back to sea. He had discovered that an easier living than actually going to sea himself was to advise others about their voyages. He worked for various British and Chinese merchants in Macao, telling them, on the basis of his own experiences, how best to load their vessels; which cargoes should not be carried in the lowest holds, for they might catch fire if not allowed access to air, and so on. After a year, Jones had travelled to Singapore, and here he had remained for two more years, being helpful to visiting American captains, and drawing a monthly retainer from a Welsh merchant who was homesick for the valleys and the accent of his youth. Presumably Jones would now remain in Singapore, for he had just been appointed Honorary American Consul—an appointment that some merchants, who had enjoyed the benefits of a classical education, declared was the most unexpected promotion since Caligula had made his horse a consul.

'What brought you the distinction of representing our country here, sir?' Jerome inquired.

'My present position as Honorary Consul of the United States of America was, as you might say, pure chance,' Jones admitted immediately. 'I was playing dice with some American merchants, right here in this city. A Mr Silas Carter, who owns an important company, running regular clippers from Salem to Macao, which call here on their homeward journey, was of our company and at my table. We partnered to win—not a vast sum as the *taipans* would account it, but important enough to me. Several hundred dollars apiece, in fact.

'After the game, we shared a bottle of rye whisky which one of his captains had brought along, and Mr Carter was saying how he had long urged the American Government in Washington to appoint consuls in some of these distant parts, so that the needs and rights of our nationals could be zealously and honourably guarded.

'Why should the damn British and the Portuguese, or even the Frogs, have it all their own way out here? Can you tell me that, Mr Jerome? A handful of Europeans can create a monopoly of whatever they like, from sago to opium—even powdered rhino horn, as an aphrodisiac for these heathen Chinese who desire sexual connection to a demented degree. And before

73

you can look round, they are all *taipans* with great houses, and scores of servants.

'And, goddam' it, in the background they have the British Navy or a Dutch frigate or some other goddam' gunboat, always ready and willing to protect their interests and safeguard their profits.

'All Europeans are looked after by their own governments, directly or indirectly, but who the hell looks after us Americans when *we* trade?

'We are on our own. We have no Navy vessels here, apart from the occasional frigate on a visit, and not even diplomatic representation. If some Chinese throws a poxy British sailor into jail, there's hell to pay. Gunboats off the coast, threats of reparations and so forth. Did you hear what happened when a handful of drunken Limeys in Macao were watching a religious procession? No? Well, I will tell you. It was, of course, a Catholic procession, and these guys refused to remove their hats, as they were politely asked to do. They said they were not goddam' papists, and much else besides, and so the Portuguese arrested them for insulting behaviour, and quite right too.

'But a British warship happened to be in the bay for some regatta, and the sailors came ashore and beat up the city and released their countrymen from the jailhouse. The locals resented this and in consequence rioted against their supine rulers, who had allowed this to happen. As a result, the Portuguese Governor was murdered.'

'If an American had been arrested, he'd have been forced to pay his fine, however steep it was—simply because he had no other option,' agreed Jerome.

'Or maybe his friends would have had to go, cap in hand, to some English *taipan* and ask *him* to intercede on the man's behalf. That is humiliating and quite unnecessary. And when Mr Carter found I agreed with him, and that I had lived here and in Macao and also had served in American and British ships, he said he would propose me for the post. And I accepted at once. It is an honour that does not fall to many men to represent their country overseas, and I am sensible of its weight and importance.'

'But what are your qualifications, Mr Jones?'

'Much the same, sir, as yours in representing an American newspaper. I, too, can string words together. I have a presence. I am not afraid to speak my mind. And I am proud of my country.'

He paused and sipped the whisky, and then smiled engagingly.

'Further, sir, to be frank, I needed a job. Does that answer your question?'

'Perfectly,' replied Jerome. 'Now, sir, if I may address you man to man, and not as a subject for an article, would you be willing to advance your own personal prospects—allied to those of your country—in a manner which I feel could bring both wealth and honour to you, and to me *and* to the United States?'

Jones picked up the Glenlivet bottle, and poured out three more fingers into his glass before he replied. The room was hot and the pores around his nose shone with sweat. His eyes glowed small and hard like brown glass beads. Jerome watched him anxiously; a lot could depend on his reaction; nay, all could depend upon it. Had he phrased his question as best he could?

Jones sipped the whisky slowly and poured another draught.

'You are not the first person to make me such proposals and extravagant promises,' he said at last. 'But promises without performance are like bottles without bottoms. Useless. I know how merchants of other nationalities often wish to sail under the American flag for all kinds of reasons. Maybe they are British carrying contraband, and fear that if they sail under their own flag a British Naval ship will challenge them. Or they are Chinese and do not wish their own customs officials to examine their cargo with zeal. Or maybe they are simply pirates and want a flag to call their own, other than the Jolly Roger.

'If your proposition, Mr Jerome, is one of these, or allied to one of these, then, sir, say no more. I am not interested in prostituting my country's flag in such a fashion.'

'My proposition is neither spurious nor shifty, Mr Jones. It is to steal a march—in the commercial sense— on the English *taipans* whom we both dislike so strongly.'

Jerome paused deliberately, to add weight to his words, but Jones said nothing. He sat, eyes on the ceiling, watching lazy flies copulate and crawl across the whitewashed cornice.

'As Consul, and one formerly actively engaged in maritime matters,' Jerome continued, disappointed at Jones's lack of reaction, 'you will be aware, to a far greater extent than me, of the swiftly growing import-ance of steamships as opposed to sail. You will also be aware of the vital need to discover coal out here, because the fleet that commands coal in this area, can also command the seas, commercially and strategically. In this connection, I believe there is an island off Borneo, near Labuan, known as the Island of the Jade Gate, where coal may be dug.'

'I know the island well,' said Jones. 'Do you know, sir, the meaning of its name?'

'Pray enlighten me.'

'The Chinese have a delicate way of describing the cruder parts of the human anatomy. That part by which we mark our manhood they describe as The Turtle Head, or maybe in deference to our religion, The Bald-headed Monk, or, more poetically, The Jade Stem.

'The Jade Gate is the corresponding part of a woman's body, most sought after by men of all degree. When one views this island from the sea, as I have, there appear to be two mountains like breasts, which the Chinese poets refer to gracefully as the Domes of Happiness. Jade Gate is a richly wooded valley that lies between.

'From this the island takes its name. Hardly an explanation with which you could regale your more puritanical New York readers, but one not without amusement to old salts like myself, who have in our time entered many a jade gate and enjoyed the pleasures we found therein.'

Jones slapped his thigh and began to laugh; Jerome nodded dutifully.

'Now, sir,' he went on briskly. 'I believe that Gunn is going to this island to discover whether it is rich with coal. The Royal Navy has already sent a surveyor who reported against the presence of coal. He did not make a detailed examination inland, but confined his attentions to the coast, although he was specially advised by a Royal Navy captain that natives inland were burning what appeared to be coal.

'I propose, therefore, that you and I engage a vessel, with crew, and sail to this island and come to some privy arrangement ourselves with its ruler before Gunn can do so.

'You are the American Consul, so why not claim it in our country's name? Or offer to the ruler advantages in return for allowing us and no one else to prospect for coal. As Consul, you could approach a bank here and seek an advance of money for our expenses, to be set against future concessions to that bank once we secure the island. Or they could enjoy a share of our profits from selling the coal.'

'This is an ingenious and not unattractive proposal, Mr Jerome, but to return your compliment of frankness, sir, if you knew the state of my personal finances, you would not think highly of my success in persuading any banker to advance money on such a highly speculative proposition. Banks do not fashion their fortunes out of dreams, sir, but *facts*. Once the banks *know* coal is to be found, and they realize we hold the right to mine it, they will besiege us with offers to invest, and on our terms. But while our enterprise lacks certainty, unless we have sufficient money of our own to match theirs, I would not give much for our chances in persuading a bank here or even individual members of the mercantile community to advance us anything at all.'

'I have one thousand American dollars, Mr Jones, which I will put down as proof of my integrity and my belief in what I propose.'

78

'A noble sum, sir, for a private person travelling alone, but, with respect, only petty cash to men who can count their wealth in millions of pounds sterling.'

'You may be right, Mr Jones, but if our ancestors had not fought against the difficulties of locomotion on land and water and so invented the wheel and the boat, we should still be living like brutes. If you feel unable to approach a bank or rich individual, I will make it my business to interest one or other to the extent of several thousand dollars. Provided you can give me your solemn word I will have your help as American Consul in this venture?'

'What would you propose as my share for such an undertaking?' asked Jones thoughtfully.

'We cannot divide the cake, sir until we have baked it. I have someone else, a European, who has advised me already on this matter, and I must divide what I make with that person. But I will suggest that we all share equally.'

'You have no contract or binding agreement with this European person?'

'We have nothing more than an idea. We are all thus as rich or as poor as each other. Surely you would agree with me, sir, that we could easily draw up contracts heavy with seals and red ribbons and signatures of principals and witnesses. But if we lack goodwill and agreement among ourselves, these papers are worth no more than the red wax and the parchment on which some clerk has so laboriously scribbled in copperplate. Give me your hand, Mr Jones. That is my contract.'

'I will do that readily, but I would still like to see something in writing. Just to show—as a representative of the American Government—that I have something written to back up your proposal.'

'Then I will write you a letter myself and deliver it to you this evening.'

'Pray do that, sir,' said Jones, pouring himself another whisky. 'Pray do that. And then we can discuss this matter in greater detail, for I am interested in what you tell me. I will also make discreet inquiries of friends who knew the island well. Maybe they can enlighten us. Time spent on reconnaissance is seldom wasted, so I learned in the Navy. And if we are in opposition to Dr Gunn, then, believe me, sir, we have no time at all to waste.'

# CHAPTER FOUR

## *In which a woman wonders and Dr Gunn prepares to land*

IT WAS THAT HOUR of evening when the whole East trembled like a night-moth's wings on the edge of tropic dusk.

Already, lanterns were lit in vessels anchored in Singapore harbour, and new tall candles glowed in the burnished carriage lamps of the rich. One by one, dark windows in the new great houses behind the town were transformed into squares of amber glass as servants lit the lamps within. To Patricia Bankhausen, standing at the window of her hotel room, overlooking the busy street, watching coolies carrying lights balanced on the end of poles on their shoulders, the doolie carriers and sweetmeat-sellers with flares above their wooden stalls, it was as though a theatre stage was being prepared for some exciting gala performance.

The sight still moved her, although she had grown familiar with it over several months. How different from the chill of her dark, impersonal house in Harley Street, where London pea-souper fogs would unroll their damp sulphurous clouds along gas-lit streets, muting even the shrill sad cries of the street-traders and match-sellers!

Here, life throbbed at the speed of a young man's heart; even the food was spiced with fire, and every day blazed with sun. On most evenings there were dinner parties and dalliances, but of late she had been unable to quell a growing discontent, even for this easy, pleasurable existence. She had been obliged to abandon one life in London, where she had grown to be accepted as a society hostess, whose invitation to dine was little short of a command. Now she was simply one of Gunn's pensioners, never seeing him, but beholden to him for her keep.

True, she was a frequent guest at rich men's tables, but was this because they knew her as a friend—or former friend—of Robert Gunn, and they sought favours from him through her? She had also taken lovers, some older than herself, some younger, like Jerome. But while she had enjoyed their bodies, as they had delighted in hers, she did not command their love or even their respect.

And the more she considered her situation, the more blame she laid on the man whom she believed had brought her to it. She hated him, for he had been the catalyst of her disaster. And in hating Gunn, Patricia Bankhausen also began to hate herself for being weak and wanting him.

Gunn thus became both the focus and the personification of her discontent. If she had never met him, she would still be Lady Bankhausen, the wife of one of London's most eminent physicians. Some day, somehow, she would revenge herself on him.

Now this American, Jerome. Was he becoming a man of action or simply remaining a man of words, who could only chronicle the deeds of other men who had made fortunes, subdued natives, founded empires?

Jerome was not the man she would have chosen for the task of infiltrating Gunn's company and seizing a share of it, but he was the only candidate she could find in a hurry. And to be fair, he had discovered that Gunn was interested in exploring Jade Gate Island. Only that week she had used Jerome's knowledge at a dinner party when a boring guest next to her had explained how he was a British Admiralty surveyor, and had recently carried out long and arduous surveys in India, Burma, Malaya and Labuan, and now on this obscure and unimportant island.

'Why is it necessary, Mr Partridge,' she had asked him innocently, 'to make such dangerous journeys simply to dig holes in the ground? Do you seek gold or diamonds?'

Partridge patted his soft prune lips with his napkin and then turned to her before he answered.

'Something infinitely more valuable, ma'am,' he replied, and his eyes roamed over her full figure in her white satin underdress with wrought muslin petticoat and pink satin bodice. She could read his thoughts from his hot, sweating face, and she smiled inwardly. How incongruous that such an ugly insignificant man should be moved by the same fierce lusts as the most handsome and elegant, and even more strange that they imagined they could be equally attractive to women!

Mr Partridge probably maintained a drab and mousey wife somewhere in one of the newer suburbs, like Islington or Bayswater, with a couple of servants, and a governess for their children. He was a common little man, really, but out here, accoutred with elegance, with his host's servants standing like sentries behind each chair, he assumed an importance alien to him and out of all proportion to his talent or achievement.

All the lights in the dining room had been extinguished, and dishes filled with brandy and salt were placed in the centre of the table and lit. These gave off hazy blue flames, so that the faces around the table became grotesque caricatures, with the faint ethereal light emphasizing their worst features: small eyes, set close together; greedy, predatory noses; thick, fleshy lips.

Mr Partridge's mundane voice brought her back to reality.

'We seek coal, ma'am.'

'But why coal, Mr Partridge? Surely we mine enough of that in Yorkshire and in Wales?'

'Indeed we do, ma'am—for our own needs and for the needs of many nations overseas. But the Royal Navy is going over from centuries of sail to a new form of propulsion—steam engines—and just as the new railway locomotives in England need coal, so will our new ships. Can you imagine the mountains of coal that must be transported below decks—and sometimes even above them, literally floating slag heaps—in order to keep that vessel's engines at full steam? And each ton of coal carried means that the ship can carry a ton less of armaments or stores or cargo. Even our largest naval ships like the *Endymion* only bear enough coal to steam hard for eight days.

'If we can find indigenous sources of coal near the centre of our mercantile and naval interests, then we can free that space, either for commercial cargo or more warlike material—and also release our ships' captains from being tied to little more than a week away from port at a time.'

'But there is no coal on Jade Gate Island?'

'*I* found none, ma'am. Indeed, I found it a most inhospitable place. The natives were far from friendly, although we had a naval party armed with muskets and cutlasses who stood constant guard. Altogether, a most disagreeable experience. I was glad to be away. I had the feeling that the forest, which crept down almost to the edge of the sea, was full of unfriendly eyes.

'There were certain vestigial traces of coal, of course, as frequently there are. Indeed, I have examined areas confidently claimed to be full of gold, and only discovered thin veins which could not conceivably be worked in any commercial sense.'

'Assuming that someone—say an English adventurer, of whom there seem to be many in these parts—found quantities of coal in this latitude, then the discovery would be of value to him?'

'Of far greater value, ma'am, than if he found an island of solid gold. For gold can only be allowed on the market in limited quantities or its value speedily becomes debased. Gold can be used to bolster a country's currency or to make ear-rings for a lovely woman, but its worth must diminish as more is mined, for gold is highly regarded simply because it is so scarce.

'Where coal is concerned, a month's output from a huge mine can easily be burned away in days by Royal Navy vessels in these waters. And then consider the other ships of every nation that would call regularly to replenish their stocks.

'A man who could discover coal on any island out here has assured himself and his descendants of an inestimable fortune with the first piece he digs from the earth.'

She remembered the scene now. The blue flames, the faces polished with perspiration, despite the punkahs pulled by silent bearers; servants waiting silently against the walls like a living tapestry; the glitter of silver and the ruby glow of wine in glasses. She knew then inside her that Mr Partridge had somehow made a mistake in Jade Gate Island. He had been afraid to stay and make more than preliminary investigations. He had dug a few little holes, and then scuttled away to safety like a crab to write his report for superiors to file and forget in some wooden pigeon-hole in the Admiralty.

Gunn must have better Intelligence, or else he had somehow guessed, with that extraordinary sense he possessed, that the island was rich in coal.

Now Gunn's vessel had sailed for Jade Gate, while Jerome and this other common fellow, Jones, this so-called American Consul, were trying to hire a ship of their own, still lacking help from any bank. No one in Gunn's office knew the date for the doctor's return, but then no one ever did, for Gunn was a man on his own, owing allegiance and loyalty and love to no one. He did as he wished, when he wished, as he wished. Would that he were here with her now to do with her as she wished!

Patricia's hands tightened and her polished nails dug into palms damp with sweat and longing. How ironical it was, that although their lives and bodies had touched but briefly, she remembered him, would always remember him with this strange, consuming amalgam of hate

86

and need; and possibly most of all, with genuine admiration.

As she stood, the night came alive with the familiar tropical noises of the dark; the croak of frogs, the whir of crickets and cicadas. There was an Italian legend about them that she recalled hearing at one of her dinner parties in London. Cicadas were really the souls of poets, long dead, who could not keep silence because, when they were alive, they had never written the poems they really wanted to write. Now their spirit voices spoke, and spoke to her. *We are dead a long time, and we have no second chance to do what we should do now.*

The thought somehow comforted her, and strengthened her resolve. She would not be like those mythical poets; she would do now what she wished to do, or go down in silence and without regret; at least, she would have tried.

Outside, the cicadas whirred on.

\*     \*     \*

Gunn raised the glass to his right eye and scanned the island carefully. Jade Gate lay like a huge green sea-camel, with two humps. A thin white line of surf broke on the head, and beyond this the valley ran to the sea, lined with trees. Some palms and banyans sheltered half a dozen bamboo huts, and spirals of blue woodsmoke drifted up from cooking fires.

Gunn lowered his glass, disappointed in the island's very ordinary appearance; he had expected something altogether more subtle and seductive to live up to its name. If the gardens of the eighteenth-century baronet Sir Francis Dashwood could be delicately laid out in

High Wycombe in the form of a woman's body, with mounds and bushes and peaks, what could one not reasonably expect from an entire island which the Chinese had named after one part of the female form?

'There she lies, gentleman,' he announced. 'If the Royal Navy surveyor is correct, then Jade Gate is a useless island, peopled by Dyaks, head hunters and probably cannibals.

'If, on the other hand, coal exists on it and can be extracted, this island will be one of the most valuable in the East. And not only to us, as traders, but also to our country and to all other maritime nations, whose steamers could coal here on their way back to North America and Europe.'

'But first, we have to find the coal,' pointed out Mac-Pherson practically. 'And I have no abundance of confidence that we will. These naval people are, in my experience, generally thorough.'

'No doubt you are right,' said Gunn. 'But it is also your experience—as it is mine—that a man working for his own profit and advancement does a more thorough job than someone simply hired by a government department, without any personal interest or consideration in the outcome. What do you say, sir?'

He turned to the third man on the afterdeck, a tall sallow-faced Midlander, Josiah Castle, the geologist he had brought with him from Singapore.

'I feel you have a strong point there, Dr Gunn,' Castle admitted. Gunn had promised him two hundred golden guineas for his services, with as much again if he could locate coal in commercial quantities.

He was a quiet man, of middle height, not given to

much conversation, preferring his own company in his cabin, and Gunn had been fortunate in securing his services. Indeed, as he regarded Castle now, in white linen shirt, pepper-and-salt trousers and high black leather boots, glass raised to his eye, scanning the distant shore intently, Gunn thought it almost providential how they had met.

Lin Yang, his personal clerk, had sought an audience with him one afternoon before the office was closing.

'I have written all your letters, tuan,' he began almost apologetically, 'and so I know your intentions about Jade Gate Island. Might I have the honour of introducing to you someone of your own race who, in my most humble and unworthy opinion, could help you in your search?'

'Who is he?' asked Gunn. He valued Lin Yang's opinion, for Lin Yang was a hard-working man. He had many children to support, and nothing was ever too much trouble for him; he arrived early each morning, and invariably he stayed last in the office.

'An Englishman, tuan, who was lately with James Brooke in his vessel, *Royalist*. I understand from his servant, who is my second cousin, that he was ill of scurvy and put ashore here to be restored to health.

'He is skilled in the art of discovering what riches the earth contains. My cousin tells me that in his hotel room this man keeps whole tea chests filled with strange rocks that glitter as though they contain glass. Some shine blue in the light and others green. He is a learned man, tuan, who has made a study of these matters. Could he not also help you to find whether coal exists on Jade Gate?'

'It is possible. How is this man employed in Singapore?'

'He waits for the *Royalist* to call in three weeks' time, when once more he hopes to join the White Rajah in Sarawak and continue with his work for him, searching for I know not what.'

'Please be so good as to speak to your cousin and ask this gentleman to call upon me.'

Gunn opened a locked drawer in his desk for which he alone held the key. He opened another box inside, took out six gold sovereigns and gave them to Lin Yang.

'This is for your interest,' he told him. 'There will be as many more if we engage this gentleman and he proves his worth.'

Lin Yang stood for a moment, holding the coins in his open palm. He looked down at them and then up at Gunn. His lips moved as though he wished to say something, then he bowed his thanks, backed away to the door and left the room.

That was the last time I saw him, thought Gunn now, remembering Lin Yang's strange reluctance to leave. Two days later, his body had been found floating in the harbour, eyes picked out by fish, fingers nibbled away, the corpse only recognizable by a leather belt that had his name branded inside, and M-G on the buckle. Curiously, the six gold coins he had paid the clerk were still in his linen purse, so he could not have been killed for its contents.

Maybe he had aroused the enmity of one of the Chinese secret societies that flourished in Singapore? Or he might have been killed simply because he knew someone else guilty of this offence, for by the harsh rules of these Tongs, if a member could not avenge an evil deed on the person responsible for it, he should avenge it on the perpetrator's friend, rather than let it go unpunished. Perhaps Lin Yang had wished to seek Gunn's advice, or even his protection, when he had paused before leaving the room? Perhaps so many things; so many questions that presumably would never now be answered. Gunn made a note to check that Lin Yang's successor had carried out his orders, that Lin Yang's widow and family were to receive an adequate pension.

Anyway, this fellow Castle, whom Lin Yang had introduced, seemed extremely competent. He was an acquaintance of Mr Partridge, the Navy surveyor. Well, very soon now, they should all know whether Mr Partridge's opinion was justified.

Captain Fernandes approached Gunn. 'I have ordered the longboat for six in the morning, sir.'

'Good.'

Gunn turned to Castle.

'You have your shovels and axes and all other equipment you feel will be necessary?'

'I have, doctor. Initially, I will use an auger, which I can screw into the earth. This is hollow and will extract a cross-section of the layers of soil and other strata that will be forced up inside it. I have studied maps of the island, such as they are, and propose we first go inland just beyond the sandy part of the shore, which could be the most promising area to commence operations.

'Then we can make our arrival known to whatever savages are in control, give them trinkets you have brought to show we come in peace and as friends, and begin to dig.

'I suggest we return to this vessel every evening before dusk, in preference to making camp there, since the real nature of these inhabitants will be entirely unknown to us, and we would therefore be unwise to trust ourselves to them after dark.'

'I agree,' said Gunn approvingly. 'The longboat can wait off shore for us until we are certain we will be received in a civil fashion. If we meet opposition, the crew can cover our retreat with muskets, although I do not expect the natives will be other than cautious and friendly. After all, so far as I am aware, they have not yet met any Europeans whose behaviour could dispose them against white people. Let us endeavour to do nothing to alter that amiable state of affairs.'

*      *      *

Bonnarjee lay on a rattan mat in the longhouse, three hundred yards from the breaking waves. Mosquitoes hummed and whined around him incessantly. Pressing in on the walls of his hut from the darkness outside, the ceaseless noises of night—the hoarse croak of marsh frogs, the whir of unseen insect wings, the rustle of creeping things in the dry warm undergrowth—accentuated his loneliness. He was surrounded by life in a milliard forms, but his mind was consumed with images of violent death.

The room was lit through a small woven wick supported by a hollow metal disc floating in a brass bowl of oil. Its feeble glow barely illuminated the rich dark carpets that hung on the walls, or the shrivelled blackened heads crowned by wisps of brittle hair which proved the house belonged to a man of consequence who had killed, and so must be respected. These trophies and badges of achievement appeared more sinister because they could only be seen indistinctly.

Bonnarjee shivered slightly beneath the ageless, eye-less sockets. What thoughts had once burned behind that wizened, blackened flesh? Had the brains these skulls shielded ever plotted the downfall of another—as he was plotting now? If so, where had they failed? How had his absent host overcome their machinations?

To one side of the rafters three logs were suspended by strips of pliant cane. The first was thick as his thigh, the second was smaller and the third barely an inch and a half thick. A chisel was on a shelf nearby, and every time one of the Sultan's family came into the room, they picked up this chisel and, in a kind of automatic action, shaved off some slivers of wood. Each log had a hole bored through its centre and this was smoothed by running a strip of cane back and forwards down the hole.

Bonnarjee knew that these logs were half-finished blow-pipes, and, after months of such casual efforts, they would be ready for use. These pipes had been begun long before he had become interested in Jade Gate, and work on them would continue long after he had left the island. Something here disturbed him; he could not quite say what. Maybe it was a reminder of the permanence of craftsmanship, compared with the transitoriness of the human condition.

Bonnarjee prided himself on being a man of peace, a stranger to fighting and all physical assault. But while his plump hand would never wield the dagger or the club, his cunning was behind every blow struck in his interest. His money meant he could pay others to do the deeds that sometimes, however regrettably, needed to be done, so that his business might prosper. Not infrequently, this could involve a death; a body dumped in the sea, a knifing in a stinking back-alley in Macao or Singapore, where prowling cats and starving dogs would lick blood from the victim's wounds and beggars would strip whatever trinkets his assassins had left on the corpse. This violence at second-hand, this pain and death unseen, was reported to him in his sumptuous home as he sipped a glass of mint tea under the discreet punkahs. Thus he never felt personally involved; his conscience was clear and his sleep unsullied, for blood was always on other men's hands, never on his.

Such events were therefore as remote to him as coins in his counting house were separated from the clerks who totted them up. After all, he told himself, not for the first time, as he lay alone on this hard floor, a death or a birth is but a debit or an entry in some celestial account. He had once celebrated a birth, and then he had learned that his seed did not run in the body of his son. The boy's bones, his blood, were not his, but grown from the act of the English merchant, Robert Gunn.

The thought nagged at him, and like a thorn in his foot, he could never be free of its pain. Now Gunn would pay with his life and his fortune. Within weeks, nay, within days, it would be as though Mandarin-Gold had never existed. And Gunn's memory would be as a hole dug in deep water.

Bonnarjee put out his right hand and rang a small brass bell. A servant climbed up the notched pole that acted as a stair from the ground outside, and bowed. The air in the room hung heavy with cheroot smoke and sweet scent; the servant was contemptuous of his master, but he feared Bonnarjee's petulant temper, his sudden vicious bursts of anger, and so stood like a mute creature.

'What is the hour?' Bonnarjee asked him curtly.

'Midnight, master.'

'Is there any life aboard the vessel *Hesperides*?'

'Nothing new to report, master. We are keeping the vessel under constant watch. As you already know, lights in the main cabins went out about three hours ago.'

'Then they are retired early, so that they can land early?'

The man inclined his head, neither agreeing nor disagreeing. Bonnarjee pulled his lower lip as another thought stung him. Could that creature Gunn have a woman out there? Might he not be mounting her in the darkness, tearing into her soft sensual body to slake the burning heat of his lust? The thought burned into his brain like a branding iron. How he hated the man! He ground his teeth together to force the thought of him, even the name of him, from his mind.

'Is there anything else, master?'

'Nothing,' said Bonnarjee quietly. For how could he begin to explain to this creature, this senseless being, this brute in the form of a man, that so far as he was concerned there was everything?

When Bonnarjee had learned from Lin Yang that Gunn planned to explore Jade Gate Island, he had immediately consulted his father-in-law, who was visiting Singapore from his home in Macao. Bonnarjee could not bring himself to mention what he had also heard about his father-in-law's involvement with Gunn; this was not the moment for such an admission, which would be painful and embarrassing to them both. The moment to mention that matter would be when Gunn had been destroyed.

His father-in-law, although old in years, was still alert in mind, sharp as a leather-honed blade. He immediately understood the importance of thwarting Gunn and if possible at the same time securing the coal for their own company.

Anything that could cut down so serious a rival was obviously a first charge on their resources.

His father-in-law had immediately sent for a Chinese contractor of his acquaintance, one Tu Sung, whose services he had often called upon in the past, and never in vain. Bonnarjee remembered their meeting with distaste. Tu Sung aped the Chinese aristocracy, deliberately wearing his nails long to show he did no manual work, walking with a stoop as though he were a scholar, bent-backed after hours over his books. But he was at heart a crude, cunning bully to whom Bonnarjee took an instant, animal dislike, because he feared him.

Ostensibly, Tu Sung contracted to dig drains, or to build walls, to repair roads and excavate pits. For these purposes, he employed a cohort of Chinese labourers. Many were ex-convicts, condemned to this wearying life of drudgery because no other employer dared to trust them; others were unwanted sons, sold by their families into Tu Sung's bondage when they were boys. It was known also that these hard men comprised his private army; they could be hired to enforce a promise or to collect a difficult debt from a man who might hold himself above the law.

Bonnarjee's father-in-law had been implicit in his instructions to Tu Sung, treating him with politeness but as an inferior.

'It is my wish that you take a group of your labourers

96

to Jade Gate Island aboard a junk. There, you will set them digging in places my son will mark out for you.'

'As always, your whim is my instruction, your thought is my command,' Tu Sung replied. 'Great is my personal happiness in working for you again, as I have so frequently been favoured by your honoured instructions in the past. But I need to know one thing. Tell me, master, what do you seek to find?'

'That is our concern, Tu Sung. Yours is but to dig the holes. The master does not tell the hireling the reason for his orders. It is enough that he wishes them to be carried out.'

'Pray do not think that vulgar curiosity prompts my question, master. I only ask so that I may know what type of spades may best serve your noble interests.'

'Take what equipment is required to dig deep but narrow holes. Not wide pits, or trenches. That is enough for you to know. And do not speak of this to anyone. Only you and my son-in-law and I are aware of this commission. My lips and his are locked. For us, it is as though the reason does not exist. See that you also keep silent about the matter.'

'My tongue shall be as a broken bell, and utter no sound whatever,' promised Tu Sung, inwardly deciding to treble his original price for the work. This vile Parsee and his fat capon-like son must know that a fortune was buried on Jade Gate Island, or surely they would not insist on such secrecy?

'If anyone does learn of our plans, Tu Sung, we shall know that you have told them,' said Bonnarjee warningly, and was instantly surprised that he had spoken his thoughts aloud. His revulsion at Tu Sung had somehow forced the words from his mouth. Tu Sung turned and looked at him, his eyes cold as stones; it was as though he was seeing him for the first time. Bonnarjee's stomach knotted like rope at the look, and he feared him all the more, because now he realized that Tu Sung guessed he was afraid, that he did not trust him.

Bonnarjee's father-in-law looked at him angrily, too; he should not have interrupted a discussion between older men. Now, as Bonnarjee remembered his shame, his face burned anew with mortification. And worse, his flesh crawled with fear at what might happen if something went wrong, if Tu Sung should suddenly challenge his authority on the island. Bonnarjee lacked the hardness and power of his father-in-law. He had not made his first fortune himself, like the old man; he had only married the old man's daughter, and he guessed that Tu Sung despised him. Also, Tu Sung's army of coolies easily outnumbered Bonnarjee and his few servants. And there was something else; the difference in character between the two men. If Tu Sung had been numerically outnumbered, he possessed strength of will and muscle that would never voluntarily surrender. He might be beaten, but he would never give in.

Bonnarjee lacked this essential quality of courage as he lacked the ability to get his wife with child. He had other abilities; he could drive a hard bargain and wring the last fraction of profit from a deal. But this was only one attribute of a man; there were others more important. Bonnarjee liked to think of himself as a golden man. But was he really just a golden eunuch?

# CHAPTER FIVE

## *In which a landing is made, with unexpected results*

THE LONGBOAT'S BOW, white as newly laundered linen, and bearing the red and gold markings of Gunn's company, slid up the sand through the clear and shallow sea. Four barefoot sailors leapt out expertly on either side and held her firm. Gunn, MacPherson and Castle climbed out more slowly and began to walk up the beach.

The sand felt soft, like finely sifted flour. They sank into it over their ankles with each step, thankful that their supple leather boots came up just below their knees. They were deliberately unarmed. Captain Fernandes had concealed loaded pistols and cutlasses beneath a tarpaulin in the longboat, and Gunn had left them there. It would not do for the natives to imagine that they were a raiding or marauding party, when they came on a genuinely peaceful mission.

Gunn carried a whistle on a lanyard, to blow in an emergency, to signal the longboat crew to seize the arms and rush to their assistance. He also carried a green canvas bag full of metal bracelets, and a cheap German clock that ticked like an angry imprisoned insect. MacPherson wore a silver flask of whisky strapped to his belt.

A wide-brimmed straw hat shaded his face; he hated the sun on his skin for, with his red hair, it invariably burned him badly. Castle carried an auger, a long thick varnished cane with a polished brass thread at the bottom and a T-shaped handle at the top. The crew had packed shovels and picks in the longboat to use if they were needed, but Gunn felt it unwise and unnecessary to arrive carrying these implements, in case the natives imagined they were weapons of attack.

As he reached the rim of the jungle that had marched to within yards of the sea he saw the delicate pigeon orchids cascading like a waterfall of white blossom from the trunks of the trees. A dark figure stepped out from between the thick fleshy leaves. He carried a polished sharpened stick in one hand. Bright metal ear-rings, a necklace of shark's teeth, and hammered brass bangles around his ankles, marked him as a warrior, possibly a man of high degree. Gunn stopped, bowed, and held out his right hand to show he came unarmed. The native did not move.

'I am here on a mission of peace,' Gunn began in Malay. 'You understand me as I speak?'

The man nodded.

'I understand, tuan,' he replied in the same language.

'I have brought presents for you, for your wife, your children and your friends,' said Gunn, and gestured back towards the longboat, where the sailors waited.

'Why have you brought us gifts when we are quite unknown to you—as you are to us? What is it that you seek from us in return?'

This reply surprised Gunn. He had expected an hour of mutual compliments and expressions of esteem, followed by a detailed, even critical examination of his gifts. Then there would be a ceremonial drinking of lemon tea or fermented coconut milk before the object of their visit was mentioned, and even then it would be touched on delicately and with deliberate casualness. Haste was a stranger to the East; only the basely born would reach the core of the discussion at once. And this man did not bear himself like a slave, but as a leader.

'I seek your permission to dig some holes in the sand,' Gunn replied.

'And for this alone you have sailed in your great ship to our small island? What do you seek to find in the sand, tuan, that you could not discover nearer home?'

'We wish to examine the quality of the earth beneath the sand.'

'How could that be important to you?'

'In my country,' replied Gunn, 'we have wise men learned in many matters, not only regarding birds and beasts and fish, but also in different kinds of soil. They calculate what crops grow best in them and what elements they may contain. It is to add to their knowledge that I have sailed here from Singapore, the Island of the Lion.'

'Your mission seems worthless to me, tuan, but then white men's ways are not our ways, so what may seem important to you need not arouse envy in my heart.'

'Then we have your permission to begin?'

'Mine, yes. But I am only one of several princes here. You must also obtain permission from the elders. I will lead you to them. It is for them to say "yea" or "nay".'

'We are making progress, doctor,' said MacPherson approvingly, grateful for the shade of the thick plantain leaves, as they began to walk forward along the faintly marked track.

'I am not certain that we are,' replied Gunn thoughtfully. 'This fellow has an insolent air. And he has not even asked to see our gifts. That to me is very unusual.'

'To many, our whole way of life would seem odd, did they but know of it,' said MacPherson philosophically.

The native led them in the strange local way, not by looking at any track or at landmarks, but by observing the tops of the trees. Each top had its own distinctive shape which he could recognize. The only trees Gunn could identify were camphors, through their smell and long tall trunks, which soared up smoothly for a hundred or more feet before they put out their branches.

He wondered how far they would have to walk. The humidity beneath these tall trees was oppressive; the air felt damp and warm, like steam from one of Mr Bridges' engines.

A sudden cry made him turn. Huge leaves flapped about them like green wings. Castle was staggering in a circle behind them, crashing blindly into clumps of young bamboos, reeling back, hands out, grasping for support.

He fell heavily on the matted floor of the jungle and lay, moaning and writhing in pain.

'What is the matter? Are you bitten by a snake?' asked MacPherson urgently, kneeling down beside him.

'No. It is my ankle. I have twisted it. I caught my foot in a creeper. These confounded things are everywhere. I beg you, watch out for them.'

'Have you broken a bone?' Gunn asked, and made as if to remove the surveyor's boot.

'No!' shouted Castle hoarsely, his face contorted like a gargoyle in his agony. 'I beg of you. Do not touch my boot.'

'Can you move the foot?'

'Barely.'

Castle's voice was only a whisper now; veins in his forehead had knotted like great blue ropes just beneath his skin. His lips were drawn back over his teeth as though he could barely endure the pain.

'I have no laudanum here to ease your suffering,' Gunn told him. 'But my chest of medicines is aboard *Hesperides*. Let us carry you back to the longboat. I will accompany you to our vessel.'

'I beg of you, leave me here. Do not prejudice your whole enterprise because of me.'

'We most certainly will not abandon you, and you cannot possibly make your own way to the shore.'

Gunn turned to the native.

'How far away are the elders?'

The man stood looking down with contempt at Castle on the ground.

'Only a matter of paces, tuan,' he replied. 'This person will come to no harm in this place. We can send some of my people to lift him and bring him after us.'

'We will go on then,' Gunn told Castle. 'But only in order to arrange a litter for you, so that you can be borne more comfortably to the longboat.'

From the surveyor's agony, Gunn considered that he could have broken his ankle instead of simply spraining it, but he did not voice his thought. Beads of sweat dripped from Castle's brow. He lay back slowly and carefully on the ground, and closed his eyes. A few flies

103

buzzed around his nostrils, and at the corners of his mouth, but he paid them no heed.

'This is very bad joss,' said MacPherson gravely, concerned at Castle's condition. Joss was a corruption of *deos*, the Portuguese word for God, and loosely applied to mean good or bad luck. MacPherson had known other men fall down and apparently give up the ghost under minor complaints that in England would pass unnoticed. Years in a hot, humid climate had eroded their constitution, and constant drinking had weakened them, just as termites and worms bored into bamboo from within, without giving any outward sign.

Gunn nodded.

'But we will have him patched up directly, once we can return to the ship. Now, to our task ahead.'

They marched on, and soon the trees thinned, and they were in a small clearing, surrounded by stumps of once-tall trunks. A huge longhouse dominated the square. A wood fire had been burning outside it and had dwindled to a mound of red ash. Over the embers, a beaten metal cooking pot was suspended from a tripod of three nibong palm trunks.

'If you will wait, tuan, I will fetch the elders,' said their guide.

'I would also appreciate it, if you could ask your people to fashion a bier on which we—or they—can carry our comrade back to the shore. I will reward them richly for speedy work.'

The man nodded briefly, as though this matter was of little consequence to him. He walked to the longhouse and called up to the open door. Two men, barefoot and dressed like him in loin cloths, wearing bright brass rings at their ankles and wrists, came tinkling like bells down the notched tree, followed by a smaller plump man in a white dhoti edged with gold.

He might have been a Roman in a toga, thought Gunn; there was something imperious and cruel about him. Could he be the sultan, or the senior elder? This man's face was the colour of creamy coffee, and his oiled and scented hair shone like new tar. He approached Gunn, who bowed and held out his right hand in greeting. The man made no motion to shake it.

'I have come on a mission from the sea,' Gunn began gravely, 'which I have already explained to your colleague here. I seek your agreement to make a small investigation into the nature of the soil on this island, so that learned men in my country can write the know-ledge they discover in their books, and so benefit us all.'

The small plump man looked up at him malevolently; his eyes were heavy-lidded like a serpent. Naked hatred burned in the intensity of his gaze.

'I will reply to you in your own language, Dr Gunn,' the man said in English. 'You come here for no scientific purpose whatever. You are not concerned with what learned men in your country write in their books. The only books that interest you are the books that list your company's profits. And it is to add to these profits, not to the sum of scientific knowledge, that you have sailed here.

'You have come to dig for coal so that your new steam-ships can be more speedily and more cheaply fuelled than those of your competitors. You have come so that your navy will enjoy a similar superiority over the navies of other countries. So that more power and glory will accrue to your Empire, and more gold to the treasuries of your country and your company.'

'You speak my language very well,' replied Gunn, surprised by being addressed in English almost as much as by what the man said—and the astonishing fact that he even knew his name. 'Also, you speak the same language of directness with regard to my business affairs.

'I *do* seek a source of coal, and, of course, I intend to enter into solemn agreement with you or with the other elders of this island, or the paramount sultan, if such there is, so that all may benefit—if indeed there is coal to be found here.

'But before we discuss this matter further, I would beg that you instruct craftsmen to fashion a bier from bamboos so that we can carry back to our vessel a third member of our party who has seriously injured his leg. We have had to abandon him on the way, because he could not walk.'

Bonnarjee smiled.

'I think you may assume that he has already made his own way back to your ship.'

'That is impossible, sir. I am a physician, and from the pain he was suffering, the poor fellow was scarcely able to speak, let alone walk.'

'Were I unwell, with you as my physician, Dr Gunn, then I would be wise to seek another opinion. That man is as able to walk as you or I. The only pain he bears is in the thought that you are rich and he is not. But even that will soon be adjusted. And at this moment, he enjoys one infinite advantage over you, that you may not quite appreciate.'

Bonnarjee snapped the fingers of one hand as he

spoke, and, on the signal four natives, who had been creeping up behind Gunn and MacPherson, their bare feet making no sound in the soft, powdered dust, suddenly seized them. They gripped them at the wrists and behind their elbows so that neither could move without the risk of breaking an arm.

'Is this how you treat visitors who come here to discuss matters of concern to you as well as to them?' asked Gunn, wincing with the pain. Bonnarjee spat at him. The phlegm ran greenly down Gunn's cheek on to the collar of his shirt.

'This is how we treat dogs of Englishmen, defilers of other men's wives, corrupters of our cousins in China.'

'I do not understand your meaning, sir. You have the advantage of knowing my name and my business, while to the best of my knowledge I have never seen you before. What is the reason for your insults and this rough greeting?'

'The reason, doctor, is one you have no doubt forgotten in the midst of other lusts and conquests, and so I will remind you. Do you remember getting with child the daughter of a Parsee merchant in Macao nine or ten years ago, when you had but recently arrived in the East?'

'I do,' admitted Gunn. How could he ever forget? From this act of love stemmed his whole success: his clipper fleet, his factories, his offices in Macao, on Hong Kong island, in Singapore and Calcutta. 'I remember.'

'So do I. Every waking moment of my life and in my sleep, too. Especially in my sleep.'

Bonnarjee hit Gunn across the face, a slack punch that drew blood, splitting the doctor's lip.

107

'I will give you cause never to forget it,' went on Bonnarjee bitterly. 'She was and is my wife. The boy I called my son is not my son at all, but yours.'

'I was young and she was lovely,' said Gunn quietly. 'I was new to the ways of the East, and to the ways of women. I can understand how you must feel, and I apologize for the pain I have unwittingly caused you.'

Bonnarjee hit him again, harder this time.

'You have come here too late,' he said, his voice clotted with rage and hatred. 'Like your insincere words of sorrow and regret, your journey is empty, without purpose or truth. I have conducted my own surveys here while you were still on your way. I am satisfied that the extent of coal on this island is enormous.'

'In that case,' said Gunn, 'can we not come to some arrangement whereby my vessels could transport it? Maybe my company could also assist in marketing it. Call off these ruffians, and let us talk like mature men of affairs.'

'Your vessels will certainly carry the coal, Dr Gunn,' agreed Bonnarjee, smiling now for the first time. 'But they will not fly your flag when they do so. They will fly mine. For I will own them, and with them I will possess every ounce of gold in your treasury, every credit in your banks.

'For all of us comes the hour when life is at an end, when our brief day approaches night and the eternal darkness we call death. You stand now at that moment. You are finished, Dr Gunn. As a merchant and as a man.'

\*　　　\*　　　\*

Captain Fernandes lit a cheroot, flicked the lucifer far over the edge of the deck, and watched it float away on the translucent sea. The water was so clear he could see shoals of pink and golden fish, fins fluttering like gaudy feathers, dart over buried seaweed trees and coral caverns. He exhaled the rich smoke and leaned on the wooden rail, enjoying his leisure, listening to the shouts and snatches of song from barefoot sailors as they scrubbed the decks and polished the ship's brasswork.

*Hesperides*, as Gunn's flagship, was always the smartest in his fleet. Fernandes was proud of her and of his crew, and also of his own position as captain. For a Goanese, half Portuguese, half Indian, he had prospered exceedingly, and most important, in a job he loved. He glanced now towards the shore, wondering how Gunn and Castle and MacPherson were faring. He saw, without much interest, half a dozen native canoes coming towards him, water glistening like glass on their long bamboo paddles. He called down to the first officer.

'Allow no one aboard until I give the order. But on no account will anyone show these natives any active discourtesy.'

'Aye, aye, sir.'

Fernandes focused his glass on the leading canoe. It was carved from a huge tree trunk and the bows were daubed with bright red and blue paint. A white man crouched in the stern of the tiny craft, waving furiously to him. As the canoe approached, Fernandes recognized Josiah Castle, the surveyor. What the devil had happened? Why was he coming back? Fernandes snuffed out his cheroot and hurried down the companionway, and waited by the white landing steps. The canoe drew alongside. Castle called up to him, cupping both hands to his mouth.

'Permission to come aboard, captain?'

'Of course. But only you for the moment. What brings you back here so soon?'

'Dr Gunn has sent me. He is making speedy progress with his negotiations and is eager to show friendship. Since these natives appear anxious to sell us fresh fruit, he deemed it wise to ask you to allow them aboard so that they can spread out their mats to display their plantains, melons and yams.'

'Let them come aboard,' said Fernandes. He turned to the first officer.

'Line up the crew on the after-deck to buy what fruit they will.'

'Are any women among these natives, sir?'

'I know not. But if there are, they must not be allowed below decks. They will probably carry the pox. Or if they do not bring it, some of our crew will doubtless give it to them to take away.'

'Very good, sir.'

The natives came up on deck, chattering excitedly among themselves, pointing in astonishment at the pipe-clayed ropes, the painted rails and high, varnished superstructure. Some carried rolled rattan mats to spread on the deck, edge to edge. Others bore huge bunches of bananas or giant melons, paw-paw, and yams. The crew gathered around, bartering. A twist of Virginia tobacco for so many yams; ten beads and a piece of thread for an armful of bananas; a walnut shell whittled into a face for half a dozen melons.

As the other canoes arrived, more natives came up

the gangway and waited patiently for their comrades to sell their produce. The first man to sell all his fruit rolled up his mat, and bowed deeply to Captain Fernandes as though to take his leave. As he straightened up, he suddenly flung both arms into the air and uttered an enormous yell. At this, all the newcomers threw away their rolled-up mats. In their hands they held sharpened swords. Too late, Fernandes realized how he had been tricked; the mats had been wrapped around these weapons to conceal them. These men were not native traders; his ship was alive with pirates.

Fernandes punched the nearest man out of his way, raced up to the wheelhouse, and kicked in the door of the emergency arms locker. As he seized the two pistols he always kept there, ready primed, a pirate leapt at him, scimitar flickering above his head, like a silver crescent in the sky. Fernandes fired. The man's face disintegrated in a mass of bloodied pulp; he sank to his knees and collapsed at Fernandes's feet. The captain flung away the now useless pistol, seized two swords from the locker and shouted a warning to Castle.

'Protect yourself, man! We've been boarded by pirates.'

But Castle remained leaning against the rail, smiling at him sardonically. Fernandes was astonished. Did Castle not realize the danger? Could he not hear him?

Fernandes flung a sword to him. The fellow was probably unarmed, a man of peace, and unacquainted with the rough fierce ways of the East. The flat side of the blade hit Castle in the chest. He made no attempt to grab the hilt; the sword clattered down on to the deck. Castle glanced at it indifferently, and then up at

Fernandes, who was still shouting to him. Slowly, Castle bent down, picked up the sword and held it away from his body as though it was distasteful to him. Then he deliberately tossed it backwards over his shoulder and into the sea.

'You are the pirates, you and Gunn and MacPherson!' Castle shouted back to the captain. 'These natives will pay you in your own coin. If you surrender your vessel now, I will give you my word you will not be harmed. I have no quarrel with you. Like me, you are only one of Gunn's hirelings. But if you refuse, Fernandes, or continue to fight in this futile fashion, I cannot help you. What is your answer, captain?'

'Damn your guts, Castle, that's my answer! You're nothing but a traitor, man, and a bloody fool! Do you imagine this scum will let you go free if they kill us? Here's my answer to your treachery!'

Fernandes fired his second pistol at him, but the ball went wide. He threw away the weapon and gripped his sword, surveying the scene through narrowed eyes. The crew were staggering about the decks, bewildered by the unexpected turn of events. They searched frantically for any weapon with which to defend themselves; a length of rope, a marlin spike, a piece of wood. They did not know why they were being attacked so suddenly, and the ferocity of the onslaught bemused them. Already, decks were slippery with blood and trodden fruit. Several of the crew had been brutally decapitated. Their headless trunks pumped blood into the scuppers.

Two thoughts burned into Fernandes's mind. Why had Gunn allowed Castle to return? Or had Castle led Gunn and MacPherson into a trap—which meant they were already dead? Clearly, he could expect no help from them, or the crew of the longboat, who must have been overpowered.

For a moment the whole terrible scene before him resembled the engraved sketches of distant battles he had seen in magazines. And then he saw wounded and unarmed sailors run blindly across the deck, to leap into the sea in a desperate attempt to escape the terribly scything razor-blows of the pirates' swords.

And to think he had been fooled so easily! To imagine a true-born Englishman could be such a traitor! Rage, regret, revenge poured like fire through his body with every beat of his angry heart.

Two pirates charged at him. Fernandes swung his sword, but did not see the blade descend. A third man had crept behind him on bare feet and felled him with a blow from a block of wood. Fernandes dropped down on his hands and knees, amid the dead and the dying. His sword clattered and rolled away out of his nerveless hand, and he sank silently into deep and solid darkness.

\*     \*     \*

MacPherson unscrewed the solid silver stopper from his flask of The Glenlivet whisky and handed the flask to Gunn.

'Have a dram, doctor,' he said. 'I always find that the wine of Scotland settles the nerves wonderfully.'

'Thank you, my friend.'

Gunn filled his mouth with whisky and rinsed the spirit round his parched tongue and gums before he swallowed, savouring the taste as it burned his dry throat like fire.

They were in a native hut on the edge of the clearing, their hands bound loosely with rattan. Their pocket knives had been removed, and they stood in the hot dimness of the hut with its rattan door rolled down, still barely able to comprehend what had happened, and totally unable to accept what would almost inevitably happen within hours. Their captors were presumably head-hunters, as were the vast majority of islanders in that latitude. And what greater prize could such men claim than the heads of Europeans?

And that fellow, Castle; was he still alive, or had the Parsee been making some dreadful jest in claiming he had returned to the shore?

Maybe if Castle had escaped, he could reach *Hesperides* and Fernandes would turn the ship's five-pounders on the island? They might not do much damage, but they would frighten the locals and drive them into the jungle, and so give Gunn and MacPherson a chance of escape. It was a comfortable cheering thought, but as the minutes stretched to an hour without any firing, it lost credibility. Either Castle had been killed or somehow he had feigned injury because he wished to betray them. But why? In God's name, why?

'It is odd to think that our trading company has prospered for nine years and now will die with both its founders,' said MacPherson lugubriously, squinting down the mouth of his flask to see how much whisky remained.

'I do not entertain such thoughts,' Gunn retorted. 'We are not dead yet. Remember what Shakespeare wrote? "Cowards die many times before their death; the valiant never taste of death but once." '

114

'With respect, doctor, and brave as those words are, the immortal bard was never in our particular situation. Speaking for myself, I taste death in my mouth every time I think of those savages out yonder with their human heads hanging up in their huts and their sharpened knives, and that foul Parsee Bonnarjee leading them, full of venom as a viper's bladder. This is not a situation from which I can see a happy way out, or even any way out.'

'The Lord got us into it. Maybe He will show us a path?'

'I never knew that you were religious?'

Gunn was about to reply, when the door suddenly dropped away from its cord bindings. Three natives with dahs in their hands had cut it loose. Bonnarjee stood behind them.

'I notice you do not approach too close,' said Gunn sarcastically. 'You are like a captor of lions who employs keepers lest they should maul him, even in captivity. Clearly, courage, like honour, is not your watchword.'

'Brave words, Englishman,' replied Bonnarjee with equal sarcasm. 'Well, we shall soon see how long your valour lasts. Come out now. You have a journey to make.'

'Where to?'

'To your vessel—my vessel, rather—*Hesperides*.'

'You mean . . . ?'

'Yes,' replied Bonnarjee, savouring every second of the situation, weighing the word carefully, as if against his own gold, to extract the maximum satisfaction from the situation.

'I mean that we have taken her over. Your captain

is wounded, and for all I know, may now be dead, as, indeed, are many of your crew. However, I must congratulate you on their toughness and calibre. Some leaped unhesitatingly into the sea when my people attacked them, hoping to swim to shore, no doubt in order to warn you.

'My men allowed them to treasure that illusion for an hour, and then gave them the option of coming back aboard immediately to work the vessel, or of being shot and left for sharks to eat. So they returned, reluctantly enough. We need them for the time being, for my people are not yet fully acquainted with all the niceties of European rigging and high sails.'

'So where are we going in my ship?'

'*My* ship,' corrected Bonnarjee gently. 'You and your crew will make a journey beyond the reef, three miles out. We shall then open all sea-cocks, and the flagship will sink with all hands, including the British founders of that remarkable Far Eastern trading company, Mandarin-Gold.

'We shall hasten to Macao, bearing news of this sad accident at sea, and at the same time I will make a bid for your company's assets, which, of course, will be vastly diminished without your acumen, Dr Gunn.'

'I can accept, Bonnarjee, how a man like you may seek to murder a more successful business rival. There are unfortunately other instances of this in the annals of eastern trading. But what harm have the crew of *Hesperides* ever done to you? They are simply sailors, concerned with matters of the sea. They are not in any commercial competition with you. If Mr MacPherson and I have to die at your hand, then that is written in

116

our stars. But I ask you most earnestly to spare the lives of these innocent men.'

'You are in no position to bargain, Englishman. Some of these British tars whose fate seems of such concern to you might spread rumours about my actions to Singaport or Macao. While, of course, they could never prove such stories in any court of law, they might still conceivably damage our interests or our relationship with others.'

'You mean, with your wife? The woman you were not man enough to get with child?'

The Parsee swallowed hard and said no more. He nodded to the natives, who prodded Gunn and MacPherson with the points of their dahs. Beads of blood started from the tiny cuts their wafer-like blades inflicted as they began to walk across the clearing, hands still bound in front of them.

Other natives came to the doors of huts to watch the procession: women suckling babies; fishermen mending nets; old men wrinkled and bent, loose dry flesh hanging in folds on withered bodies that had once been supple and young.

The longboat lay waterlogged, axe-holes hacked in her hull. The bodies of the crew, puffy and pale in the sea-water, floated near her, heads down. Gunn guessed that they must have been surprised and then murdered. Maybe Castle had lulled them into a state of false security so that the natives could kill them? God rest their honest souls, he thought. And may Castle rot for ever in hell for his treachery.

Three canoes waited in the shallow water. Bonnarjee climbed into one, and Gunn and MacPherson were prodded into the second, with several guards. Slowly, they moved out across the calm sea. A faint and unexpected breeze barely ruffled its glassy surface. Here and there, a fish leapt like a silver flash and fell back again and was gone.

The deck of *Hesperides* was lined with dark, grinning faces. Gunn guessed they were Malay pirates Bonnarjee had hired for the voyage. This belief was confirmed when the strong morning sun glinted on earrings, on metal necklaces and swords. Streaks of bloodied water stained the side of the ship from her scupper drains. Fernandes had anchored her fore and aft by chains so that she would not swing with the tide, in case he needed to open fire on the shore, should the inhabitants prove hostile to Gunn and MacPherson. Now she strained impatiently against these moorings, for the tide was turning. Within minutes, they could be away. The canoes bumped against the hull, scraping and scoring white paint with the carelessness of men who had no pride in the vessel's appearance.

A pirate ordered Gunn and MacPherson up the landing stairs. They stood on a deck still littered with corpses. No attempt had been made to move them, although someone had thrown buckets of sea-water over the most mutilated to drown the blue-bellied flies and the sickly stench of violent death.

Bonnarjee waved to someone behind Gunn. The doctor turned to see who this might be. Castle was standing, hands on his hips, smirking at him.

'I thought you were injured,' said Gunn slowly.

'Only by association with you,' replied Castle, and spat on the deck.

'What do you mean by that remark, sir?'

'I mean, that I tricked you. I mean that I have been working for your rival, Mr Bonnarjee, and his company.'

'Then what was your object in coming with me, in accepting my commission and my coin?'

'To lead you directly into this situation, Dr Gunn. To deliver you into the hands of a man who has the best reason in the world to hate you. You have grown rich as a result of lying with his wife. Now it is his turn to seek revenge. And my turn to become wealthy.'

'I see. Truly it is written, love of money is the root of all evil. Not money itself, Castle, for you have little, and will gain no more from your murderous treachery, but the *love* of it that led you into becoming a murderer.'

Gunn remembered his Chinese clerk Lin Yang mentioning that Castle was unexpectedly in Singapore and might help him search for coal. Had he deliberately done this—or had Bonnarjee or someone else forced the introduction on him?

Gunn also remembered how Lin Yang's body had been found floating in the bay. Surely these two events must be connected? Had Lin Yang used his position and the confidence Gunn had placed in him as a lever to enrich himself? Or did he just need a little more money to feed his large family—and then had paid for this need with his life?

Gunn turned to Bonnarjee.

'You had a Chinese clerk killed,' he told him bluntly. 'Lin Yang, one of my employees.'

'I am not concerned with the fate of unworthy persons of low degree,' replied Bonnarjee evasively.

119

'I am concerned with your fate, Bonnarjee, when news of all this reaches Singapore.'

'It will no more reach that city than you will, Dr Gunn. Harbour no illusions on either matter.'

'Illusions do not concern me—although they appear to be valued by your creature, Castle.'

Gunn turned to the surveyor.

'Do you sincerely imagine that this Parsee will ever allow you to return to Singapore or Macao, lest you speak in your cups about what you both have seen and done? Do you seriously believe you will ever see any safe harbour again? If you do, that is an extremely dangerous illusion, Castle. A deadly illusion, too.

'Your throat will be cut and your body thrown over the side as food for the sharks, as happened to my clerk, Lin Yang. I hope for your sake that you are dead before the sharks reach you. As no doubt Bonnarjee's merciful nature made sure Lin Yang was dead before your master's minions threw him into Singapore harbour.'

Castle's face tightened. He had not heard of Lin Yang's death before.

'You lie in your teeth, doctor,' he said hoarsely.

'I speak the truth, Castle. No one honours a traitor. Traitors are like rotten branches in a high tree—untrust-worthy and deadly dangerous. And how, pray, will you ensure *your* survival, when you are surrounded by men who have everything to gain by killing you?'

'Say no more, doctor, or I will kill you here and now.'

'As one apparently about to die in any case, that threat does not alarm me. So I will say this, Castle. If I die now, as seems likely, you will swiftly follow me into the mists of eternity. And may the Almighty treat your soul with mercy. If, however, I survive, I shall pursue you without any mercy whatever—or rather, as much as you allowed the crew of my longboat. Think on these two alternatives, Castle. They are your only ones.'

Bonnarjee came up between the two men.

'Enough of words,' he said brusquely. 'To action instead. What, in your opinion, Mr Castle, as one who knows this vessel, is the best place to incarcerate these two countrymen of yours for the short time they have remaining in this world? The crew are presently detained in the fo'c'sle, apart from two men we need in the wheelhouse, and four more standing by to go aloft to deal with the sails.'

'Up in the bows, beneath the main deck, in the chain locker, Mr Bonnarjee. That has but one small means of entry, and no portholes. There is also barely enough room inside for a man to stand upright when the chain is out. When the bow anchor chain is wound in on the capstan, these creatures will be crushed by your invincibility, Mr Bonnarjee. That is a parable which I find fitting.'

'I agree. It is also not unpleasing to me.'

'Lash them to the anchor chain,' Castle went on. 'Then, with each turn of the capstan, they will be drawn farther on to the spindle, first crushing their wrists, then their arms and shoulders, and finally their trunks. They should just be dead before they drown.'

Gunn's words had frightened Castle. He had assumed that Bonnarjee was his ally, and even if he was not drawn to the man, he had the promise of a share in his enterprise on Jade Gate Island. But now that Castle had delivered Gunn and MacPherson to him, he realized that Gunn had spoken the truth. He could be an embarrassment, an unnecessary witness who might prove awkward, even dangerous, unless his tongue was silenced.

But surely Gunn was only attempting to terrify him because of his own desperate situation? So how better to consolidate his standing with Bonnarjee than by condemning his two countrymen to a hideous and agonizing death?

There was a quality of Chinese cruelty about it—and yet he bore no deep animosity towards Gunn or Mac-Pherson. They had not quibbled over his fee. All that had driven him to these terrible extremities of treachery and murder had been envy of their wealth, greed for their gold. He looked away so he would not have to see contempt in the doctor's eyes.

Bonnarjee turned to the pirates, and spoke rapidly in an unknown tongue. Four of them immediately drew swords and prodded MacPherson and Gunn along the decks, past fallen men, and up and down companionways, until they reached the door of the chain locker in the bows.

On the fore-deck, directly above, was the main anchor capstan whose axle passed through an iron bearing in the decking planks. A small cogged wheel on this axle meshed with a large wheel on a second spindle that ran down to another bearing in the keel.

When the crew applied their weight to the capstan bars on deck, chanting in rhythm to gain momentum, these wheels meshed and turned and slowly wound in the rusty anchor chain until the links lay coiled like a giant thread on a cotton-reel the size of a tree trunk.

A pirate opened the locker door, and the two captives stood looking into the small triangular room. Its tarred walls smelled strongly of rust and salt and crude grease used to lubricate the bearings and the gears. Strips of seaweed were coiled like blackened ribbons around the rusty spindle. The floor was black with tar. A few lengths of rope and a pot of grease filled most of the little space. There were barely two feet clear on either side of the spindle; this space would shrink dramatically with each turn of the capstan.

The pirates kicked Gunn and MacPherson into the room. One bound the rope already around their wrists to a link of the chain. Another insolently rifled their pockets. Then they slammed the door behind them, and Gunn and MacPherson were alone in the stinking tarry darkness.

For a moment, they could see nothing. Then they made out a faint rim of light around the ill-fitting door; more light filtered in through the anchor chain opening on the starboard side of the bow. By craning their necks they could see the chain curve down into the water, and the bright hard glitter of sun on sea.

Gunn moved against the chain, and the rusty scaly metal, rough as a rasp, scored the flesh of his wrists. If it was so rough, then surely it should also cut his bonds? He began to saw his wrists to and fro against the link. The rope smouldered and frayed. He jerked his wrists until the last strands snapped, and then massaged feeling back into his wrists and forearms.

Then he freed MacPherson, and the two men crouched in the airless heat, sweat pouring down their chests and backs, awaiting the commands on deck above their heads that would start the chain to move and the spindle to turn.

Already they could hear shouted orders and an excited chatter of voices just outside the locker. The pirates who had brought them down must still be waiting on the other side of the door, in case they thought they might somehow escape. Or maybe they hoped they would attempt to, for this would provide them with the chance to cut them down. Within minutes, at most, the capstan must turn and they would be as good as dead. Unless . . . unless. . . .

Gunn whispered urgently: 'Give me your flask.'

'It is empty,' replied MacPherson, also in a whisper.

'I do not need the contents, only the container.'

MacPherson handed over the flask silently and watched as Gunn held it above his head, feeling in the gloom for the huge iron cog wheels. They formed a simple reduction gear to increase the power of the capstan, so that the crew could raise the anchor from the deepest sea-bed, even if it had fouled in seaweed roots or rock formations. Gunn calculated which way each cog would turn, and then he forced the flask between the teeth, jamming it with a piece of wood. As the capstan gear began to revolve, the flask would now be squeezed and flattened. But such was the small tolerance between the two toothed wheels that the ball, nearly an inch across, would jam between the teeth and prevent the gears from turning. This by itself could not save them, but it should delay their death. And in their situation a minute extra was worth a king's ransom, for all the unmapped darkness of eternity gaped ahead.

Bare feet drummed on the deck only inches above

124

their heads; planks moved, one against another; a little dust filtered down on the heads of the two captives. Gunn heard an iron slam as the safety ratchet on the capstan was thrown off. Now the small cog began to revolve, squeezing the silver flask to the thinness of a coin.

Four feet of anchor chain came in before the cog jammed on the silver stopper. The two wheels strained against each other and stopped turning. Men shouted first in surprise, and then in anger. Other feet padded on the deck; the teeth jerked sharply as more weight was flung against the capstan arms. A small piece of flattened silver detached itself from the crushed flask and tinkled down between the two captives. But still the wheels refused to turn.

'Now,' whispered Gunn urgently. 'Scream as though we are in pain. They'll think our bones have jammed the capstan.'

He began to yell as he spoke, MacPherson joined him in the long drawn out cries of men in intolerable, unendurable agony.

'Save me! Help, I pray you! Have mercy on us!'

Between shouts, MacPherson listened at the door. Bare feet padded on wooden planks outside. He moved back to the chain. The door opened a few inches, and a pirate peered in cautiously, accustoming his eyes to the darkness. He could make out Gunn and MacPherson, both apparently still bound to the chain, leaning over it, moaning and sobbing in their pain.

The man came in.

Gunn looked cautiously over his shoulder. The deck outside was momentarily deserted. The other pirates must have gone up to help turn the capstan. The man looked up at the jammed cogs, saw the flattened flask and the stopper and instinctively reached up to remove them. As he stretched, arms above his head, Gunn whipped round and punched him in the stomach with all his force. The pirate collapsed forward like a huge hinge closing. MacPherson lashed the pirate's arms to the chain and ripped out the flask.

'The wheels are free now! Heave ho!' roared Gunn in Malay. On the upper deck, the crew flung their bodies against the capstan's thick spokes. Slowly, inexorably, the wheels began to turn, and the rusty dripping chain screamed up through the iron-edged hole in the bows.

Gunn ripped off the pirate's loose linen shirt, pulled it over his own and crammed the man's round straw hat on to his own head, then backed to the door.

MacPherson removed the half-conscious pirate's knife from his belt. And all the while they both kept screaming as though in agony, as the chain coiled around the spindle.

'Help! Save me, I beg you! Mercy! Aah!'

The pirate now began to moan, too, as his arms were pulled slowly, steadily, from their sockets. His moans changed to harsh shrieks of delirious agony as the huge links crushed the bones in his wrists.

The chain stopped moving momentarily. Feet drummed on the deck outside, and the door opened. Another pirate, seeing a bent back in the semi-darkness wearing a familiar shirt, asked in Malay: 'What's the matter? Why are you so long?'

Gunn spun round, punched him hard in the stomach, and as he went down, hammered his head on the wooden

126

boards. Then he ripped the knife from the pirate's belt and, half crouched like animals, he and MacPherson came out from their foul, cramped locker into the glaring sun, almost blinded by its brilliance. Behind them, the chain began to move again; the pirate's cries increased to an animal bellow of mortal agony.

They only had seconds before they would be discovered and overwhelmed—unless they could release the crew. Down a wooden companionway they raced, past huge sail lockers and oak barrels of lime juice lashed on deck, down steps to the fo'c'sle. Gunn tried the door; it was locked.

'This is Dr Gunn,' he said in a hoarse whisper. 'Anyone alive in there?'

'We are, doctor,' a West Country voice replied, buoyed up with hope, trembling with relief at the prospect of rescue. 'Twelve of us.'

'Stand away from the door, then,' ordered Gunn. 'We're going to kick it in.'

He flung the whole weight of his tall body against the lock. It held. MacPherson kicked with his boots. Still the lock would not give way. Gunn cast about, and found a marlin spike in the scuppers. With this he smashed the panels around the lock, then together they threw their shoulders against the door. It collapsed with a great splintering of wood. The crew were crammed inside, wrists and ankles tied. Gunn cut the ropes with the pirate's knife, and the men massaged blood back to numbed limbs, and hopped about clumsily to bring feeling to their feet.

'Seize what weapons you can. Anything,' Gunn ordered. 'But hurry. The pirates have pistols.'

The crew kicked open lockers for sail knives, and metal spikes; others tore long, jagged strips of wood from the door for clubs. Already there were shouts of alarm and anger from the upper foredeck; the deception in the chain locker must have been discovered.

'This is life or death for us all,' Gunn told them urgently. 'Do not strike to wound. Strike to kill. But save two men. The surveyor, Castle, who is a traitor, and a fat Parsee in a white dhoti. Wound them if you must, but do not kill them. I will deal with them myself.'

'What about Captain Fernandes, sir?' asked the mate. 'He was badly hurt and thrown into a cabin.'

'He will have to wait, poor fellow, until we can overcome these pirates. How many are aboard?'

'I would say about thirty, sir.'

'The odds against us are therefore roughly two to one —a pretty fair ratio for success, gentlemen. And we must succeed, because death is our only alternative. Now— to arms!'

Gunn climbed up the steps, sprinted back along the deck, and leapt up the next companionway. A pirate lunged at him with a sword, missed, and for a second almost overbalanced with the force of his thrust. Before he could recover, Gunn ran the man through the chest with his knife, turning the blade expertly under his rib cage and driving it hard into the man's right lung. The pirate screamed with a terrible choking, bubbling sound; he was drowning in his own blood.

Gunn left the dagger in his body, seized in its place the Malay's cutlass and pistol, and raced on to the foredeck.

MacPherson went directly to the stern of the vessel; he felt it was easier to try to pick off pirates one by one, instead of attacking the group around the main capstan.

Two Malays stood uneasily near the smaller stern capstan which held the second anchor chain, awaiting the order to wind it aboard. They had both heard shouts and screams from the bows, but did not know the reason for them. MacPherson crept carefully along the deck, dodging from bollard to bollard, until he was within feet of them. For the last three yards there was no cover. He gave a great roar, and as the pirates swung around in alarm, he hacked the right hand off one and gouged at the neck of the other, before they could draw their swords.

He seized a musket which one pirate had placed by the capstan, but did not have the chance to lift, and a pistol from the other. Then, pushing his own sword back into his belt, he ran along the deck. Half a dozen pirates were now coming down from the bow capstan. For a second they stood, regarding MacPherson in amazement and disbelief. How could these Red-Bristled Barbarians possibly have freed themselves, when only moments before they had been screaming in agony, tied to the main anchor chain?

As the pirates paused, irresolute, MacPherson fired at them, first with the musket, then the pistol. Then he tossed the empty weapon at them, and gripping the musket by its hot, reeking barrel, swung it like a huge club, hitting arms, trunks, heads. Other members of his crew were with him now. One drove a giant splinter of wood like a lance through the throat of a pirate;

another hacked off a native's sword arm as he raised the blade above his head.

Both sides were fighting with a terrible, tireless ferocity. A death for a life, a death for a death; they could afford no mercy, no second chances. Some men fell groaning in the extremity of their pain—and immediately their adversaries lifted them and flung them over the rail into the sea. Every man out of the fight was one less on the other side.

Gradually, the fury of the fight diminished; surprise had been Gunn's greatest ally. MacPherson leaned wearily against the base of the mainmast, feeling the warmth of the varnished wood through his sweat-soaked shirt. Wounded men, some hideously maimed, with hands lopped from wrists, and sinews severed at the shoulders, lay on the deck like bales of crumpled, bloodied rags, still writhing feebly. Others seemed like the dead with head wounds; several had bled to death in silence.

Three or four pirates still fought on, swords reddened like butchers' cleavers, eyes wild, lips drawn back over their teeth with the effort of their exertions. But gradually these individual fights also ended; the air was thick with the moans of the mutilated.

The first mate came up to MacPherson and saluted.

'Are all the pirates accounted for?' MacPherson asked him hoarsely.

His mouth felt dry as the bricks of a baker's oven. He would willingly have given a fortune for a glass of cold, fresh water.

'So far as I know, sir,' the man replied.

'Then go below and seek out Captain Fernandes. Take

someone with you to report his condition to Dr Gunn while you stay with him. And bring back as many flagons of drinking water as you can find.'

Gunn approached them, relieved to see that his partner appeared to be uninjured. Gunn's right arm was red with blood to the elbow, and his shirt in tattered ribbons. His back had been scored in a dozen places, but none was serious, although blood from the shallow flesh wounds had stained the sodden cotton. He flung away his sword, tied a bucket on the end of a rope, threw this over the side, hauled it up and doused himself with sea-water, wincing as the brine bit into his raw, cut flesh.

A steward arrived, carrying two flasks of water by their necks in one hand, and gripping a reddened marlin spike in the other in case any hidden pirate should attack him.

Gunn and MacPherson drank greedily, their parched bodies thankfully soaking up the tepid, brackish water.

Four crew members now approached them, man-handling Castle across the deck.

'You asked us to keep him alive, sir,' one of the sailors reminded Gunn.

'I thank you for that. But whether he will is altogether another matter. Now, let him stand free.'

The two men fell away on either side. Castle stood facing Gunn and MacPherson, shoulders drooped, head down in defeat.

'I can understand the Parsee plotting against me,' Gunn told him, 'for he has reason. But you, sir, who we engaged as a professional person, a man of our own country, who took both our money and our commission,

and carried hate and murder in your heart all the while
—what can you say in your defence?'

Castle raised his head.

'I envied you both your riches, sir,' he replied quietly.
'I thought that if I could depose you, I might also become
rich. Indeed, the Parsee promised me as much.'

'As convincing an excuse as our first ancestor, Adam,
gave to the Almighty when asked to explain why he had
eaten the fruit of the Tree of Knowledge: "The woman
tempted me, and I did eat." Envy is no excuse for
murder, and the punishment for taking another's life
is to lose your own.'

At that moment, others of *Hesperides*'s crew now
appeared, frog-marching the Parsee. His face shone with
the sweat of terror, and his brown skin glistened like
varnished teak. As he faced Gunn and MacPherson, his
eyes flickered nervously from one partner to the other.
Incongruously, amid all the blood and filth of the deck,
Bonnarjee's *dhoti* still appeared crisp and well laundered. He might have just received it back from the
*dhobi* man moments before. Clearly, he had not been
in the fighting, but had sheltered away somewhere.
Gunn's contempt for him rose like bile in his throat.

'Now, Bonnarjee,' he began coldly, 'barely an hour
ago, you were full of your own triumph. You spat at me
when I was your captive. You reserved for my partner,
Mr MacPherson, and for me—as well as for innocent
members of our crew—a peculiarly terrible and linger-
ing death.

'Shall I reward you as you would have paid us, in the
same currency? Or shall I hand you to my crew who
will deal with you in even cruder and more painful

fashion? You have killed many of their comrades, and nearly all in the vessel bear wounds inflicted at your command. I fear you will have to produce a stronger and more convincing defence than your creature Castle, if you seek to escape the solemn consequences of your actions. Speak! I offer you an opportunity which you denied my partner and me.'

'I am a rich man,' said Bonnarjee, and his voice sounded hoarse and rough, the despairing tones of a man whispering against the bleak winds of eternity.

'I will make over to you any share of my company you desire, if you but spare my life.'

'And what about the life of this traitor, Castle?'

'He was a hireling,' replied Bonnarjee quickly, imagining that Gunn was interested in his proposition. 'He has been paid his fee.'

'I do not wish to accept your offer,' said Gunn. 'I am not interested in acquiring any part of your company by letting you go free, no doubt only to afford you opportunity to plan my murder by other means.'

'Well said,' interrupted MacPherson. 'Let us cut down these bastards by a head and then set about tending our own wounded. We have had enough treachery for this day.'

'Your suggestion has attractions,' agreed Gunn, 'but I propose another punishment. We will spare their lives. But all your wealth, Bonnarjee, will be of no avail to save you.'

'Then?' asked Bonnarjee, half hopeful, half despairing.

'We sail on this tide to Singapore, and our way is scattered with islands. Some lie on the trade routes, others are some distance off. I intend to maroon you and Castle on one of these small unknown islands. There you can live—if you can catch fish or cut down coconuts—and always assuming he does not kill you or you murder him. Or maybe natives on that island, or on others nearby, may take their own vengeance on you simply because your ways are not theirs.'

'But my family,' protested Bonnarjee, 'my business. Listen! I will make everything that is mine over to you. Everything. Only let me return to my home. Give me my freedom, I beseech you.'

Gunn shook his head, and turned to the first mate.

'Have these two murderers searched thoroughly for arms, and then set them the task of cleaning our decks. Maybe the act of swabbing away the blood of young men they have murdered will help to cleanse their own souls.'

'It is unclean for me to touch the blood of the dead,' said the Parsee quickly.

'Then you will have to make it clean,' Gunn told him roughly, and nodded his dismissal.

A cabin boy approached and saluted.

'First officer's compliments, sir,' he said respectfully, standing in awe of the owner. 'And could you kindly come down to see Captain Fernandes? He is very poorly.'

'Of course. I will collect some physic and be with him immediately.'

'I will join you,' said MacPherson, 'but first I must go back to the chain locker.'

'To see how that pirate fared?'

'Not so. He will now be far beyond all human aid. I go in search of my whisky flask. I would hate to lose that

134

now. After all, we owe our lives to it. I wish to preserve it as a memento of our providential escape.'

He paused and grinned, and then slapped Gunn on the back.

'And, as a Scot, Robert, I'd have you know, that stopper is solid silver!'

# CHAPTER SIX

## *In which others set sail and also carry out a landing*

HIRAM JEROME and Abner Jones, the American Consul, looked around the small eating-house with disfavour. It was clean enough, to be sure, for the floor was freshly scrubbed, the bamboo tables and chairs well wiped, and neat bead screens hung across doorways and windows to keep out the heat and the flies. But Jones had eaten in too many similar places when he was on the lower deck to feel any enthusiasm for them. And now that he was promoted Consul, even if rather unconventionally, he felt he belonged to a higher level of society, where servants should stand behind each guest, and wines were poured from crystal decanters, and there was silver on the table, not bone-handled knives and porcelain spoons and tin mugs.

'Why did you bring me here?' he asked Jerome irritably.

'Because the proprietor is an Englishman, or, to be accurate, a Welshman, like your ancestors, one Able Seaman Jenkins. He was formerly in the employ of Dr Gunn and served in the *Hesperides* for three years. He was telling me the other night that when he informed the doctor he wished to start his eating-house, Gunn advanced him money, and at the same time took a share in his enterprise. Thus Gunn showed his skill, even in such a petty matter. He will draw a monetary dividend if the eating-house prospers, and he keeps his former employee as a grateful partner.'

'Very shrewd, no doubt, Mr Jerome, but I trust you did not bring me here simply to enlarge on the business acumen of Dr Gunn?'

'Of course not. I asked you to what may appear to be an unfashionable—although entirely reputable—eating-house because I believe that the owner, as one who holds Dr Gunn in understandably high regard, may be able to help us, even if unknowingly. Possibly unknowingly.'

'That puts a different complexion on the matter. Will you introduce me as North American Consul, or as a friend?'

'I will wait to see what turn the conversation takes.'

There was a rustle of beads over the doorway and Jenkins came into the dining room from the kitchen. He was a dark-skinned Welshman, sturdily built, with a starched white napkin neatly folded over his right arm.

'Good evening to you, gentlemen,' he said. 'And what may be your pleasure? Might I recommend a fine dish of fresh prawns to start with? They were swimming off shore only this afternoon. Then could I suggest a mild lamb curry or what back in Wales we used to call olla podrida, a stew of meat and vegetables? And my wife informs me that we have just received a new consignment of bottled beer from Mr Perkins's brewery in London, which arrived by clipper this week. Or we have some of our own home brew, which, I am proud to say, yields to no other brand in strength and quality.'

'Will you join us for a pint of your home brew?' Jerome asked him.

'You are very kind,' replied Jenkins. 'It will give me pleasure, gentlemen, while you make up your minds.'

He called over his shoulder and a Chinese serving man brought in three polished pewter tankards of ale, set them down on the table, bowed, and withdrew.

'To the success of your enterprise here, Mr Jenkins,' said Jerome.

'Thank you, sir. And the success of whatever you gentlemen are engaged in. Being a writing gentleman must be a most interesting life. Meeting all types and classes of people, learning about different trades.'

'That is one of the rewarding aspects of my life,' agreed Jerome. 'As you know, I am presently engaged in meeting some of the more distinguished members of the mercantile community in this city so that I may present their considerable achievements before the wide audience of my readers in New York. And in that connection, I hear that Dr Gunn's vessel is due this evening.'

'She has already docked. I have had some of my former companions from *Hesperides* in for a drink this afternoon.'

'I must meet the doctor,' Jerome continued. 'His career is a legend out here. It is a pity he has been away for so long, but I had a most interesting talk with a compatriot of yours in the Royal Navy, Lieutenant Blackman.'

'Oh, yes, sir. My brother, who now works with me here, served with him. A fine gentleman, and a brave highly regarded officer.'

139

'He spoke most highly of Dr Gunn.'

'You will find that most people here are of the same opinion about the doctor. Unless, of course, they are his rivals.'

'That is to be expected,' said Jones sagely, lighting a cigar. 'Let me introduce myself. Abner Jones. I am also desirous of meeting Dr Gunn because I have recently been appointed North American Consul in this city, and as he is one of your country's most important *taipans* I wish to present my card to him as soon as possible.'

'He will be pleased to see you, sir, I am sure.'

'Where has he been on his last voyage?' asked Jerome casually, putting down his half-empty tankard and wiping his mouth with the back of his hand.

'To be quite honest, sir, I am not altogether sure of all the ports where his ship may have called, but my friends did say they had visited Jade Gate Island. I believe they met rather a hostile reception on the part of certain natives, and there was bloodshed. Seafarers lead a rough, dangerous life in the East, gentlemen. Would that we were more concerned with wielding the pen rather than the sword!'

'I would second that,' agreed Jones. 'I must explain, I served for a number of years in the American vessel *Bulwark.*'

'Did you now?' said Jenkins, his face lighting with interest. 'I remember hearing about her. It was said that she traded with the pirates along the coast of Borneo. But no doubt that was after you had left her?'

'Not so. I was first mate aboard her when we were involved in that matter. A strange trade, Mr Jenkins, a very strange trade.'

Jones sighed and shook his head to emphasize its strangeness and how much more he could tell if he felt constrained to do so.

'Indeed, sir? The opium trade, in which Dr Gunn was primarily involved some years ago, was also strange.'

'Not so strange as ours.'

'What were you carrying?' asked Jerome.

'Powder,' replied the Consul briefly. 'The pirates needed something with which to charge their muskets and their cannon. The British were understandably reluctant to supply them with any, so we Yankees produced it for them. They paid a high price.'

'A price in blood,' said Jenkins shortly. He did not care to be drinking with a man who had once helped to supply pirates with the means to attack harmless merchantmen and maim or kill their crews.

'No higher a price than that extracted for your opium,' retorted Jones.

'I would say, sir, rather substantially higher. Our mud brought peace and dreams to thousands of wretched peasants who worked long hours every day up to their thighs in water in the paddyfields. Their joints literally locked together with pain. Our mud helped them to forget their misery, if only for a few hours. Your powder helped murderers to raid or destroy ships—including those of their own country.'

'It is easy to philosophize,' said Jerome soothingly, kicking the Consul's ankle under the table. What had made the fool give away this part of his background so soon? Was it his aim to establish a rapport, a common ground with this eating-house creature? If so, he was not succeeding.

141

'Happily, your Royal Navy has now virtually dealt a death-blow to piracy here, helped by Dr Gunn and James Brooke,' he went on. 'And of course you will be able to eradicate pirates completely when the new steam vessels come into service. Their swiftest sailing ship will stand no chance whatever against a ship powered by such an engine.'

'Agreed. But steamships also have a weakness,' said the Consul, as if on cue. 'The coal that fires their furnaces. How much can they carry—and how far away are new stocks? I have discussed this matter with many merchants in Singapore. A number would buy these steam engines, if they could only be assured of a local source of coal. But at present it has to come all the way from mines in India or even Wales. My ancestors, like yours, come from the Principality, so I know what an immense undertaking that would be.'

'There will be ways of overcoming it, you will see,' said Jenkins confidently. 'Dr Gunn and the Royal Navy have already made their own surveys. Indeed, I am giving away no secrets when I say that the doctor believes Jade Gate Island contains quantities of coal just beneath the surface of the soil, so my friends tell me. There is apparently no need to dig deep mines and put men and ponies underneath as we do back home. You can almost scratch the stuff out with your hands. At least, that is what the natives inland are said to do.'

'This would make the basis of a most informative article for my newspaper,' said Jerome slowly.

'Ah, I am sure it would, sir. But unfortunately I cannot give you chapter and verse. You should ask Dr Gunn. He will doubtless be willing to help you.'

'Did he take a surveyor with him?'

'I believe he did,' said Jenkins. 'But I do not think that he came back. I cannot give a reason, gentlemen, I only run an eating-house here. I am not privy to what goes on among the owners, as you must understand.'

'Of course not. But you have been most helpful, Jenkins, most helpful indeed. Now, I think we will take your advice and order the prawns to begin with, and a lamb curry to follow.'

Jenkins nodded, and went out to the kitchen.

By now, half a dozen other men had come in; Norwegians, Portuguese and British sailors with black beards, all looking incongruous in shore-going clothes intended for a cold climate. When Jenkins returned he called one of them over to Jerome's table.

'Gentlemen,' he said. 'I would like to introduce a former shipmate aboard *Hesperides*. Jim Rudkin, sailmaker.

'Jim, this is Mr Jerome, who is a correspondent for a North American newspaper, and Mr Jones, the newly appointed North American Consul in Singapore. Can you enlighten these gentlemen on any aspects of your voyage?'

'I do not know what I can tell you, gentlemen,' said Rudkin doubtfully, looking from one to the other. 'I am engaged only in sail-making and repairing, you understand.'

'That art in itself would make a most interesting subject for my readers,' Jerome assured him. 'Would you join us for a mug of ale?'

'I would rather have a grog, sir.'

'Then pray bring Mr Rudkin a treble measure.'

When the rum arrived, the sailmaker swallowed it instantly, smacked his lips, and placed the empty glass ostentatiously on the table. Jerome nodded. A waiter returned with a full bottle of local rum, the colour of creosote.

'I do not wish to discuss my employer's business, gentlemen, as I am sure you will understand, and really I know very little to tell you,' said Rudkin dubiously.

'Naturally, we would not seek to ask details of your employer's business, Mr Rudkin. That would be ungallant, and is of no possible concern to us. My newspaper is read by many people on the East Coast of North America, who are interested in the sea and ships and the men who sail them—especially in foreign parts. I am therefore seeking any recollections you might have of incidents that occur on your voyages.'

'Oh, I can tell you one of those,' said Rudkin, relieved. He was a loyal and simple person. 'We had a bit of trouble on the island where we called first—Jade Gate. We stopped to prospect for coal. Pirates came aboard, and some nigger Parsee called Bonnarjee. They had a dispute with our guv'nor. In fact, gentlemen, they tried to take over the vessel, but Dr Gunn was a match for them all. He was a doctor before he became a merchant, and he gave them a bit of physic they'll remember.'

'It sounds an adventurous voyage. Can you tell me in greater detail what happened?'

'We dropped anchor, sir, and natives came out with fruit—yams and melons and suchlike—to sell us. Only they were not genuine natives but pirates in disguise. They tried to seize our vessel. And I reckon that if it had not been for the doctor they would have damn' well succeeded. They were a crafty bunch of devils—pardon the expression, gentlemen.'

'I understand. I was also a seafaring man in the American ship *Bulwark*.'

'Oh, yes, I have come across her. We were anchored side by side in Macao harbour not long since. A tough crew, sir. Most of them time-expired sailors from the Royal Navy. Or deserters from the same.'

'That is true,' the Consul agreed. 'Britain, as the premier maritime nation, can teach her competitors a great deal.'

'What lesson did your people teach Mr Bonnarjee?' Jerome asked and poured another rum for the sailmaker.

'I know what I'd have done with him,' Rudkin replied. 'Put a long knife up his black arse. But Dr Gunn was too merciful. He dropped him and some surveyor fellow, who I thought was a gentleman until I learned different, on an island on the way back. Left them there to cool off.

'I suppose the doctor knows what he is doing, but my whole experience out East has been that if you do not kill your enemy, eventually he will kill you. No time for mercy. Can't afford it, either. Revenge here is like the fever. Quick and final.'

'What is the name of the island where they marooned these rascals?'

'I cannot rightly say, sir. So far as I know, it has no name, but it is three days' sailing from here. We were on a north/north-west bearing most of the time, so you could work it out backwards easily enough. Why? Do you plan to rescue them? They'll only cut your throats.'

'Of that, you leave me in no doubt. I think it would be

safer if I contented myself with writing about the deeds of others.'

'Nice way of putting it, sir, and nice drop of rum, too. Now with your permission, gentlemen, I'll rejoin my party. I'm sure you would be welcomed aboard by Dr Gunn, if you cared to ask him for any details of the voyage. He is a most hospitable gentleman—as you are yourselves.' Rudkin bowed, and carried the rum bottle back to his own table.

'What do you make of that?' asked the Consul.

'Bonnarjee is a well-known family here, Mr Jones. And even better known in Macao. Parsees. Moneylenders, usurers, general merchants. They also have some clippers of their own. Dr Gunn, so I heard, started his company by seizing one of their vessels under rather peculiar circumstances.'

'I have heard the same. What he has done, we can also do. And, my friend, we will.'

*     *     *

Patricia Bankhausen poured out two glasses of claret, handed one to Jerome, and raised her own in a toast.

'So you are sailing tomorrow?' she asked.

'Yes. We now have some idea of the area in which Bonnarjee and his English surveyor, Castle, are marooned. I have hired a vessel and crew with all the money I have over here—one thousand American dollars.

'We will land on each island until we find our men. Our price for rescuing Bonnarjee will be that he finances an expedition to Jade Gate Island so that Jones, as American Consul, can enter into a formal agreement with the ruler, whoever he may be, to give us the sole right to the coal, and, indeed, any other minerals of value the soil may contain.'

'Am I right in assuming that you have not sailed in these waters, save in the vessel that brought you here from Salem?'

'That is correct.'

'Then I must warn you that you may be disagreeably surprised. You have a naïveté about you, Hiram, that in a younger man would be endearing, but which distresses and depresses me to find in a man of your years.

'You are accustomed to North America, to small, close-knit, rather Puritan communities. Hard work, honesty and integrity are their constant watchwords—if not yours. Out here, different philosophies prevail.

'Our sea is not like the safe Atlantic along your East Coast. It contains sharks, giant rays, poison fish that can kill a man. Our land swarms with tigers, wild boar and elephants. And the people here, both native and European, are cunning because the prizes are the highest in all the world. You can have a man murdered in Singapore for a few Malay dollars. The price comes less in Macao, or on Hong Kong island. Not the sort of situation, I imagine, that obtains in New York City?

'Life is cheap here because life teems everywhere. You imagine you can land easily on some lonely island or out-crop of rock and search for a Parsee and a renegade Eng-lishman—and find them. But what makes you think they are still alive? It is most probable that they were killed within hours of being marooned, and eaten by cannibals. Their heads will now be decorating some chieftain's hut, and their private parts have probably been a delicacy at a dinner for the chieftain's favourite concubine.

147

'How long will your thousand dollars last with a crew you have never met before? And what type of men will they be? Chinese cut-throats and deserters from the Royal Navy who dare not return home. They are for hire to the master with the deepest purse. They will outnumber you, obviously, and they will be armed. So even if you do miraculously rescue Bonnarjee and this surveyor, do you not think that they will then take orders from the Parsee rather than from you—simply because of his wealth and power?

'You attempt a brave mission, but it can only have one end—failure—because neither of you appreciates the strength of the forces against you—both natural and human.'

'You list all the difficulties eloquently, ma'am, but we have energy and need and ambition on our side. When I was first introduced to you at the dining table, I thought that you were a cool, self-controlled English lady. Then I saw a smoulder in your smile and from your warm glances I divined that this was but a concealment, necessary in the civilized society in which you move, for burning depths of passion and desire. Yes, and hatred of one man, who, in a strange, perverted way, you wish to destroy while still admiring him—some would say, even loving him.

'So you, ma'am, are not entirely as you seem to be to the casual outward view. Perhaps I am the same. Perhaps I am done with chronicling the great deeds of other men and am about to attempt some myself. Maybe their example has inspired me. Or maybe you have, Patricia.'

'When you speak like that, the words move me strangely. I can almost believe them.'

148

'Then let us speak no more,' said Jerome, gently taking the glass from her hand and placing it on the table. Then he gripped her roughly by the arm and pulled her to him, feeling her body warm and willing against his own.

'I could almost love you,' said Patricia dreamily.

'We are of a type, born under the same star. Love may not be for us. But this is.'

Jerome forced her back against the wall. She did not resist, but closed her eyes and arched her back as he seized her clothes. Her hands were already undoing buttons. There and then he had her. Jerome was now not just a recorder of other men's acts; he was a man by his own accounting—and by hers.

*     *     *

Jenkins climbed up the gangway of *Hesperides*, nodded to the sailor on duty at the top, and turned to a steward.

'I wish to see Dr Gunn, he told him.

'You know the way, then,' his former shipmate replied. 'But I had better announce you.' He led him down to Gunn's cabin and tapped discreetly on the door.

'Jenkins to see you, sir.'

'Show him in.'

Gunn stood up, came forward, hand outstretched to greet the Welshman.

'How pleasant to see a friendly face,' said Gunn warmly. 'Yet you have an air of worry and concern about you, Jenkins. I hope that your eating-house prospers and your wife is well? I hear the highest reports of her cooking.'

'You are too kind, sir, but as I tell everyone, you are a gentleman.'

'Who is everyone?' asked Gunn sharply.

'I am thinking about two American gentlemen who called at my eating-house two days ago. I tried to visit you that night, but you were at a private engagement, and I spent most of yesterday at the market.'

'Who are these gentlemen?'

'One is a Mr Jerome, sir, the correspondent for a North American newspaper, *The New York News*. He is writing articles, so he tells me, about *taipans* in this city, and he was interested in you. He did ask me one or two questions about you, sir, but I told him nothing.'

'Very wise. He can address himself to me directly. Indeed, he has already sent me a letter, and I will be pleased to see him. Who was the other inquisitive gentleman?'

'A Mr Jones, sir. Says he was born in Wales. Now he is North American Consul in Singapore.'

'Never heard of the fellow. What does he want?'

'He was also interested in meeting you, as you are such a distinguished merchant.'

'That can equally readily be arranged. I am sure you have not come to see me on these two matters alone?'

'No, sir. Several members of the crew were in the eating-house and I introduced one of them to the two gentlemen. Mr Jerome said he was compiling an article about voyages here. They plied the man with rum and I overheard him say he believed you had discovered coal on Jade Gate Island. And also that you had endured hostility from pirates there, and a Mr Bonnarjee and some English surveyor whose name I did not catch. He said you had marooned these two persons on an island.'

'Who was this talkative member of my crew?'

'I would rather not say, sir. I sailed with him for three years, and saying who he is would not stop his mouth now.'

'I would stop any man's mouth whose loose tongue can harm my business. What else did this anonymous and garrulous man tell two inquisitive Americans?'

'He said that Bonnarjee and this other man were marooned on an island three days' sailing from here, and from that island you had taken a course roughly north/north-west.'

'Could the two Americans make any use of this information, such as it is?'

'That is not my province to say, sir. I am a Mandarin-Gold man, or rather, a Dr Gunn man, and I thought I should tell you what happened, just in case it might affect you.'

'You did right,' said Gunn. 'Tell me if they call again.'

'I do not think they will, sir. I understand now that they have engaged a vessel with a local crew and a half-caste, who speaks the lingo, as captain. They sailed today on the morning tide. I do not know their destination, but it would not surprise me if they are aiming for this island.'

'What speed has this vessel?'

'I understand, ten knots under full sail.'

'Thank you. I will discuss the matter with Mr Mac-Pherson. Please say nothing of this matter to anyone.'

Jenkins bowed, closed the door quietly behind him and walked along the deck and down the companionway to the shore. He felt content, for he had kept faith with two friends, Dr Gunn and Jim Rudkin. He had warned the first and not betrayed the second. One good turn can be difficult enough to achieve; but when a man can help two people at the same time, surely that is a moment to remember?

*        *        *

Bonnarjee crouched on his haunches like a caged beast under the crude shelter he had built of split bamboos.

Ahead of him, the sea stretched in an infinity of dazzling, splintering liquid light, so bright that when he closed his eyes the glare still burned like flame on his raw and reddened lids. His once-smart *dhoti* was now foul and torn. He had ripped strips from its hem to make bandages to bind up the ulcerated cuts which sharp edges of the bamboos had scored in his soft brown palms when he was making his hut. The largest strip of linen he had wrapped around his trunk like a loin cloth. His skin was dry and pocked with sun-blisters. Here and there, the flesh had split right across the raw festering weals around which flies gathered and buzzed. Bonnarjee was so used to their pain now, he hardly noticed them.

A few yards from him, in a similar shelter, but slightly larger and more skilfully fashioned, lay the Englishman, Castle, still asleep. Bonnarjee did not like the man, but at least he was a fellow creature, and without Castle he would be alone and prey to even worse hallucinations and imaginings than those which tortured him every evening in the dark.

But the Englishman was not content to stay, marooned, sustained only by the hope that one day a vessel might sight the spiral of smoke from the fire they kept burning day and night. He had constructed a raft of large bamboo poles, bound them with jungle creeper, and then had laboriously carved water containers from the thickest bamboos, plugging the tops with leaves. On this raft, with the supply of water, he intended to attempt to escape.

Bonnarjee hawked in his throat and brought up a gobbet of green phlegm as an expression of opinion on this scheme. With lack-lustre eyes he counted the notches on the main bamboo pole that supported his hut. He carved a new one every evening as the sun went down; they were beginning their eighteenth day. He could scarcely recall any incidents that marked one day as being different from another; only a growing accumulation of misery and hunger and discomfort and fear.

Gunn's longboat had brought them ashore from *Hesperides*. The crew had tossed out a pair of knives, a couple of tin pannikins for drinking, two metal plates from the lower deck mess, and half a dozen empty grog bottles for their use, and then tipped the two men over the side like garbage. They stood up, and watched the sailors' oars dip and flurry in the shining sea, and the longboat diminish as it drew out towards *Hesperides*.

'You bastards,' said Castle softly. 'May you rot in hell. I will escape from this island and, as God is my judge, I will see you suffer for this.'

He spat into the sea in the extremity of his rage; it was the only way he could show his hatred. The oarsmen rowed on, unheeding.

Bonnarjee remembered the scene as he walked down to the edge of the sea. He had killed a snake with a stone the night before, and with Castle's help he had built a small cage of split bamboos in the shallow water of a rocky pool, using half the snake as bait. He hoped to find

153

that some crustacean had crept in after food and was unable to escape.

If not, I will eat the other half of the snake myself, he thought wretchedly. What have I come to, eating serpents, unclean, crawling things? But yet, it is better to devour their flesh than to pine in hunger; better to preserve one's strength by any means in the hope of ultimate rescue than to let it dwindle and finally die. For somehow he would escape from here. Then he could follow Gunn to the edge of the world and even beyond, if that were possible. He would inflict on Gunn all the tortures his wealth could command, his influence procure, and his loathing devise.

He reached the pool. The crude cage was empty except for part of the snake, its speckled skin eaten away by sharp-toothed fish. Bonnarjee's disappointment was so great that he almost wept. He had imagined his teeth sinking into the succulent pink flesh of a young turtle or the white meat of a baby lobster, grilled over their simple fire. He could not face the thought of swallowing the remnants of this reptile that even the fish had refused; he would have to climb a palm tree and tear down some coconuts, gouge them open and then drink the sparkling juice, and spear out the milky pith with the edge of his knife.

On several occasions, he and Castle had managed to catch some fish, literally with their hands, but somehow Castle was much better at this than he was. He had explained how he used to catch trout by tickling them when he was a boy in England. Castle was stronger physically, and also the more enterprising. This explained why he was not content to wait in a supine way for rescue;

why he had built his raft and was going to attempt to reach the mainland or at least an inhabited island.

I'll be alone tonight, thought Bonnarjee, and dug his nails into his palms, fighting back waves of terror that threatened to engulf him at the thought. What if this island did contain savages, who would murder him slowly, once they knew he was on his own? Or might it not be the home of wild beasts? He had heard from boyhood how tigers had swum almost unbelievable distances in the warm sea from one island to another. Was it so unlikely that they had also reached this place? If so, he would be defenceless against them. Death would be terrible; but even worse would be to be left mutilated and alive, in an agony of fear, limbs half devoured, waiting for the animal to return at his pleasure to finish his feast.

I have enough wealth to buy this island, thought Bonnarjee despairingly, and every other island within a thousand square miles, and still have money in my treasury, but here gold is like dross; here, I am on my own, a castaway. My wealth now is measured in terms of my will, my determination to survive. And in this currency, I am a pauper. . . .

Castle was dreaming. He was not on this deserted island where poisoned coral cut his hands and feet and left sores that would not heal. He was with Bonnarjee in the Parsee's house overlooking the quay at Singapore. He had been astonished to receive a hand-written invitation to meet Mr Bonnarjee, of whom he had never heard, and even more surprised at the nature of Mr Bonnarjee's request.

'I hear reports of your prowess as a surveyor, Mr Castle,' the Parsee had assured him, leaning forward in his green leather chair he had imported specially from England. 'I wish to engage you for a secret assignment. I have a ship standing off harbour and would like you to take passage to an island. You will be escorted by one of my staff and, of course, servants will be at your disposal. On the island I want you to search for traces of coal. For this I am prepared to pay you one hundred golden guineas, half now and half on your return.'

'James Brooke's ship *Royalist* is due within three weeks,' replied Castle. 'I have half-promised to return to his service.'

'If you find coal in any quantity,' said Bonnarjee, 'I will make you another offer. That we join forces to extract it in the most economical fashion. This offer may cause you to think again before returning to the service of the White Rajah, Mr Brooke.'

'It might indeed, sir,' agreed Castle. 'I will accept your assignment.'

'I am pleased to have that answer,' said Bonnarjee. He bent down, opened a small drawer in a bow-legged table, and pulled out a chamois bag of coins. Castle counted them out: fifty golden guineas.

'It will be in your interest, Mr Castle, to observe strict silence about this mission. I will tell you in confidence that Dr Gunn and his Scottish partner, Mr MacPherson, are also interested in seeking coal from this place. Should they learn that you have similar thoughts they might take steps to remove you as a potential rival.'

'You mean they would kill me?'

'I mean what I say, Mr Castle. You are a young man and not versed in the ways of the East. Keep your silence, preserve your life.'

So Castle had sailed to the island, found the traces more quickly than he had imagined, and within a week was back in Bonnarjee's house to claim the second fifty guineas. Now Bonnarjee had outlined a further scheme. Castle should join Dr Gunn, go with him to the island aboard his ship, take his commission and his coin—and then betray him. That way, they would both ensure they were without a rival.

The fifty guineas lay heavy in Castle's pocket. The thought of wealth, quite unexpected, quite unsought, now bemused him. He did not wish to deceive a fellow countryman, but such a price gilded the name of treachery. Judas Iscariot had betrayed Our Lord for thirty pieces of silver. The price for betraying Gunn was a fortune. Surely, Castle argued against his own conscience, it was not so much a matter of betrayal as a matter of business? No doubt Gunn must have deceived and betrayed others to reach his present position, so it seemed a case of the biter being bitten in turn.

'I will do it,' he said to Bonnarjee.

'You make a wise decision,' replied the Parsee. 'When you land with the doctor, fall behind a little way and then cause some commotion. Pretend to swoon. Twist an ankle—anything so that you can be left alone to make your way back to the ship.'

'On what basis shall we share the profits?' asked Castle, and was instantly surprised at his own question. How quickly the love of money had become paramount in his thoughts!

'We shall decide that on the island,' replied Bonnarjee suavely. 'In the meantime, here is my hand, and we go forward together as partners. . . .'

Castle stirred on the sand as the sun burned its way up over the sheltering trees. He put a hand over his eyes, but sleep had already gone, and with sleep, had vanished his dream. He was back with Bonnarjee; back in exile, marooned. He must sail today, or he would never leave. Every day of delay diminished his determination.

He stood up, and stretched himself and yawned and hawked and spat. Then he rubbed his hairy armpits with the backs of his hands in a manner that disgusted Bonnarjee.

The man was foul and crude, and his habits constantly repulsed the Parsee. And yet Bonnarjee knew he would miss him when he went more than he had missed the departure of anyone else in all his life.

Castle was a rough stinking Englishman with a reddish beard; a man careless of exposing himself. He would walk naked and unashamed, with the stench of his unclean body causing him no embarrassment, while Bonnarjee bathed twice a day in the sea, and dutifully scrubbed his body with sand.

Bonnarjee was desperate to maintain his cleanliness, for he felt that his honour was somehow inextricably involved. But whereas Bonnarjee would religiously reserve one hand for clean duties, such as cutting up food and putting it into his mouth, and the other for necessary bodily functions, Castle was entirely without any such hygienic or religious scruples. The man would defecate like a beast, tearing off leaves from a bush to wipe his backside—and the next moment use the same hand to select a cube of coconut. But, even so, he was a companion; without him, Bonnarjee would only have his thoughts for company.

'You are still leaving, Mr Castle?' Bonnarjee asked him, still hoping that somehow his reply would be in the negative. It was odd how they still called each other 'mister'; the civilities of life had not yet deserted them. How would they behave when they did?

'I have to, Mr Bonnarjee. If I delay any longer, I fear my resolution will slip away. I will grow weaker on this wretched diet, this confounded coconut and damned inedible half-cooked fish.'

'You will be burned and scorched by the sun on that raft. Its heat may soften your mind.'

'I realize that, so I have constructed a screen from bamboo,' replied Castle.

'You have been meaning to leave for five days, and always, on the eve of your departure, we have discussed the matter, and you found it expedient to delay your departure. Why not do so today, one more time?'

'Because it would be, as you say, one more time, one more postponement. I must go, because to be honest, I fear going, Mr Bonnarjee, and the longer I wait, the greater will be my fear, and the less my chances of success. But I promise you truly, that when I make land, my first concern will be to send a vessel to pick you up.'

'Urge on them the necessity for speed,' implored Bonnarjee. 'Tell them not to count the cost. If you have to buy the vessel, then do so and purchase the crew. Promise them prize money, anything they wish, so long as you persuade them to come here.

'I will keep this fire lit day and night, with new damp wood so that it smokes and they will be able to see it from a distance. Remember, this island will not be on any chart, for it has no name.'

159

He paused, still praying that Castle might change his mind, but when the man said nothing, Bonnarjee continued in a flat, defeated voice.

'If you must go, then let me help you launch the raft.'

Together, and in silence, they carried the unwieldy creaking sagging mass of bamboos down to the sea. Ants still crawled over the smooth green and yellow wood; the sap smelt sharp in their nostrils; a little drinking water spilled out from the crude containers.

'Leave me but one bottle of water,' said Bonnarjee. 'Take the rest and fill them at the river. Your need is so infinitely greater than mine.'

'Thank you, sir. I am most grateful.'

Castle filled the grog bottles at the trickling stream, hacked down a young bamboo, cut it into small plugs and sharpened these to a wedge shape with his knife. Then he rammed them into the necks of the bottles. He also had twenty coconuts tied with jungle creeper and two large stones to smash them open.

'Are you utterly convinced it would not be better to leave at evening and so sail with the stars and the cool of the night?'

'That time of departure has its attractions, Mr Bonnarjee, but then I would be condemned for at least twelve hours aboard this raft before I could hope to see a ship, or they could see me. I would rather risk the heat of the sun, because some lookout may spot me. And then all our troubles would be at an end.'

'And Dr Gunn's about to begin,' said Bonnarjee bitterly.

Castle had erected a crude mast roughly in the centre of the raft, supported by bamboo struts lashed at each corner. The top of the mast was split and into this split he had pushed a pair of linen drawers. They fluttered like the two prongs of a strange white pennant. Maybe some lookout high in the crow's-nest of a merchantman would see this flag and urge his skipper to change course to investigate?

The raft was floating now, moving heavily on the uneasy surface of the sea. Its edge bumped against their bare legs; the rough serrations in the wood scratched Bonnarjee's flesh.

'May your gods bless you and grant you a safe voyage,' he said hoarsely. 'I will pray to my gods, Mr Castle, and you must pray to yours.'

'Perhaps they would all be more eager to answer our prayers,' replied Castle dryly, 'had I lived more according to their teachings.'

'We are as we are because the gods have made us thus,' Bonnarjee assured him. He held out his hand. Castle gripped it. His palm was wet with salt and soggy and split with cuts that would never heal in that climate. Castle put on a conical hat he had made from leaves, then carefully climbed on the raft and knelt in the centre.

Water slopped over its surface. The sun was stronger now, reflecting off the sea as though from a giant mirror, dazzling, blinding; its fierce heat and light and power mocked his feebleness.

Castle took a bamboo paddle he had made and dug the blade into the water. The little raft spun uneasily in a circle, righted itself, and began to move jerkily with each thrust of his paddle.

'You should have had a sail,' called Bonnarjee. Anything to delay the man's departure, to postpone that moment of utter loneliness when he would be on his own. 'Wait! We can make a sail somehow from leaves. I can cut down some bamboos. Wait for one more day. Only for a day.'

Castle shook his head. He had already tried to fashion a sail from leaves and it was impossible. His only hope was to paddle out into the trade currents, and trust that they would carry him into the clipper routes; or if not, at least take him to an island where the inhabitants would understand and help him.

He turned cautiously, for the raft rocked alarmingly at any movement, and waved to Bonnarjee, and then applied himself to his task of paddling. Sea-water ran down the smooth edges of the paddle, stinging his raw hands and his sun-burned arms, and the sun blazed on his back like a furnace. Then he was gone beyond hearing Bonnarjee's call, and finally, drifting like an ever-diminishing dot, he shrank on the edge of the horizon.

Bonnarjee turned slowly and walked up the beach, shoulders bent, his whole body trembling with dejection and reaction.

'Oh, God, save me,' he prayed aloud, his voice cracked with emotion. 'Deliver me, I pray, from pestilence and the fear of death. From unknown enemies, from the wild beasts of the land, the carrion birds of the sky, from the deadly fish that swim in this accursed sea.'

He sank down on his knees, sobbing from his heart, and then lay on the fiery sand, careless of the heat, lost in a welter of loneliness and misery. Presently, wearied by weeping, and crouched in a foetal position of subjection, Bonnarjee slept.

\*        \*        \*

The oiled hide whip flickered in the harsh sunlight and cracked like a gun. At the sound, the Chinese coolies, most of them naked save for black plate-shaped straw hats, and strips of rough canvas around their genitals, wielded their picks and axes with redoubled vigour.

Thirty of them, spread in a long line across the baking scrub, inland from the shore of Jade Gate Island, were working under the hard eyes of a Chinese overseer. Dust swelled and swirled, a sand-coloured cloud, choking them, irritating their eyes, coating their slim-muscled, smooth, hairless bodies. They hacked on, fearing the lead tip of the whip scoring their flesh more than the heat of the sun and the suffocating dust. A cut from that whip would never heal, but fester indefinitely, suppurating and open, attracting flies. A cut could kill, not immediately but slowly and with ever-increasing pain.

Tu Sung, the coolie-master, watched them impassively from the top of a small mound of sand they had already dug. A servant held an umbrella of plaited plantain leaves above his head to shield him from the sun. His face looked unusually rosy for a Chinese because of high blood pressure and his love of rice wine. This colour also gave him a benevolent appearance entirely alien to his character.

On the instructions of Bonnarjee's father-in-law, Tu Sung had transported his private army to Jade Gate Island in the junk which he kept moored close inshore, so that it could not be readily seen from the sea.

The old Parsee had given him a down payment of 1,000 silver dollars and the promise of three times as much, plus all their food and wages when they had dug certain holes at the direction of a Red-Bristled Barbarian

163

who had made a study of the ground. The Barbarian had driven special hollowed rods into the earth to examine the texture of the soil, and had decided where Tu Sung's men should dig. Speed was necessary, for this Barbarian, Castle, could only stay for a few days before he had to return to Singapore.

Tu Sung had not liked this Barbarian, Castle. He hated his smell, his roughness, his bristled beard. The Chinese preferred smooth skins and delicate manners, and Castle possessed neither of these attributes. Also, he had shouted at Tu Sung in his own language, and when Tu Sung, while understanding that the Barbarian was angry, could not quickly comprehend what he meant, Castle had pointed with his stubby nail-bitten fingers, and even jostled the coolies, pushing them this way and that.

Tu Sung hated him then and despised him, and also feared him, for his strength was great, and so was his power with the Parsee. Worst of all, Castle had almost caused Tu Sung to lose face, and therefore he would like to see Castle stripped as these coolies, and working with a shovel, digging out samples of this black coal by which the Parsee set such importance. But what had happened to Bonnarjee and Castle and their plans? Where were the pirates who had accompanied them? Was it not said that they planned to take over the other Barbarian's vessel, *Hesperides*, and sink it and claim that Barbarian's goods, and his company, as their own? But words are one thing, and deeds are quite another, and in this instance the two had not been equally matched.

Tu Sung, hiding inland, had watched from a treetop through the magic glass Bonnarjee had left, and he had seen Bonnarjee capture two other Red-Bristled Barbarians, one said to be a physician, and the other a former sailor in deep seas, through the treachery of their countryman, Castle.

They had all rowed out to *Hesperides*, and from across the water, Tu Sung had heard shouts and the clang of sword on metal, the crack of muskets and pistols. Then the vessel had unexpectedly sailed away, leaving bodies floating in the water to be eaten by sharks and killer fish whose teeth were so sharp they could skin the flesh from a body in minutes, and leave only clean and separate bones.

Bonnarjee had not returned to him; neither had Castle, and nor had the Barbarian's vessel. Could it be that Bonnarjee, whom Tu Sung despised, had tricked him—just as Castle had deceived the two Barbarians, who believed he was their friend?

If this were so, Bonnarjee would cause him to lose infinitely more face than even the wretched Barbarian Castle with his uncouth manners, his hoarse voice, and the flecks of spittle that sprayed from his mouth as he bellowed his Barbarian instructions. If this was indeed the truth, woe would fall upon the head of Tu Sung as heavily as holy rain on the celestial plains behind Peking, when the heavens opened on the Emperor's prayers.

He would then have to transport his coolies back to Macao, and although he would pay them in rice instead of money, word would soon spread that a Barbarian had swindled him; that Tu Sung the great, the wise, the infinitely cunning, had been made to look a fool at the hands of an unbeliever. His enemies would trumpet this news with the glee that bad news always gives to inferior persons who delight in the downfall of those who have set themselves above them.

Tu Sung had already been on the island for three weeks, and to stay for one more week would be too long. He had decided to wait here for another two days, in the hope that Bonnarjee would return, and prove his worrying thoughts were foolish as the anxieties of young wives who suspect infidelity in old and withered husbands.

But what an absurd and impossible situation for a man of his achievement and shrewdness; to be laughed at by aliens, by the sons of Barbarians from over the outer seas! Never would this happen again. Tu Sung prayed it was not happening now, but he still felt doubtful and concerned, and unease lay heavy as a hammer-head in his stomach.

He therefore ordered his overseers to whip the coolies to make them work harder and faster, sucking some sour modicum of comfort from inflicting humiliation on these wretched creatures. A messenger approached, bowed low and patiently waited Tu Sung's permission to raise his head.

'Speak,' Tu Sung ordered him.

'A small boat is approaching the bay, master. It is no larger than a raft of bamboos. It has no sail and no crew, only one Barbarian with a paddle.'

'Fetch me the glass, so that I may examine this craft myself.'

The man sped away, and returned with a brass telescope which he extended, and handed over to his master. Tu Sung raised the glass to his right eye and focused on the raft. He recognized Castle, although he was nearly half a mile away. The Barbarian seemed exhausted, and crouched on his hands and knees, head forward. His skin was red as flame. No doubt he was in too great pain to lie on the waterlogged bamboos, for the sea-water would sting his flesh like etching acid.

'It is the Barbarian with the trumpet voice,' said Tu Sung, lowering his glass. Where was Bonnarjee? Why was this one man approaching on a raft? What could have happened to *Hesperides* that she did not return— or even send back a ship's boat? A raft smacked of shipwreck and catastrophe.

'Take four men to the beach. See that sweetmeats and lime juice are available for him. Maybe his vessel has met with some disaster.'

The messenger bowed again, retreated, head down, for three paces, and then ran to the beach, shouting to an overseer as he ran.

From the raft, Castle saw the white rim of breaking surf, then the brief spread of sandy beach, and the emerald green of jungle, and uttered a prayer of thankfulness. He did not recognize the island, but beyond the haze of spume from the breaking waves, he could see men waiting for him on the sand. Relief flooded through him, so that he forgot the agony of his burned and blistered back, and the huge areas of flesh which the sun had fried hard as a hog's crackling. His lips had split with heat and dryness, and he had long since drunk all the water in the bottles. The salt he felt in his throat was the taste of his own blood.

The tide took Castle's waterlogged raft, now floating inches below the surface. Trailing bamboos, which days and nights of sea-water had weakened, hung down and scraped the sandy bed of the shallow sea.

Four coolies stepped forward to steady the raft while another picked him off and carried him through the breaking waves and up the beach. He could smell sweat on their bodies, overlaid by the sweet scent of their perfumed hair. They laid him down on scrubby grass in merciful shade. One held a gourd of water and lime juice to his lips, and Castle drank greedily, choking and coughing in his desperate desire to force his dry parched throat to swallow it. He felt sweat sting the sores on his back, and greedily held out both hands for some paw-paw served up to him on a wide flat shell.

The brightness of the sun reflected from the sea had damaged Castle's eyes, so that at first he had difficulty in focusing them on his rescuers. Gradually, their features resolved from hazy yellow blobs into human faces. With surprise, he recognized one man. He had somehow returned to Jade Gate Island. He felt that now he was among friends, or at least people who knew him. Truly, his prayers had been answered. He began to speak in pidgin, very slowly because his tongue was swollen with thirst, and his mind still seemed miles away.

'Fetchee number one chop, full time speed, head man Tu Sung,' he ordered the nearest coolie.

'No way fetchee you number one man. Must quickly runee fetchee you him along,' came the answer.

The coolie signalled to some other coolies, who now appeared, carrying a crude stretcher they had quickly made from bamboos lashed together with creeper. They lifted Castle on to this, and with two men at each end, they began to run in their tireless jog-trotting way. Castle held on tightly with his cut, split hands lest he was thrown off into scrub and prickly thorn.

Each step they took was agony to him, but he bore it stoically. He was alive and safe, and within the hour he should be aboard Tu Sung's junk and heading back to the island to rescue the Parsee. Then he would do what he had planned all along; agree terms with the Parsee before he sent in a boat, so that Bonnarjee would make over to him a significant part of his company and his treasure in return for rescue. Then Castle would come into his true destiny. No longer would he be a surveyor, working to other men's commands, carrying out examinations of soil or sites that would make them rich; at last he would be rich himself.

The thought comforted him, and he was still thinking about this agreeable future when the bearers stopped running, and gently deposited the litter on the ground at Tu Sung's feet.

The Chinese contractor looked down at Castle contemptuously. So the wild Barbarian who had shouted so arrogantly at him, who had frequently addressed him as if he was a yellow-eyed cur, now lay defenceless at his feet, skin burned as though in a furnace.

'You remember me, no?' asked Castle hopefully. 'I here short time along Bonnarjee sahib.'

'No more speak pidgin,' replied Tu Sung coldly. 'Only Cantonese talking or both tongues keeping silence as fish in deep pool.'

Castle dredged in his mind for the Cantonese phrases he needed. He could only speak a little. Why the devil could not this Chinese swine converse in pidgin? Was he on his dignity?

'I have come from Bonnarjee sahib,' said Castle slowly in Cantonese. 'He is marooned on an island. He needs your help. I wish you to take me in your junk and we shall rescue him. You will be richly rewarded. I pledge you his word on that, and mine.'

'Where is this island, and who marooned him?'

Castle explained how far Gunn had sailed, and by what stars. Tu Sung nodded. The island could be barely two days' sailing, and was possibly even less. He would easily find it, for he would see the smoke signal when he was still miles away. He had no problem there, and no doubt Bonnarjee would reward him.

But why take Castle with him on the voyage? What part had he to play in the deal he would force on Bonnarjee? Castle was beaten, defeated, humiliated, as useless to Tu Sung now that he told him the whereabouts of the island, as a shattered gong or a broken drinking vessel. Why therefore should he now take this foul, salt-stinking creature and make him rich? Surely Tu Sung's dead illustrious ancestors would cry from the happy land that this was madness and folly beyond belief?

Instead of such foolishness, he should kill Castle now, and feed his body to the fish.

But that could have dangerous consequences, because these Red-Bristled Barbarians held power of a strange kind that commanded his respect, if not his liking. One of his coolies might talk too much when he returned to Macao or Singapore, and as a result Tu Sung could be flung into jail or given over to the torturers. He had many enemies who would rejoice at his downfall, and who would willingly speak truth or lies about him if they thought that they could assist at his downfall.

He would not kill Castle; instead, he would humiliate him in the most devastating way a man could be humbled. He would deprive him of his manhood, re-move what the Chinese poets delicately called the Jade Stem or The Turtle-head. In crude terms, he would castrate him, and send him as a eunuch to Macao, and then along secret trade routes, over the snowy peaks, to the forbidden city of Peking.

There the Chinese Emperor, God of Gods, King of the Lands and the Air and the Waters, would greatly wel-come the gift of a Barbarian Eunuch. Castle would be a living example of the fate reserved for those who offended his subjects. Might it not also be that the Emperor would reward Tu Sung for his loyal kindness, by sending him his Imperial felicitations, thus giving pride not only to his humble servant, but to the shades of his ancestors?

And would not the fact that he had carried out this ultimate degradation on Castle also weigh heavily with the man's employer, Bonnarjee? He would be infinitely more eager to come to any terms with Tu Sung when he learned how fierce he was, how ruthless. Tu Sung would not be a paper lion or tiger, as were so many with loud mouths and soft wills, but truly a man of action, a man to be feared, in whose presence lesser beings trembled as the branches of the casuarina tree flutter in a high wind. Truly, it was written, he who climbs a tall tree can lay claim to its fruit. And Tu Sung felt that this was his opportunity to climb high—and to climb alone.

There were three ways in which Tu Sung could de-prive the unspeakable Barbarian of his manhood. First, and easiest, he could perform Hsing-Ch'en, which meant Total Loss, removing the man's penis and severing his testicles at their roots. He could accomplish this easily enough with a sharpened knife and then crush the Stones of Life with tongs until they burst like almonds from their flesh.

Alternatively, he could sear them with red-hot irons or even tear them physically from Castle's body, leaving only his male organ to remind him that once he was a man.

More subtly, he could remove this organ but deliberately leave the testicles unharmed, and this was the cruellest punishment of all, because a man thus cut would still feel the warmth of sexual desire. And although he might insert a bamboo or straw tube into the hole where once the stem had grown to carry away his urine, nothing he might do could ever quench the heat of accumulating lusts that would burn his flesh like fire.

The Vital Essence could not find natural release, and so the eunuch would be forced to seek relief from the impotent fury of his needs by inflicting pain and even death on others. He might elect to be cudgelled insensible himself, or he could beat to death the young and unwanted children of unworthy persons, or carry out enormous cruelties on animals.

Sometimes a eunuch in this situation would split the skulls of lazy servants with an axe and eat their brains, for it was written in the books of legends, that only thus could the Flame and Fire of his soul be assuaged, and the ferment driven from his blood.

For centuries, senior eunuchs at the Emperor's Court in Peking, who had suffered this deprivation had his authority to decapitate the Emperor's enemies and certain groups of criminals. Invariably, they ordered that the dead men's skulls should immediately be split open, and their brains carried to them in silver ewers, still steaming, in the hope that they could gain release from their own extremities of desire by eating the thoughts and memories of men newly murdered.

How the mighty would be humbled if Tu Sung dealt thus with the Barbarian Castle!

In Castle's screams of agony and despair, in his desperate appeals and prayers for mercy, Tu Sung would hear the echo of his arrogance only weeks before.

'When can we sail?' asked Castle impatiently, scattering Tu Sung's pleasurable imaginings like newly ground grain in a sudden breeze.

Castle saw that the Chinaman was still staring at him and doing nothing. Did the fool not understand what he was saying, or could he not comprehend the urgency of his mission? Or perhaps Tu Sung did not fully understand Castle's halting Cantonese? But this possibility brought another question to which Castle could find no comforting answer: why would not the fellow converse in pidgin as he had been pleased to do throughout the time they were working together?

Castle felt frustration flood through his veins, as it always did when confronted by natives who would regard him sullenly, not carrying out his orders, but apathetic and stubborn as oxen.

'I will sail when my vessel is made ready. And I will sail alone,' Tu Sung told him.

'But you will need me. I am fit to travel. And I can tell you exactly where the island lies.'

'You have already told me where it lies and how I will recognize it. I have a glass that Mr Bonnarjee gave to me. This extends my sight for many miles. You will stay here.'

'But I must return to the island, and then go to Singapore or Macao. There is nothing for me here.'

Something in Tu Sung's attitude suddenly alarmed Castle. The man was speaking coldly, as though to someone of low degree.

'You must take me,' he shouted, standing up, and swaying weakly with the unaccustomed movement. 'Cannot you understand what I say?'

'I understand,' replied Tu Sung, relishing his position. 'You are the one who lacks comprehension in this matter. I do not trust Mr Bonnarjee. He had done to death a relation of mine, Lin Yang, who worked for the Barbarian physician turned merchant, Dr Gunn. You are Bonnarjee's creature, and so I do not trust you. Nor do I relish your loud voice and your crude habits, or even the sharp smell of your body. You will stay here.

'Mr Bonnarjee has dishonoured his agreement with me. He has sailed away rather than pay that which he owes for my coolies. As a result, I have lost face in their sight, and become to them lower than a carrier of dung. No doubt he has sent you back to see me because, as a Barbarian, he thought you would be spared my anger? He believed I would fear the ships of your Navy, and the voices of their guns, for Mr Bonnarjee is a devious man with a cunning mind. Is it not written: "No man ever lost himself on a straight road?" But he has lost himself now in the convolutions of his own imagination, his own avarice. Now he is confounded, like a lamb abject before the slaughterer, a pig squealing before the sharpened knife.'

'What do you mean?' asked Castle in amazement. 'You cannot believe this. Let me sail with you, and I will prove that what I say is true. Mr Bonnarjee will honour all his debts. He is a man of his word, a man of wealth and power.'

'I am not prepared to be fobbed off by a lying Barbarian messenger. I will teach you how we treat traitors, and those who murder honourable Chinese people.

'Bonnarjee is not man enough to father his own son. I know the stories of the Englishman, Gunn, and I know why Bonnarjee hated him. Bonnarjee's Jade Stem is weak and feeble, soft and useless as a cut vine stalk. His Vital Essence is thin as acid from the root of the Lin Sing tree. So we have contempt for him; he is a creature who wears the clothes of a man, but he is nothing, a neuter. And as a warning to him, and others like him, we shall make you as he is.'

'What do you mean?'

Castle's voice was taut with worry. The man was mad, of course; these bloody Chinese were all mad, when they had a little power or when they felt insulted. Bonnarjee must have crossed Tu Sung in some way—but that was surely no reason for Tu Sung to take out his anger on him? Of course not. But while Castle fully convinced himself of the total incongruity of this attitude, could he convince Tu Sung?

The Chinese did not deign to answer him; he had already said what he meant. Now was the time to translate words to deeds. Tu Sung called instructions to his overseer; the coolies stood up, straightened their backs thankfully and dropped their picks and pengahs, grateful for any lull in the weary drudgery of their work. Their overseer cracked his whip twice in the air, and like circus animals, trained to move on the signal, the coolies obediently formed a wide circle around Tu Sung and Castle.

There was something expectant in their attitude. One or two were even grinning, and what had these poor brutes to smile about? It was almost as though they were gathered to watch a rare and entertaining spectacle. The circle had the vague appearance of a boxing ring; was Tu Sung going to challenge him to some form of combat? Castle's flesh crawled with foreboding. He was too weak to fight. Surely Tu Sung was not going to murder him ceremoniously as a diversion for his slaves?

Tu Sung produced a small curved knife from the folds of his robe and tested the blade on his thumb. The overseer tore a shirt from the back of one of the coolies and ripped the cloth into long thin sweat-sodden strips like bandages.

'What are you going to do?' Castle asked; the action seemed menacing. What in the name of God was about to happen? His voice was hoarse, and his heart fluttered and hammered like the wings of a wild bird trapped within him.

'Wait!' he shouted. 'I speak the truth! Let me prove my words.'

'You and Bonnarjee have had the opportunity to prove your honesty. Now I will prove *my* words,' replied Tu Sung. 'I will cut you, as I would cut a colt. I will deliver you of your manhood, but not of the urge to love and couple. That will still burn on as you Christians believe the eternal fires burn sulphurously in hell. This will be your hell.

'You will still desire women or boys and will endlessly search for any relief, as a man dying in the desert under

176

the sun craves for any drop of water. But your fountain of Vital Essence will be denied a way into the world. It will be as an underground river, forever bursting to be free, and forever failing to escape.'

'But why punish me in this way? What can you possibly gain by it? Nothing. Yet if you allow me to accompany you to Bonnarjee sahib, you will instantly see that what I say is true, and you will have your debt paid, and infinitely more treasure besides. He will give you his whole fortune if you will but deliver him from the isolation of that island.'

'Some debts cannot be paid by money. They are debts of honour. Bonnarjee has broken his word to me. He has used me and gone his way. He has caused me to lose infinite face with vastly inferior persons. He has defiled me and insulted my noble ancestors. If he were not as despicable as a yellow-eyed dog, he would have come here, to settle my debt in person.'

'But I tell you, he cannot,' screamed Castle. 'He is marooned on an island.'

This was a nightmare come to life, overwhelming him. His body ran with sweat and his joints trembled uncontrollably, as though with ague. All strength left his legs and he sank down in a kneeling position on the sand, like a supplicant, his cracked split bleeding hands raised beseechingly.

'I beg you to listen.'

'You have spoken enough,' Tu Sung told him briefly, 'I have listened enough. My ears are stopped with your words.'

Castle watched with horror as Tu Sung plunged his knife three times into the hot sand, and again drew the ball of his thumb across the honed blade. Castle tried to stand up, hoping in his delirious terror to flee he knew not where; to plunge into the sea and swim away and risk death between the jaws of sharks rather than at the hands of a heathen. But his legs were too weak after his voyage on the raft, and he pitched forward humiliatingly. Immediately, coolies seized him under the armpits and lifted him up, and once more his nostrils were filled with the smell of their scented body oil and his own fear.

The overseer cut away Castle's trousers. The breeze felt surprisingly cool on his hot sweaty body. Coolies pressed forward to examine his private parts, exclaiming at his body hair. Castle cried out in rage and fear, struggling against the wiry little men who held him, once even tipping them off their feet, so that they all rolled like a human pyramid on the hot sand.

'Listen, you fool!' Castle screamed at Tu Sung. 'You are throwing away a fortune. I will take you to Bonnarjee. Just give me the chance, I beg of you.'

He turned to the overseer and coolies and shouted to them in Cantonese.

'Save me! I will make you all rich, if you help me.'

They looked at him with empty eyes, as keepers examine a caged animal they have never encountered before but which they believe to be dangerous and deadly. And what was the depth of the words he uttered? They were only shallow promises, empty as a summer sky when the south wind whisks away the clouds.

The ranks of the coolies parted and a man appeared, carrying a bowl of hot water. It steamed slightly and had been sprinkled with hot pepper, so that the bearer coughed and sneezed, and his eyes ran with its fumes.

At the sight of this ritual cleansing vessel, Castle began to weep and then retched in his misery, vomiting out bile and gobbets of fruit which stuck to the hair on his chest.

A coolie kicked his ankles from under him, and as he dropped down on his knees, others bent back Castle's body so that it was held in the shape of a curved bow. The overseer prised his legs apart, wedging his knees open with a piece of bamboo which he had whittled into a sharp point at each end. A coolie sprinkled hot peppered water on his flesh and Castle screamed with the pain. Tu Sung took a strip of Castle's shirt, soaked it in the cleansing water and then wiped the area to remove sweat and sand.

'Now, Barbarian with the trumpet voice,' he said, intoning the words like a pagan priest at some primitive religious rite, 'with this swift motion of my knife I take you across the frontier from manhood to a world of men who seek women but who can never possess them.

'In that new world your place will be with women, but your thoughts will remain with men. It is a half-world, a hinterland of light and shade, of longing without release, of need without fulfilment. Truly this is the hell on earth of which the ancients speak.'

Four coolies forced back Castle's head upside down so that his hair was rammed down into the sand. Blood flooded his brain, diffusing his skin the colour of a purple plum. His vision clouded. He gasped for breath, gouging his raw hands into the hot sand. Veins swelled in his neck and temples like blue cords. He choked, sobbing entreaties to men who did not understand. 'Help me! Jesus! Mercy! I beg of you!'

Tu Sung bent forward with his knife, poised it for a second and then swung the blade down with a swift, precise and circular motion. The instant spout of crimson arterial blood was quenched by a sheet of rice-paper that the overseer produced. He pressed this against the round, pumping wound. Instantly, the white paper turned red; another was placed above it, and then a third, and the strips of shirt were bound tightly around Castle's waist and his legs.

He sobbed in his immeasurable pain and the coolies released him slightly but would not let him collapse. Instead they lifted him up and bent his body forward. A rope of vomit streamed from his mouth; blood ran down the inside of his legs and reddened the sand, sticking to the sweaty flesh.

The overseer now produced a sharpened bamboo and prodded this into Castle's buttocks. Blindly, like a captured beast still held by his hunters, and in a red raw mist of pain, Castle staggered forward and fell, sand encrusting the bloodied rice-paper. The coolies pulled him up to his feet.

'You will be kept walking for two hours,' Tu Sung told him. 'It is now the Hour of the Serpent. By the Hour of the Rat you will be allowed to lie down.'

Castle was in too great pain even to speak. All strength had sapped from his body. He could only keep upright because two coolies supported him. He was like a statue, forced to move without will or life. His legs sank up to the ankles in the soft sand, and the three men stumbled in a reeling irregular line down the beach, and then back across their tracks.

Tu Sung regarded Castle with detachment. He felt

proud of what he had done. Now, any other Barbarians who might present themselves to him under guise of friendship or trade would know he was not a man to be trifled with. He was no longer a base-born person, a driver of coolies, a barterer of slaves; he had proved himself a worthy descendant of his ancestors. But he still had to keep Castle alive, and it was therefore essential that the wretched creature was made to move for several more hours. If he was allowed to rest too soon, blood might congeal in his body, and, according to the teaching of the ancients, the man would die.

Castle would not be allowed to drink anything for three days, and in this time he would endure agonies of delirium from thirst. His lips would crack, his tongue swell like a bull's pizzle, and his whole throat burn dry as the inside of a chimney. And not only this, but the tightness of his bandages would stop him passing out water already trapped in his body. So, desperate to accept water at one orifice and unable to release it from another, he would endure almost unbearable pain until the bandages could be removed. And even then the Barbarian faced one last risk that could prove mortal.

The wound might heal so thoroughly that the small hole from which the imprisoned urine should spurt was permanently blocked and Castle would be condemned to die, his passages swollen, bladder distended to the size of an ostrich egg. Ironically, he would drown in his own water and yet be crazed with thirst. Truly the ways of the gods with men were as inscrutable as the Emperor's eyes.

Tu Sung turned to the overseer and ordered him to gather up the remaining strips of cloth and the porcelain

181

bowl. A coolie scattered fresh sand over the bloodied mess where Castle had lain.

The overseer's whip cracked angrily, like a dry tree splitting.

'To work, you dogs,' he shouted. 'You have seen enough entertainment for the day. Be thankful your manhood remains. Poor as you are, you are still richer than this Barbarian will ever be.'

# CHAPTER SEVEN

*In which the Governor wishes Godspeed
to a mission, so long as no responsibility can
rest with him*

TWO INDIAN SEPOY SENTRIES presented arms smartly
as Gunn stepped from his doolie and walked up the wide
stone steps of Government House in Singapore. Inside
the doorway, the butler bowed.

'His Excellency is expecting you, sir,' he said gravely,
and led the way down a long cool corridor with a marble
floor. The lime green walls were hung with oil paintings
of English politicians. Tapestried punkahs creaked at
intervals. The butler paused outside high double doors
painted in matt dark green, tapped on them gently,
waited for a moment and then flung them open. He
bowed to the only occupant the vast room contained.

'Dr Robert Gunn to see you, Your Excellency,' he
intoned, and closed the doors silently, leaving the two
men on their own.

The Governor stood up slowly from behind his desk.
It was three o'clock in the afternoon and he had been
dozing in his high-backed chair after a heavy curry
lunch. The sudden opening of the big doors had
awakened him, so that his heart raced, and he leaned on

the desk to steady himself and regain his breath. He was a small, bald man, with a dark splayed beard flecked with grey, and eyes set too close together.

'It is a pleasure to meet you, doctor,' he said warmly, as though he had been waiting all his life for this opportunity. In fact, he had forgotten Gunn's name, and only the butler's prompting reminded him. Who the devil was this fellow Gunn anyhow? Just another merchant or opium-runner who had struck lucky and was now a *taipan*. The only thing that marked him out from a dozen similar upstarts was that he had originally been a sawbones. If there was any justice in the world he would be flogged as a drug pedlar, instead of being granted a private interview with Her Majesty's representative.

'Please be seated, doctor,' said the Governor, indicating one of two green armchairs with button upholstery. 'Would you take a glass of port with me? Or perhaps a glass of claret? I am happy to say that a new consignment has only just reached me—possibly aboard one of your vessels?'

'Thank you, sir, but I do not drink so early in the day,' replied Gunn. 'My mother was a Presbyterian, and as a result my habits are somewhat abstemious.'

'A wise rule of life in this climate, but one which my official duties do not always allow me to observe.'

The Governor opened a carved ivory box of cigars and handed it to Gunn. He selected one. They both lit up. The Governor sat down behind his desk, his heart calmer now. He had not known who or what to expect when he heard that Gunn wished an interview with him, and had vaguely imagined some kind of pirate creature, uncouth and rash. Instead, the fellow was personable

184

enough, almost a foot taller than he was himself and with a grave face and the demeanour—if not the background —of a gentleman.

'You wished to see me about some important matter, doctor?' the Governor asked Gunn. 'Something that can only be discussed privately?'

'That is true,' said Gunn. 'Since you represent Her Majesty and her Government here, I wish to bring to your notice an opportunity which has been brought to mine, and which, if we do not take, we may never be given again. You probably know, sir, in far greater detail than I do, that the Royal Navy is going over to steam propulsion for their more important vessels, and eventually for all of Her Majesty's ships.

'This will be of incalculable benefit to our nation— as will be the change to steam from sail of those of us who maintain merchant fleets. Our vessels will be faster and more manœuvrable than those of our rivals—but at a price. For the one weakness in an otherwise overwhelming argument in favour of steam rests on the source and availability of coal to fire the ships' boilers.

'As you will also know, sir, the Royal Navy has sent a surveyor to Labuan and Jade Gate Island in attempts to discover local supplies of coal. He is more hopeful regarding Labuan, but I can tell you I do not accept his negative findings as regards Jade Gate.'

'You have absolutely definite proof there is coal on that island, sir?'

'Not as categorically as we both might wish, Your Excellency. But I am sufficiently convinced to spend my own money in proving my private conviction. What brings me here especially is that I have also learned that other parties are of the same opinion and seek this coal. One group has been organized by a Parsee merchant possibly known to you, Mr Bonnarjee. While the Parsees are traditionally friendly to the British, it would not be ideal if our prime source of naval fuel in this hemisphere relied on their continual goodwill.

'I know for a fact that Mr Bonnarjee is ill-disposed to me personally, and therefore my assumption is that he would actively hinder any enterprise with which I might be associated.

'The other party interested involves Americans. I need not tell you, sir, how strange are the ways of Americans in the East. Without, of course, any official backing from their Government, they have for long supplied pirates with arms and powder which enabled these murderers to maintain their nefarious trade in these waters.'

'It has been said, doctor, that the Americans, as our trans-Atlantic cousins, have actually helped our efforts to subdue the pirates because the powder which they sold them was of such poor quality that it did not always explode!'

The Governor smiled at his own joke, and tapped the end of his cigar into a silver ashtray.

'I have heard that, too, sir. But from my own experience, I must report with feeling that American powder is as strong and fierce as ours. However, that is another subject. If the Americans should gain suzerainty over Jade Gate, they could hold to ransom any fleet in these seas, whether mercantile or naval. They could also combine here with the French or the Dutch, as they did in their so-called War of Independence against British rule.'

The Governor nodded solemnly.

186

'I accept your points, doctor,' he replied. 'I am not unaware of these movements myself.'

This was, in fact, the first time he had heard of even a search for coal in any island in the area, but he had not risen to his present eminence without being able to combine the role of actor with that of diplomat.

How much safer and more rewarding it was to pretend foreknowledge when you had none; to nod your head sagely, or shake it sadly at the folly and presumptuousness of others infinitely more subtle and clever! You thus acquired a reputation for wisdom, and became a man widely known and respected for your vision, and your readiness to hear all kinds of opinions. In fact, you held no strong opinions of your own and the last view you heard was the one you invariably adopted.

'Then, sir, since you agree with what I say, I have no doubt you will agree with what I now propose?'

'That depends, doctor, on your proposition. You have the reputation of being a man of mettle, if I may say so, whereas here in government, we must proceed slowly. *Festina lente*, as my old Latin tutor at the House used to say.'

'I have learned the wisdom of that saying myself,' replied Gunn. 'But I have also learned the even greater wisdom of anticipating a rival's move before he makes it.

'What I wish from you, Governor, is the granting of papers so that when I sail to Jade Gate, as I intend to do speedily, I can proceed immediately to the Sultan or other native ruler of that island, and enter into an agreement with him so that Mandarin-Gold, in conjunction with Her Majesty's Government, can secure sole rights to prospect for coal, and then extract coal and sell it.'

'You are asking for a great deal, doctor. I would have to send a message to London before I could agree to such a proposal, and as you know, that takes a long time. Assuming the Foreign Minister received it within six weeks, that would take us to August. And no doubt he will be spending the latter half of that month on the grouse moors, shooting.'

'No doubt, sir. But out here we could spend years shooting, not grouse but other human beings unless we can secure agreement on this vital matter.'

'I have not the power to commit Her Majesty's Government to take control over any further areas of land. As you know, our present Empire, which was largely unsought, is ruinously expensive, with little enough return to the national exchequer.'

'All the more reason, sir, for us to acquire all rights over Jade Gate, which would secure a guaranteed return.'

'Guaranteed by whom?'

'By me.'

'Your proposition sounds undeniably attractive, doctor, but I would be seriously overstepping my authority if I gave you permission to negotiate any treaty on behalf of Her Majesty's Government without their prior knowledge and agreement. I would naturally be pleased if you could extract the coal for the sole use of our Navy and merchant vessels propelled by steam engines without such a treaty. But what would the natives on the island require in return?'

'I could offer the ruler a percentage of all net profits on the coal, after all expenses, of course. Therefore, the more coal they dug and we sold, the greater would be their revenue. If they produced nothing, then they would receive nothing.'

'A most ingenious proposition, doctor, but again, while I applaud the sentiments and patriotism that lie behind it, I cannot accede to it officially. You must understand my position. I am not like you, a free agent in such matters. I am a servant of the Crown.'

'If you will not give me any authority, sir, then if I make my own arrangements with the ruler of Jade Gate to extract coal from his island, I assume you would set no hindrance in my path?'

'So long as you do not commit Her Majesty's Government, Her Majesty's Navy, Her Majesty's armies, or any of Her Majesty's servants, such as myself, to any fixed involvement or guarantee, I could—unofficially at least —give you my blessing.'

'But you wish to have no active part whatever in this enterprise?'

'What I wish, doctor, and what I can agree to, are two different things.'

'In that case,' said Gunn, 'I will sail to Jade Gate and negotiate the best deal I can on my own, since you specifically wish to stay totally uninvolved. Of course, you would not then expect any share of the profit—assuming we make any—to be subject to any Governmental levy or taxation?'

'That is a different question, doctor. Again, it is not one I am qualified to issue a firm opinion on immediately.'

'It seems to me then, Governor,' said Gunn dryly, 'that you wish to take no risk, to make no decisions, to give no answers, except general aphorisms of goodwill and Godspeed. By this abdication of authority you also hope to make sure none of the shot falls on you should the guns begin to fire.

'However, if—despite your firm lack of help or involvement—our enterprise is blessed with success, you wish to reserve the right to tax our efforts which, sir, we will make at the risk of our lives. Is that not a correct assessment?'

'It is an assessment, sir, that I must say offends my senses deeply.'

'I regret that just as deeply, Governor, but your total lack of enthusiasm and your temerity of purpose also offend my sensibilities as a true-born Briton.

'We have a chance here to acquire something of value, not only for our native land, but for the good of all merchant vessels and Royal Navy vessels in this area. I intend to take this opportunity, which you affect not to see. And at your express instruction, I will specifically exclude you from all involvement in the enterprise.'

'But what, doctor, if things go wrong? What will happen if your vessel is seized?'

'Nothing, sir, that could conceivably concern you,' said Gunn, and bowed his farewell. 'If we fail, forget we ever attempted to succeed. Blame our failure on greed and opportunism. But if we succeed, sir, then I will feel at liberty to advise a wider audience concerning the amount of official help our enterprise attracted. Now, sir, since you doubtless have many claims more important on your time than mine, I will wish you farewell.'

Gunn bowed stiffly and let himself out of the high doors.

\*　　　\*　　　\*

Castle writhed feverishly in the sand. His flesh was raw and blistered and burned dry and hard as a turtle's shell. His tongue stuck to the roof of his mouth, and flies buzzed and settled and buzzed again unheeded around his half-closed, gummy eyes. He lay beneath a crude shelter of plantain leaves supported on four thin bamboo poles.

On either side of him, two coolies squatted, watching him, eyes like brown glass beads, faces empty of all expression, all feeling.

Their orders were to prevent the Red-Bristled Barbarian from removing the bandages, soaked with brown dried blood, from his groin and between his legs. For three days and nights, relays of coolies had watched over him thus, with orders that if they did not keep their watch closely they would suffer a similar fate.

Tu Sung knew that three days was the minimum time which bandages must cover this fearful, pulsating wound. It was also the maximum time that any man could hold his water without the likelihood of internal rupture, haemorrhage, and a swift death. Castle had endured the waiting, but for most of the time he had been semi-conscious or in total coma. He still faced the last hazard to survival. When the bandages were removed, it would be known whether they had been bound so tightly that the new scar had completely grown over the whole area. If that had happened, nothing could save his life.

Tu Sung looked down at his victim. Castle lay in the foetal position, knees drawn up to help support the enormous pressure on his bladder, his stomach tight, the tenseness of his muscles drawing away some of the pain from his wound.

This was the Barbarian Englishman who would be Tu Sung's living passport to preference among the Chinese nobility. For who of all his contemporaries and rivals could deliver into their Emperor's hands a live Barbarian eunuch?

Anyone could persuade the poor father of an unwanted boy that the lad might secure some preferment if he lacked his manhood; but this was a fully grown man from over the farthest seas. He would thus be worse than a slave, for while a shrewd Chinese eunuch could wield power by being given a position in a rich man's harem, and play one favourite against another, manipulating suppliers of grain and foodstuffs to his master's estates, drawing his commission from this one or that, a Barbarian lacked sufficient skill in the language to aspire to such a position.

He would be a curiosity which mandarins would travel many miles to see and examine with amused interest: the only eunuch Barbarian in all the East.

And who would receive the credit for this rare prize? Why, Tu Sung, his humble and unworthy self. Upon his meek and lowly head would be heaped rich words of praise and honour. He would be accepted by those who now held him in contempt because formerly he had worked with his hands, because he dealt in slaves, and because he was not born of aristocratic lineage. Now he would be raised to greatness and his name would be a name of honour.

The overseer saw Tu Sung approach and ran with an umbrella made of plantain leaves, and held this over his head lest the sun should harm his skin. Tu Sung gave no outward sign of pleasure at this mark of great respect, but it warmed his whole being. Already, he was being treated as a mandarin. Before long he would be a mandarin, would wear his nails longer, stoop his shoulders even more and be preceded by an umbrella carrier whenever he left his home.

Tu Sung extended his right hand in silence. The overseer placed his curved knife in his palm. Tu Sung's fingers closed over the hilt. He spoke sharply to the overseer who called two coolies from the beach. They kneeled down on either side of Castle's bent wracked body and straightened his limbs, now thin from lack of food and scaled with sand and salt, scarred by suppurating sores and hot with fever. Castle writhed feebly, threshing with his hands, his mouth open.

'Be gentle! Have mercy!' he beseeched them.

His bladder had swollen to the size of a huge imprisoned balloon in his groin; the flesh was so distended that it shone as though polished.

Tu Sung bent over the filthy bandages, wrinkling his nose with distaste at their stench. Then he slit them expertly with the point of the blade. It would not do for him to soil his hand by touching the filth they might conceal. The overseer poured a little sea-water over the strips of cloth to loosen the encrusted blood, and then pulled them away.

In the centre of a patch of dark hair, matted with blood and filth the round wet raw wound pulsated as with a heart of its own. A little urine trickled through the blood and spouted, and then a strong ammoniac straw coloured stream sprayed uncontrollably into the air.

The swelling in Castle's groin subsided. He moaned with relief and tried to sit up. The overseer handed him half a coconut shell of fresh water. He drank greedily and looked about him for the first time more clearly, as the fever left him. He glanced down at his wound and began to sob with humiliation and misery and exhaustion.

Tu Sung handed back the knife to his overseer, rinsed his hands delicately in a metal bowl a coolie presented to him, shook them dry and stood examining his victim.

'See that he is fed,' he told the overseer. 'Give him some kind of clothing and if you can find any mud on the person of any of the coolies, let him have a pipe, so that he may sleep and dream.'

All this man's life is now a living nightmare, Tu Sung thought to himself, comparing Castle's terrible future with his own. Why should I deny him one hour of drugged dreams?

\*     \*     \*

In the small cabin of the vessel that they had hired with Jerome's thousand dollars, Jones poured two measures of The Glenlivet into a silver beaker, swallowed them and smacked his lips appreciatively. The tiny craft bore down through an unexpected profusion of islands. They sprouted on either side into the infinite haze and beyond with amazing prodigality.

Some were small, little more than reddish rocks, lapped by waves, with sea birds flying around them. Others were several hundred yards long, with palm trees bent against the prevailing wind, shaking feathery fronds as a housemaid shakes a morning duster.

He wondered how the seeds of these palms had been carried out so far from the mainland. Possibly in the beaks or claws of birds, or maybe a whole tree had been carried away in a storm and washed up on that shore? Truly, the ways of the Almighty were strange and beyond human deciphering. He would therefore waste no more thought on attempting the impossible, for what Jerome had asked him to do was proving difficult enough. This was to use his knowledge of the seas to calculate on which of the islands they would be most likely to find Bonnarjee or the Englishman.

Each day at dusk they dropped anchor in shallow water near one of the larger islands, lest they should pass their target in the dark. At dawn, they sailed on slowly with a lookout in the crow's nest, and Jerome on deck with the most powerful glass that he could borrow in Singapore. How ironic that he lacked money to buy the telescope, and so had been obliged to borrow it from the mate of an American clipper lately docked from Salem, and delayed in Singapore for four weeks because of a warped keel!

On some islands both men thought they saw movements, but when they landed they could find no evidence of human life. Perhaps the movement had been the wind in distant bushes or a wild animal moving or a bird's wings spreading as it prepared for flight?

Jones had sailed on a directly reverse course to the one Rudkin had given, and now they were traversing islands in a wide circle. A horrible almost unthinkable thought nagged him. What if Jim Rudkin had deliberately given them the wrong bearing? What if he and the Welshman in the eating-house had made up the story together, contemptuous of the American because they did not believe he had ever sailed before the mast, because they thought he was boasting?

Jones knew that unless they sighted the island soon, they would have to sail back to Singapore. One thousand dollars might sound a lot of money on land; at sea, it was very small change. Jones, legs braced wide against the dip and roll of the vessel, refocused his glass on an island to port. No sign of life. Nothing.

He lowered his glass, and the lookout called down from the crow's-nest.

'Smoke ahoy! On the starboard beam.'

*       *       *

Bonnarjee stood on the shore, transfixed with terror, sweat pouring down his back, his whole body trembling.

A vessel was approaching the island, and incredibly, instead of welcoming the thought that soon he might meet fellow countrymen, the prospect now filled him with horror. How could any ship conceivably come in friendship to such a remote island? Might they not be pirates or other predators come to seize him or torment him? In a blind panic, he stamped out the fire he had so carefully kept lit day and night since Castle sailed away. Perhaps, when the smoke died, these newcomers would also leave without landing?

He screwed up his eyes against the blaze of sun on sea, trying to recognize faces on the ship's deck, but without success. He saw two white faces; the rest were Malays or Chinese.

Perhaps Gunn was coming to mock him—or to kill him? Maybe Castle had managed to reach help. But then surely he would also be aboard one of these vessels, waving to him? He must hide and watch them secretly and discover who they were before he admitted his presence, lest his rescue proved worse than his abandonment. Decision unlocked his muscles, and he began to run, slowly at first, and then more speedily as his strength grew, up through the powdery sand into which his feet sank over his ankles, then into the forest, careless of the prickly edges of leaves, and sharp spearing thorns, until he was in the foothills.

Bonnarjee paused once and looked back towards the sea. His heart thundered like a hundred drums and sweat ran down into his eyes so that he could only make out vague figures landing from the ship. Whether they were black or white or yellow he did not know, and now he did not care. He had no friends left; only enemies who would pursue him to torture him further, to humiliate him more. But if he hid in the heart of the island, they would never find him.

He began to run again, blindly, sobbing for breath, never noticing the whipping branches and thorns, only eager to escape and reach a hiding place where no one could find him.

*     *     *

Jerome lit a cheroot and flicked the lucifer over his shoulder. Sand burned through the leather soles of his boots, and the heat was so intense that the trees above the shoreline shimmered.

There was no one here, yet he and Jones had both confirmed a tall column of smoke, although by the time they landed, it had disappeared. He had also seen a movement through his glass; he could have sworn a man had fled inland from the edge of the sea. Of course, this might have been some native, a cannibal, but would such

197

a person keep a fire burning? Equally, would they extinguish the fire when a ship approached? This seemed more likely to be the act of a lonely terrified man who hoped to be rescued—but only by those friendly to him.

Jerome shouted, cupping his hands to his mouth: 'Mr Bonnarjee! We are your friends! Mr Bonnarjee!'

The name echoed hollowly, *Jee, jee, jee,* and died.

Insects droned and the heat burned his flesh. He must have been mistaken. No one was here. Once more, they had landed on the wrong island. He turned to the Consul.

'I thought I saw a movement,' he said. 'But I must have been wrong. The heat plays the devil with your sight in this climate.'

'I am certain I saw a man, too,' agreed Jones. 'And there is no doubt whatever about the smoke. Maybe he is afraid of us. After all, if you are a native marooned by Europeans and you see more Europeans arrive, would you not assume that they have some evil purpose in their visit?'

'The same thought occurred to me.'

'Then let us pull offshore for a little distance, beat down the coast a couple of miles, and lie up till dusk and return when the sun goes down. Maybe by then he will have forgotten his fear and come back to this beach.'

'Shall we not search first and see if he has a lair? We could leave a message for him, protesting our friendship and goodwill?'

'No,' said Jones. 'We will do as I propose. You, as a scribbler, are understandably keen on writing messages and letters and stories. I prefer we should catch him when he least expects it.'

'As you say,' said Jerome slowly. He realized he was now not above the Consul, as he had appeared in Singapore, but subordinate to him. For while Jerome was a man of words, Jones was proving himself a man of deeds.

\*         \*         \*

'The moon will rise in exactly one hour, sir,' the hired captain reported to Jerome. 'It will take us about twenty minutes to anchor at the same bearing we reached this morning.'

'Then another ten for you to row inshore, and ten more minutes to find our man?'

'You will need more time than that, sir. If he is still hiding, I doubt you will ever flush him out at all.'

'That's as maybe, captain. We intend to do our best. Kindly put the vessel about and anchor near as you can to the shore, and quietly as you are able.'

The darkness was so thick that Jerome could almost feel it; the night wind was a warm dampness blowing off the island. He was sweating, partly from the humidity, and partly at the thought of going ashore. What might he find there? It was one thing to listen to Blackman's accounts of punitive expeditions in the safety of an anchored *Aeneas*, to hear of marines being landed, longboats rowing ashore full of reinforcements, and hostile guns firing. It was altogether another to know that you would be rowing ashore yourself within minutes with one other of your countrymen, and a handful of hired sailors, the riff-raff from a dozen paid-off crews in Singapore who would instantly abandon you on an unknown beach if the whim moved them.

What guarantee existed that they would not be left

there, at least until they agreed some inflated sum for rescue—as indeed they planned to do with the Parsee?

Jerome could feel his stomach knot like a muscle at the thought, and he gripped the wooden rail, peering through the darkness as though to force his eyes to make out the outline of the island.

The Consul joined him. He had been drinking. Jerome smelled rum on his breath, and Jones swayed slightly, slapping his hand angrily on the back of his neck to kill mosquitoes.

'We are going in now,' Jerome told him. 'I hope this fellow has come back to the beach. Otherwise we will have to wait another day.'

'He will be back,' replied the Consul reassuringly. 'You imagine what it must be like for him on that island. He must wish to get as far away from the centre as he possibly can, for there it will be even more dark and frightening. Down by the sea, he can feel he is nearer escape.'

The ship creaked and dipped and creaked again, timber on timber; ropes groaned in pulleys; there was a slack flapping from a loose topsail. The captain approached them in the darkness.

'We are riding without any lights, gentlemen. I hope there are no other vessels in the vicinity, for this is against all the rules of seamanship.'

'The sea is very wide, captain,' replied the Consul. 'I have sailed all its oceans, and so I know. I would discount any risk of collision.'

'What we need to do,' said Jerome, 'is to collide with someone on the beach, never mind the sea.'

'How far in are we now?'

'As close as I care to come, gentlemen. According to my charts, we have about three fathoms' depth and then the sea-bed shelves quickly. It is difficult to be precise.'

The ship turned gently. A boat was lowered; four sailors sat at the oars. Jerome could smell their sweaty stinking bodies, but could barely see them. As the oars dipped, phosphorescence in the water clung to the blades and reflected off the boat's hull, like some phantasmagoric spectacle in a theatre.

The men rowed steadily and tirelessly. The only sound was the dip of their blades, the creak of rowlocks, and their breathing. Ahead, the faint luminous rim of breaking waves showed they were near the shore. The crew shipped their oars. One held a bamboo vertically in the water and dug it into the sand.

'About two feet depth, sir,' he reported.

'Right,' said Jerome. 'Wait for us as close in as you can. We may be an hour or more. But do not return to the ship in case you cannot find us again.'

'We'll find you,' the man assured him. 'The moon will be up in minutes.'

Jones and the American Consul waded ashore. The water felt surprisingly warm through their trousers. As they squelched up the beach, the moon began to rise behind them. Trees grew to within ten feet of the water. Somewhere within those trees was a man they wished to rescue—at a price. A man who wanted rescue but feared all strangers.

Jerome began to call: 'Mr Bonnarjee, we are your friends! We have come to help you! Come out, we are unarmed!'

Both men held up their hands in the moonlight, and

Jerome felt increasingly uneasy. It seemed foolish to admit they were weaponless. What if Bonnarjee had others hiding with him in those trees? What if head-hunters or cannibals with poisoned darts and arrows were waiting for just this moment?

They lowered their arms and stood sheepishly, sweating in the warm night, their feet and legs still cool from the sea. A bird of some kind flew out of the deeper darkness that marked the trees and fluttered up against the moon, wings spread wide. Other creatures were chattering in the forest. Jerome guessed they would be monkeys and baboons, but he would not venture inside to find out. Then he heard a sound of crashing branches and a voice cried out in English.

'Who are you? Do not approach me, but give your names and speak your business.'

'We are Americans, sir,' cried Jerome, addressing himself to that part of the darkness from which the voice had come. 'We have landed to rescue Mr Bonnarjee.'

'I am he whom you seek. But how did you know I was here? Who informed you?'

'We met a seaman from Dr Gunn's vessel, *Hesperides*. He told us of your plight, and how evilly Dr Gunn had dealt with you.'

'Prove you are who you say you are.'

'That is impossible at this moment, and in these present conditions, sir, but I will light a lucifer and you can see my face, that I am white. And you will already appreciate I do not have an English accent, and that the cut of my clothes is not that of a Singapore tailor. My colleague, Mr Jones, is the American Consul for the South China Seas.'

'Let me see your faces. But, remember, one move of treachery and you both die.'

'I am putting my hand in my pocket to find a lucifer,' said Jerome. His right hand grabbed the box. He opened it, selected two, felt the sulphur heads were close together, then struck them on the sole of his shoe. In the brief flare of flame, he could see the Consul's shadow long on the ground.

He held up the lucifers to his face, sniffing their pungent smoke, then he held them in front of Jones's face. They died quickly; he threw them away.

'How did you reach here?' asked the voice.

'We hired a ship in Singapore. We tried to land this morning, but missed you, so we lay offshore. We did not wish to alarm you.'

'Your voice has the ring of honesty,' said Bonnarjee, and he left the shelter of the trees.

Jerome struck another two lucifers, and saw the wretched Parsee, unshaven, his hair long and matted, face blotched with ulcers and unhealed cuts. His hands were swollen and his nails chipped and broken. He was also unarmed. His bold talk had been bluff.

'You are alone?' asked the Consul.

'I was alone, until you came here. Let us reach your boat as speedily as possible. I am eager to see lights again, and to hear human speech. I am also desperate to have a bath, to cleanse my body, to put on some new fresh clothes.'

'Then, sir,' said the Consul smoothly, his voice rich and sweet now as crystallized honey, 'I assume you will be willing to agree to a small condition we would make? It is that your company advances us sufficient money to

203

guarantee a project dear to our hearts. We know that Jade Gate Island contains coal. We know that Dr Gunn and others seek this coal, and a fortune awaits those who find it first. We wish to find it first.'

'But *I* found it first!' cried Bonnarjee proudly. 'I hired an English surveyor, Mr Castle. I organized a gang of Chinese coolies under their master, Tu Sung, to dig wherever the Englishman suggested. We tried a dozen places without success, and then we found what we sought. I will not yield to you what I have already made my own.'

'I can readily understand your reluctance to do so, but I would remind you that you are scarcely a free agent in this matter. Without our help, you do not leave this island. With our help and your agreement that you share on an equal basis with us whatever coal Jade Gate Island contains, you leave with us now.'

'Are you Americans any better than the British, than Gunn and MacPherson and the rest? You seek to drive a bargain for money, with blood. Am I a slave that I must buy my liberty with that which is already mine?'

'With the deepest respect, Mr Bonnarjee, you have never fled from making such an offer yourself. Have you not driven the hardest bargains of any merchant in the East—when you could do so? I regret that it is widely said that you and your company have even hired murderers and assassins to deal with people who could not sell to you for a price—your price, of course.

'I trust that these allegations are as spurious as they must seem, but if you wish to stay here and ruminate on the evil minds of men who say such wicked things, then we shall leave you alone, as we found you.'

204

He turned to Jerome.

'Mr Bonnarjee does not appear to wish to be rescued. He desires to stay here for reasons of his own, and we must therefore bow to his wishes, reluctant as we are to abandon a fellow creature to such isolation. No doubt his thoughts will prove his best company.'

They began to walk in step down the beach to the breaking waves. The tide was on the turn, and beyond the surf, in the moonlight, the boat waited, rocking and dipping.

Jones waved to it. One of the crew waved back.

'Come in to take us off,' Jones shouted.

The men bent to their oars. The boat approached the beach.

'Wait!' cried Bonnarjee hoarsely. 'Wait! You would not leave me here to die?'

'Why should you die, Mr Bonnarjee? This island is full of birds and beasts who know it as their home. They live out their lives within its boundaries. So can you. You may even be happier here than in a great city, for you will be away from the stresses of the counting house, the problems of usurers, the worries of all who deal in gold. We will therefore bid you farewell, for we shall not sail this way a second time.'

'Take me back with you,' pleaded Bonnarjee. 'I beg you, do not leave me here. You have no idea what it is like. The forests are alive with strange noises. Every night, I start up from my slumbers, wondering whether beasts or serpents or hostile natives are approaching. The whole jungle speaks with voices of danger. There are huge snakes and wild baboons and strange creatures that crawl and slither on their bellies. Do not leave me here.

I will pay you anything if you will but give me passage in your vessel.'

'We do not wish you to pay us anything,' replied Jones. 'All we wish is that you will underwrite our expedition to Jade Gate Island—and we will share equally on any coal we find.'

'I will agree to what you say. You have my word.'

'Your word on a desert island is one thing, Mr Bonnarjee. It could speak in different tones when you can brief expensive lawyers. Give us your bond now, instead of just your word.'

'But how can I, gentlemen? I have no implements to write with, no ink, no paper. You ask the impossible.'

'We have brought a document which we instructed a lawyer to draw up before we set sail. Be so good as to strike a lucifer, Mr Jerome. Let Mr Bonnarjee see what he is signing.

'You will note here, sir, a clause, that specifically says you sign at your own free will, and not under any duress, but out of your spontaneous admiration for those of our countrymen in North America who have shown how a former colony can become independent and rich. We would not like you later to suggest to anyone that we in any way forced your signature or your agreement.'

'You bastards!' screamed Bonnarjee. 'You bastards! At least Gunn came to Jade Gate himself, in his own ship, with his own men. You seek to gather wealth from the labours of others.'

'We will also go in our own ship, with our backer— you,' said Jerome. 'Here, I have brought two quills and a horn of ink for you. We can have the paper witnessed by the captain of our ship.'

'Give it to me,' said Bonnarjee hoarsely.

Jerome struck another lucifer. The Parsee read quickly, eyes narrowed in the sudden blaze of light, mouthing the words.

Jerome remembered their visit to the lawyer off Commercial Square; the small room sour with the smell of waxed parchment contracts, high windows slatted against the sun. Eurasian clerks on tall stools, crouched like round-shouldered birds writing, in careful copperplate, new deeds and mortgages and contracts for men they would never meet, for sites they would never see.

And the lawyer himself, Scottish and ageless as a granite gnome, face wizened from years of malaria, glasses pushed up on his dried yellow skin, was eager that they should know the great favour he bestowed on them by accepting their instructions.

'It is unusual,' he complained. 'Drawing up a contract without both parties being present.'

'The size of your fee is also unusual,' retorted Jerome. 'Do you wish to draft this contract, sir, or do you not? We have no time to wait upon the etiquette of the robe, if you feel disinclined to accept our business.'

'You have come at a very busy season,' muttered the lawyer, ringing the bell so that a writer could come in and take notes as he spoke. 'I am inundated with work. I have clerks away ill. One man has embezzled clients' funds.'

'You either tell us this to force up your fee or else you announce yourself as an inefficient attorney. Either way causes me displeasure in your company. Draw up this contract without more talk or let us terminate this discussion.'

'Serious work cannot be hurried in this fashion, gentle-men. The drafting of a contract is crucial. One wrong word could nullify everything else it contains.'

'If you write one wrong word,' said Jerome coldly, 'then more than a contract will be nullified, I assure you. But I also give you my word that if you draw this up speedily, while we wait, you could become—I do not say will be, I say, *could* be—the legal representative of one of the largest trading companies in the East.'

The lawyer's eyes narrowed and flickered like gold at the thought.

'You will have it, gentlemen. Give me but half an hour and it will be completed.'

And now on the beach they held the contract ready. The tide was coming in behind them and they stood with foam swirling around their ankles, legs lit by the phos-phorescence of the waves. The moon rode up the sky now, surrounded by a galaxy of stars. Bonnarjee scratched his signature on the oily paper. Jerome waved it in the air to dry the ink, folded it carefully and put one copy in his pocket.

'Here is your copy,' he told Bonnarjee. The Parsee folded this neatly and put it away in the waist of his loin cloth.

'We are now partners in an enterprise which will not only bring us wealth, but will also almost certainly assure the downfall of a man for whom none of us have any regard—Robert Gunn.'

'We will drink to that aboard our ship,' promised Jones.

'It is against my religion to drink alcohol,' replied Bonnarjee sulkily, watching the sailors beach the longboat. As they climbed in and headed back to the ship, Jerome felt a curious sense of anticlimax.

He had pinned so much on finding Bonnarjee, in persuading him to sign. And now that the man had done so; now that their wealth seemed assured, he felt that it should have all been more exciting, more satisfying. They had struck a hard, rough bargain, but then was not that inseparable from success in business?

Now the Parsee sat in the stern, head sunk on his chest. He seemed not so much grateful at being rescued, as concerned at the price they had forced him to pay for his freedom.

Jerome wondered then at the price he and Jones had paid for their future fortune.

\*　　　\*　　　\*

Tu Sung clapped his hands sharply. The overseer appeared, bowed, and stood awaiting his master's pleasure. The junk creaked and dipped and the rattan sail rattled above their head like huge beads.

'Carry the Barbarian Castle on deck,' ordered Tu Sung.

The overseer padded away over the teak boards, and within minutes Castle was being manhandled, half-carried, half-prodded to where Tu Sung stood near the cross-trees of the ship. Two coolies still supported Castle. His head lolled and his tongue was swollen. Dried blood encrusted his trousers to the knees. He wore a ragged shirt someone had found for him.

'We are approaching where you say Bonnarjee was marooned,' Tu Sung told him. 'Can you recognize the island?'

Castle did not move. He was living, yet hardly alive, his spirit broken. Tu Sung nodded. The coolie struck Castle lightly across the shoulders with a thin bamboo he had split into strips.

When the man still did not move, he hit him across the buttocks and then across his back.

'I cannot tell you,' said Castle at last. His voice, a hoarse whisper, seemed to come from far away and not from his own throat. 'I did not look back when I left the island.'

Then he remembered Bonnarjee's care in building a fire each day.

'There should be smoke. He was determined to keep a fire going, so that a passing ship might see the smoke.'

'There is no smoke here,' said Tu Sung. 'Take him below again.'

'We will sail on,' Tu Sung told the captain. 'Order every man to search the horizon every hour for any sign of smoke, however faint, however distant.'

Presently a lookout in the long high prow called back excitedly in dialect. The captain translated to Tu Sung, who came from an island province and was not acquainted with the ways of the sea or the dialect of those who lived by the shore.

'He says that a ship is approaching.'

'What of it?'

'She flies the British flag. A two-masted schooner. Not a large vessel.'

'A friendly vessel or a man-of-war?'

'It is impossible to say, master. But if her captain orders us to stop we should do so.'

'Then detain this Barbarian eunuch below decks. Bind

his wrists and stop his mouth so that he cannot shout to his countrymen.'

'He will not see the vessel, master. There are no port-holes where he is kept.'

'He might hear their voices and recognize their tongue and call to them. I will hold you personally responsible, captain, that this does not happen.'

'Very good, master.'

The captain bowed and went below deck. Castle lay stretched in a small space about eight feet square, usually used for storing rattan mats on which the sailors could sleep. He had a wooden pillow for his head and a tin caddy of water and a mug. The space smelled foul and airless. Wood creaked on every side as plank scored against plank under the movement of the ship. The captain ordered a sailor to tie Castle's hands behind his back and then bind a long bandage round his mouth.

Castle wriggled, groaning like a trapped beast, his eyes bulging onion-like from his head. What had he done to deserve the dual humiliation of castration and then be bound like a felon in this foul ship?

Oh, God, save me, he prayed. If I must die, let me die speedily, and not just exist in this tortured hell, from which there seems no relief, from which there is no end. *Oh, God, hear my prayer and let my cry come unto Thee.*

\*  \*  \*

Jerome lowered his glass and turned to the Parsee.

'A Chinese vessel on the port bow. The captain thinks we should stop her. But he warns that they may be pirates.'

'Give me your glass,' said Bonnarjee. He focused it on the deck and stood, feet pressed wide against the roll of the vessel, searching for a face he might recognize. Then he saw Tu Sung on the deck. The man had taken off his straw hat and was wiping his forehead with a silk square. Bonnarjee lowered the glass.

'I recognize one man in the vessel,' he said slowly in a puzzled voice. 'I left him in charge of coolies on Jade Gate Island.'

'Who is he?'

'A Chinese contractor, Tu Sung. He builds roads and houses on the mainland. My father has used him on many occasions. But his coolies are really a private army. He is a rough, evil man—but useful on occasion.'

'He has certainly a lot of ruffians with him there,' agreed Jones, turning the glass on the ship. 'How are you involved with him?'

'I needed men quickly to dig for coal, to know whether it was there, before Gunn arrived. He was coming with his whole crew for the same purpose.'

'Why do you think this Chinese Tu Sung has left the island?'

'I do not know. Let us draw alongside and find out.'

'Do you speak his language?'

'I speak his tongue. His language is that of an evil man who does not honour his commitments, who gives his hand and his word and then goes back on both.'

'You should have much in common,' said Jerome dryly, beneath his breath, and ordered the captain to pull over to the junk.

'How will you stop her?' asked Jones.

'We have made a signal with flags, but the Chinese

pretend not to understand,' replied the captain. 'I will have to fire across her bows.'

'That is in the English tradition, surely?'

'There is no other tradition, sir. Only by threatening them can we persuade them to stop. How else do you suggest? That we pursue them through the sea like two children playing tag? Or that we run alongside and put out grappling irons? Is not that worse than firing a warning shot?'

'I see your point. Well, fire your shot.'

A small brass cannon was brought out, powder and wadding rammed down its mouth, then a cannonball trundled on deck by a seaman. He lifted it into the muzzle and rammed it down. Another seaman lit the taper. They waited alongside the gun while the fuse burned and crackled.

The boom of the cannon came as an anticlimax. The ball surged through the lambent air, bounced once, twice off the water, and was gone in a high white gout of foam.

'Put her alongside,' ordered Jones. 'Five men stand ready with cutlasses, and five with pistols charged, in case they attack us. But no one to fire or to fight unless at my direct command. Understood?'

'Aye, aye, sir,' said the mate.

\*     \*     \*

Captain Fernandes saluted Gunn, who was sitting in a cane armchair under an awning on the afterdeck of *Hesperides*. Fernandes had almost completely recovered from the blows to his head from the pirates; his scars were healing, and only bruises remained to show he had ever been attacked.

'We will sight Jade Gate Island within the hour, sir,' Fernandes reported. 'Have you any instructions?'

Gunn nodded as he put down the document he had been reading.

'Yes,' he said. 'First, place an officer in the crow's-nest with the strongest glass we have, to report on any movement ashore. As soon as he can see the island clearly, drop anchor until dusk and then sail in before the moon rises. At dawn we must be standing offshore where we anchored last time.

'Prepare two longboats, and arm their crews with pistols and cutlasses. And have my steward lay out my own pistol with two signal rockets.'

'You are going ashore, sir?'

'At first light.'

'Even if the lookout reports that a hostile reception may await you?'

'Especially in that situation, captain.'

Captain Fernandes bowed and withdrew. Gunn took up the document again; it was a contract drawn up regarding the extraction of coal from Jade Gate Island. One copy was in copperplate, prepared by Gunn's lawyer in Singapore; the other was in Chinese characters. He put the thick parchment pages on the deck, placed his hat carefully on them to foil the wind, and crossed to the deck rail. The wood felt warm to his elbows as he leaned on it. *Hesperides* slowly rose, dipped gently and rose again under the great weight of wind in her sails. Gunn heard Fernandes shout commands and watch a young officer swarm up the rigging to the crow's-nest. The afternoon sun glinted on the polished brass-work of his telescope.

As Gunn gathered up his papers and went down to his cabin he heard the officer call: 'Land ho! On the starboard bow! Shore deserted! No sign of life whatever!'

Within hours now Gunn would know whether the coal he believed that Jade Gate contained would be at the service of his country and his company, or whether others had already secured it. He would know, too, whether the contract he carried was just another fine example of flowery legal phraseology—or the most valuable agreement in all the East.

*          *          *

The cannonball splashed so closely to Tu Sung's fighting junk that its spray drenched him as he stood in the prow. Despite the heat of the sun, he shivered under the cold salt dash of the sea. Why did this strange ship need to halt them so urgently that they must fire across their bows?

His captain had explained the meaning of the coloured flags the schooner flew—an imperative summons to heave-to—but on Tu Sung's orders they had sailed on. He calculated that if the ship really belonged to the British Navy, she would speedily overhaul the junk. The fact that her crew had fired a cannon at them instead, smacked of pirates or Portuguese.

Well, he would soon discover who they were—and what they wanted.

Behind Tu Sung, the huge triangular sail was still rounded by the wind, and the mast creaked under its weight. Tu Sung hated the noise it made, for the mast was secretly hinged a few feet from its base, and in calm weather it could be swung down, to lie parallel with the deck. This enabled the captain to alter the appearance of his ship, should he sight a potential victim at sea.

Without a sail, and lacking even a mast, his vessel would appear harmless, perhaps a small fishing boat blown off course, and so would lull any suspicions of her real role.

But the fastenings around this hinge in the mast had been known to break in other ships, and the mast swing forwards and down unexpectedly with the huge weight of the wind, killing all in its path. Tu Sung feared the thought of such a violent end. He deliberately forced himself to think of other things, for even though he was soaked, his pride would not allow him to withdraw to a safer position. Face was all; if he lost face before his crew over such a minor matter, then how could he command their respect over graver issues?

The ship's captain ran towards him, his face creased with anxiety.

'We will have to drop the sail, my master, or lose our mast. They are most likely to shoot it away next time.'

Tu Sung bowed to show that he accepted the situation and climbed down to the oar-deck. Above him, the junk's sail dropped with a great rattle, and the clumsy vessel rolled and wallowed in the ocean swell as the rowers shipped their oars.

The captain came down the bamboo ladder after Tu Sung, and bowed low before him.

'I will see what these Barbarians desire,' Tu Sung told him. 'They will doubtless assume we are some local native ship of inferior degree, which is why they have so insolently fired a ball at us. But we are not ill-equipped to answer aggressive gestures of this kind, as they may well discover, unless their armament is more powerful than it seems.'

He contemplated his two brass swivel guns, known as *lelahs*, always kept crammed with grape in case of any chance meeting at sea, where their voices could swing an argument in his favour, and now concealed by old sail-cloth sheets. Three larger cannon, mounted on either side of the main deck, the fighting deck, were also loaded and shrouded by canvas sheets so that to a casual glance they would appear to be harmless deck cargo of some kind. It would be the work of an instant for his crew to rip these covers away and fire the guns. At point blank range any of these weapons would cause terrible damage to a wooden hull.

The deck where he now stood stank of human sweat and excrement, for forty slaves were seated on wooden benches, two to each enormous oar. They were naked save for filthy strips of rotting cloth gathered about their loins, and tied in pairs by rattan collars around their necks. Muscles on the slaves' arms and shoulders were of gigantic, almost grotesque development, through pulling on the oars, but their legs were thin, and in some cases deformed and almost withered away. Many of the slaves had been tied to the oars for months; all of them for weeks. Only death or dread disease could set them free from the benches on which they sat day and night, while the ship was at sea or at anchor.

Tu Sung had captured them in raids on different islands, and even if they somehow succeeded in cutting through their neck-collars to leap into the sea, they could never escape. Tu Sung and his Chinese overseers regularly hammered their knees with flat bamboos so that they were unable to swim. Indeed, some could barely walk, and they were prisoners without hope, urinating and defecating where they sat.

If a slave fell ill and was unable to row, or if he died suddenly, as frequently happened, through an internal hæmorrhage or heart attack, the overseers simply cut him loose and threw him into the sea. The survivor of the pair had to struggle as best he might on his own until the ship put into port. Then Tu Sung would send a party of Chinese ashore to seize someone as a replacement.

Their dark, sad faces were deeply lined, and their hair matted with filth like the manes of wild forest animals. Some were blinded, because Tu Sung would throw handfuls of cayenne pepper into their eyes to force them to keep awake through the hours of darkness, when he was in a hurry to make for shore.

Others had open festering wounds on their shoulders, cruelly carved with blunt blades, and now covered with blue, buzzing flies and festering scabs. He and his overseers had deliberately mutilated them in this fashion so that pain and irritation would overcome their weariness and force them to keep awake, although their heads might loll low with weariness between their shoulders. They sat now, heads down, racked with pain, thankful for this unexpected respite from rowing.

They did not speak, for speech was an effort, and they needed to harbour all their strength for the oars; and indeed what was there to say that would not bring a blow about their heads from an overseer for disturbing Tu Sung's thoughts?

But still, in their wearied dejected minds, bemused

218

and captive as they were, flames of hatred still flickered. It wanted but one chance, however slight, and blinded, tortured, crippled as they might be, they would still tear to pieces Tu Sung and their overseers, gladly risking sudden death than continue this drawn-out agony of death in life.

Tu Sung distrusted them as much as he feared them, and so every day, at dawn and dusk, he ordered his overseers to check that their rattan collars were not frayed or loosened. And for the slightest sign of insolence or hatred in a slave's eyes, the man would be beaten around the head with thin bamboos or doused by a bucket of salt water which would open his raw scabs and burn for hours like liquid fire on his sun-blistered shoulders.

'It is your wish that we should grapple them, my master?'

The junk's captain carefully kept his eyes averted from Tu Sung's face. He feared his temper and knew how gestures of humility such as this pleased and pacified him.

'Not unless they discover we are not people of insignificance and try to elude us, all courage gone. Then grip them with our hooks and show them how we deal with insolent Red-Bristled Barbarians.'

Both men glanced unconsciously at the huge wooden beam which ran from the bows up to the masthead, apparently to strengthen the mast. By Tu Sung's right hand was a rope which, connected to a pulley at the masthead, would allow this beam to drop down parallel to the sea. The end contained several sharpened hooks, modelled on those in the head of a tapeworm. They would bite deep into the timbers of the other ship, so that it could not draw away. Then his Chinese coolies, concealed as they were now beneath the rattan shelter in the stern of the junk, could leap across and subdue the strangers with their swords.

Tu Sung raised his glass and scanned the deck of the approaching ship. To his surprise, he saw Bonnarjee and two white men standing on the foredeck. He moved the glass, focusing it on the faces of officers and crew. They appeared to be half-caste men of low degree, the sweepings of Singapore port.

He recognized none of them, and was not impressed by their appearance. The schooner was also dirty and ill-cared for. Green scum fouled her sides, her sails had patches and even unmended tears, and rigging ropes were frayed and joined. She was one of a dozen such craft available for hire in Singapore with a crew of a kind at a low price. He had nothing to fear from this vessel or from the men aboard her. Men fought best in defence of their own possessions; not to preserve the wealth and belongings of others. He turned to his captain.

'Put her alongside,' he told him. 'I will go aboard. If there is any trouble or hostility whatever, fire two rounds below their water line from our swivel guns. Then send in our fighters. But warn them not to harm Bonnarjee or the white Barbarians. I must discover who they are and what brings them across this sea.'

'Very good, my master,' the captain replied, bowing even more deeply.

The distance between the two vessels narrowed to yards, and then feet. The junk would not come too close because of the length of her oars, but by skilful helmsmanship her prow was brought directly against the bows of Jerome's schooner, where the grappling hooks could grip with maximum effect, should they be needed.

Bonnarjee called from the deck, his voice high-pitched with nervousness. He feared Tu Sung, and his back was already damp with the wringing sweat of terror. How could these Americans, innocent to the ways and cruelties of the East, possibly appreciate the gravity of their danger? He knew what the dirty sailcloths concealed on the junk's decks; and he also knew that apart from their brass cannon, Jerome and Jones only had a pair of American Colt revolvers between them should Tu Sung decide to swarm across with his own men.

'Where are you sailing?' he shouted.

'We wished to rescue you from your island, Bonnarjee sahib,' replied Tu Sung. 'The Englishman who was marooned with you brought me news of your sad and unseemly predicament at the hands of the Barbarian physician.'

'Where is the Englishman, Castle?' asked Bonnarjee.

'Aboard my unworthy vessel. But he is gravely ill, sahib, and rests from the heat of the sun.'

'Let me speak to him.'

Tu Sung shook his head.

'It is not possible, sahib. He has a fever. Let me come aboard your vessel and we can talk. It is more fitting than shouting like horse-dealers at a fair.' Tu Sung jumped across the narrow gap as he spoke, climbed over the schooner's deck rail, and bowed to Bonnarjee.

'Who are the gentlemen who travel with you?' Tu Sung asked, indicating the two Americans.

Bonnarjee translated the question, and Jerome replied in English. Bonnarjee interpreted.

'We are American citizens bound for Jade Gate.'

'I have but lately come from that island,' replied Tu Sung. 'What is it that you seek in such a remote and primitive place?'

'We are making a visit of research.'

'There is nothing to look for there but coal,' said Tu Sung, smiling.

Bonnarjee interrupted sharply.

'I have an agreement, as you know, with the Sultan to dispose of that coal.'

'And my humble coolies, unworthy as they may be, were engaged by your father to dig where it might be found.'

'For that I was grateful,' replied Bonnarjee. 'But now I will make my own arrangements for its extraction.'

'It is given to very few born of woman to make all their own arrangements,' replied Tu Sung. 'We are all like ships with small rudders. Winds and waves, the gods and other influences all bear upon us, and force us off a course we might otherwise have chosen.'

Bonnarjee turned to Jerome. His face was grave as he spoke in English.

'This man intends to be a party to my arrangement with the Sultan, whether we wish it or not. I can read it in his manner.'

'Must we accept him?' asked Jones.

'We have no alternative,' said Bonnarjee. 'He has a private army aboard his ship and could seize our vessel and put us all to the sword.'

'But why? We have done no harm to him, nor do we seek to harm him. We are citizens of a great, far-off country.'

'It is precisely because your country is so far away that he can do as he wishes.'

'What about the British Navy?' asked Jerome. 'Do they not police the seas?'

'They have no ships here,' replied Bonnarjee. 'And in any case, none of us are British subjects. So why should they concern themselves with our affairs?'

'You mean if we do not agree, we could be in danger from this Chinese ruffian?'

Bonnarjee nodded. For the first time, Jerome felt fingers of fear grip his stomach. On every side, the shimmering sea stretched away to empty infinity, and the sun beat down on them impersonally with its blinding glare. As the two ships rocked and creaked, wood meeting wood, he could see the dark faces of Chinese crouched in the stern of the junk, watching them. The canvas-covered humps on deck were clearly guns. They had stopped a pirate ship—and if they had not deliberately done so, they might now be miles away.

How many others like him, ignorant of the hidden dangers in the East, had sought wealth, and instead found an unknown and lonely death at the hands of creatures like these? For every one who succeeded, for Jardine or Matheson or MacPherson or Gunn, dozens had perished in unknown places and in unthinkable ways. He had imagined that creating a fortune was simple, because it appeared so when others did it; now he knew the truth, and the truth was heavy on his heart.

And yet, if he ever survived to write about this situation, how few of his readers in the comfortable safety of New York would believe him?

He had wilfully underestimated the risks. Patricia

Bankhausen had warned him that these Eastern seas were not like the safe Atlantic; that life was cheap, and he had refused to believe her. Now he realized how low a price he had set on his own life in venturing out so ill-prepared.

'We must be civil to this man,' said Bonnarjee. His sing-song lilting voice scattered Jerome's bitter thoughts.

'Let us agree with him, whatever he asks, because he has the means to overwhelm us. Maybe later, back in Singapore, we can come to some other arrangements if we do not like what he proposes now.'

'Do as you think fit,' Jones told him sharply. 'We are not well placed for bargaining.'

'I do not understand your talk,' Tu Sung remarked coldly to Bonnarjee, 'but from the expressions on the Barbarians' faces, it would seem that they lack enthusiasm for me as a partner. Without goodwill, Bonnarjee sahib, nothing of note can ever be achieved. I therefore suggest you all join me aboard my vessel. Then, maybe, we can grow closer in esteem and even friendship. We will sail back to Jade Gate together.'

'We are indebted to you for your gracious invitation,' replied Bonnarjee quickly. 'But we feel we should stay aboard our own ship. She is chartered and . . .'

'In that case,' Tu Sung interrupted, 'you must all prepare to swim.'

He turned towards the junk, and gave a brief nod of his head. Three Chinese leapt to the nearest swivel gun, tore away the tarpaulin, and held a lit taper to the firing-hole. Jerome and Jones watched with fascinated horror as the fuse dwindled, spluttered and died. Then the gun boomed like thunder. Sails flapped furiously in the sound waves, and their schooner jerked and reeled like a living thing. Almost immediately, she began to list to starboard. The Chinese fired the second gun, and now the deck trembled beneath their feet, and sagged and dipped.

'They have holed us,' said Jones, his voice dry with disbelief. 'We are sinking.'

'My vessel awaits the honour of your approach,' Tu Sung told Bonnarjee, smiling at their consternation.

'I must get my papers,' said Jerome suddenly, and ran down to his cabin. The floor was already tilting at a dangerous angle. Drawers had fallen open, and their contents were strewn across the polished boards. He picked up his Samuel Colt revolver, checked that it was loaded, rammed it in his pocket, with a packet of cartridges, grabbed a money belt, strapped this under his shirt, and then came up on deck. As he began to climb over the rail, two hands grabbed him expertly by his elbows and held him. Thin thrusting fingers relieved him of his Colt and ammunition. Tu Sung smiled and bowed towards him contemptuously.

'It ill becomes a guest to arrive armed in the presence of his host,' he said reprovingly.

Jerome's hired crew stood crammed in the stern, now rising rapidly out of the water as the bows sank lower.

'Take them with you,' beseeched Bonnarjee. 'They have done you no harm, they are just seafarers. You cannot leave them to drown.'

And as he spoke he remembered how Gunn had pleaded with him in much the same terms for the lives of his crew aboard *Hesperides,* and how he had ignored his appeal.

'One only,' said Tu Sung. 'That tall man.'

Two Chinese leapt upon this Malay sailor, beat him roughly about the head, to stun him, and then carried him semi-conscious into the junk.

'We have an oarsman who is ill,' Tu Sung explained. 'He will take his place.'

Already other Chinese were cutting free one of the slaves who had sunk across his oar, head down. They lifted him up roughly. The slave's face was contorted in agony, and a little green bile ran down his chin. He pressed both hands into his groin as they moved him. Jones watched with horror as the Chinese flung him out into the sea. He floated feebly, gasping and choking for air, then drifted, hump-backed and drowning.

Jerome turned to Bonnarjee.

'Tell him, I beg of you, that this is murder and abhorrent to us. Why cannot all the crew be taken aboard his vessel?'

'They are only mouths to feed,' replied Tu Sung.

'It is murder, murder.'

They watched in silence as their chartered vessel sank slowly. The crew, packed now against the stern rail by the wheelhouse for their last few moments of life, shouted to them in half a dozen tongues, throwing up their arms in supplication. And then gradually, as the water rose to their ankles, then to knees and waists, they realized their shouted entreaties were of no avail. No-one could save them. They were doomed to die.

They fell silent, awed by the inexorable approach of eternity. Some prayed, others floated away and swam around to the junk, hoping to climb aboard unobserved. But Chinese were waiting for them with flattened bamboos and beat them about their heads and knuckles as they reached up to grip the deck. Others clutched to floating spars, and hatch covers that had come adrift, grateful for anything that might prolong their lives for even a few moments. Then, circling them in the distance, Jones saw two triangular, black fins, and turned away.

'What is going to happen to us?' Jerome asked Bonnarjee. The Parsee shrugged.

'I have escaped one incarceration for another. This man Tu Sung knows I have a treaty with the Sultan. No doubt we will all be spared until we alter this in his favour, and present it to the Sultan.'

'And after that, what?'

'After that, my friends, it will depend what gods you believe in. And how we have all lived.'

\*         \*         \*

MacPherson turned to Gunn as the steward removed their empty coffee cups and plates from the breakfast table. Through the cabin window, the palm trees on Jade Gate Island fluttered long green fronds in the morning wind from the sea.

'I don't know about you,' said MacPherson dourly, 'but the sight of that island fills me with gloom and apprehension. Maybe I am growing old or timid—or simply wiser. But I have no enthusiasm whatever for returning after our last experience—even if it is built on gold, not coal.'

Gunn nodded understandingly.

'I intend to land on my own,' he told MacPherson. 'With just a few members of the crew. Your part will be equally important aboard the ship.'

'In what way?'

'I will take two signal rockets and my pistol. Captain Fernandes will anchor around the bay, out of sight from shore and sea. Should I encounter any hostility, I will fire a rocket. Then you can send two longboats, while Fernandes sails *Hesperides* back into the bay to engage the natives with her armament.'

'And if any other vessel approaches while you are ashore?'

'You will be out of sight, as I say. But post look-outs so that they can advise you of any such approach. Have all guns charged and ready for instant action. Then make what dispositions you wish, according to the situation.'

'Do you feel any foreboding about landing?'

'None,' replied Gunn cheerfully. 'If we are met with hostility, we will give the best account of ourselves we can manage. The rest will be up to you.'

Gunn buckled on his belt with his pistol and two flares, and went out on to the main deck. Two longboats had already been lowered and the crews waited, oars shipped. Gunn climbed down the rope ladder to the nearest longboat and watched the shore approach. Six sailors dragged up each boat beyond the line of pounding surf, and he motioned to the others to follow him. In single file they walked inland through the soft sand. Gunn could see no sign of any life or movement. On either side of the beach *keelongs,* long fences of bamboo stakes, marched in a maze formation so that fish, trying to swim out from the shallow water with the tide, could be trapped and taken at leisure.

This part of the beach was shaded by the strangely shaped Penaga trees, whose branches were naturally curved like the ribs of giant umbrellas. Boat builders used them to strengthen their dug-out canoes, and the tree itself often provided cover for a boat dragged up the beach. Gunn peered beneath the shield of metallic green leaves, each at least eight inches long. Sure enough, a fisherman's canoe lay on its side; and sea-water still glistened on the wood.

A couple of yards away lay a turtle with a span of several feet on its back, beak and legs moving slowly in impossible attempts to right itself. A turtle would not turn on its back unaided; fishermen must have seen Gunn's ship and carried back the news inland. So his arrival was probably being watched—but were the watchers hostile or well-disposed?

He led his men on into the jungle, to the clearing where he and MacPherson had been captured. The houses stood on their stilts, wooden doors firmly closed. Chickens and pigs rooted for scraps in the dust beneath them. A fire burned lazily near one house, and a cooking pot, on a tripod above it, bubbled like a witch's cauldron.

Gunn crossed to the largest house, from which the Parsee had come down to meet him on that earlier visit. Drawing his cutlass, he beat with the flat of the blade on the notched pole that led up to the door. The door opened a few inches and a young man looked out.

'Be pleased to give the Sultan my compliments,' Gunn told him in Malay. 'I wish to speak with him urgently.'

The door closed and then opened for a second time. An old man with a wrinkled face and grey stubbly hair stood framed in its bamboo frame.

'What is it that you seek?' he asked Gunn.

'If you are the Sultan, sir, I seek a meeting.'

'On what matter, tuan?'

'One I do not wish to discuss where the ears of others may hear us. Either in your house or down on the beach.'

'I will see you here. But only two persons. I am a man of peace and you come armed. I fear the prospect of violence.'

'I come in peace,' Gunn answered him, and motioned to one sailor to climb up the pole with him into the house. He stood on the creaking bamboo floor and through gaps in the poles beneath his feet he could see sand and the occasional white flutter of a hen's feathers. A young man and two older men stood with the Sultan. The walls were covered with carpets, and above them hung shrunken heads, blackened with age, the mark of rank of a man who had killed, and so should be respected. Gunn took off his hat and waited, accustoming his eyes to the gloom before he spoke.

'I am Robert Gunn, a subject of Her Majesty Queen Victoria of England, a physician and a merchant,' he began. 'I know, your highness, that courtesy decrees we should talk of other matters before we reach the core and reason for our meeting. But time is against me, so I seek your indulgence if I break with custom and speak immediately of the matter closest to my heart.'

The Sultan nodded gravely.

'Speak,' he commanded.

'I have sailed here in the hope that we may be able to sign a treaty together. My company—Mandarin-Gold —after payment of dues and money to be agreed, seeks the sole right to dig for coal on this island, and to sell it elsewhere for the best price obtainable.'

'Why do you seek this now when coal has lain untouched by white men's hands for centuries?'

'I seek it, your highness, because as a result of inventions in my country, ships of peace and war will soon be propelled by steam engines instead of sails. And steam engines, like the oxen that draw ploughs, require to be fed regularly. They feed on coal.'

'Have you not sailed to this island before in your great ship?'

'Your highness knows my movements well. I did indeed sail here, but was met on the shore by a man of your country who I do not see today. He brought me to this house, and then a Parsee merchant came down to speak with me. He spoke with deeds—violent deeds instead of words. He seized a colleague and me and would have put us to a terrible death in my own ship had not our God been merciful to us, and allowed us a chance to escape.'

'Truly then your time on earth is not finished,' said the Sultan. 'You have great deeds yet to accomplish, or your life would have been required of you. I saw you taken away, and I grieved for you, for I could see no means by which you could be set free.'

'But you do not know me, your highness. Why waste tears on a stranger?'

'Tears and righteous sorrow are never wasted, tuan. And while I still do not know you as a man, I know of you by reputation, which is sweet as the breeze from the spice isles. Are you not the tuan who helped Kuchin, the son of the Sultan Kuan Lung Fai,* a province on Borneo Island?'

* For Dr Gunn's adventures there, see *The Chinese Widow*.

'I am.'

'He is my nephew,' the Sultan explained. 'His father was my elder brother. You are like that other tuan, the Rajah Brooke in Sarawak. Neither of you seem to seek a fortune for yourselves. Your wish, like his, was to help others, and so to gather treasure in what you Christians call heaven.'

'I seek no fortune here because I already have one,' explained Gunn.

'Would that Mr Bonnarjee could say the same, for he is also rich. When he was here, before he seized you, as you described, he forced me to sign a treaty with him, giving his company all the rights that now you seek.'

'Can I see a copy of the document, your highness?'

'I have no copy,' replied the Sultan bitterly. 'I do not read in your tongue, but it was read out to me. I had no option but to sign.'

'What would have happened had you refused?'

'I would have been put to the sword and my island taken and my people reduced to the ranks of slaves. They are not a warlike tribe. They are people of peace, fishermen, cultivators, not soldiers. They feared the Chinese warlord, Tu Sung, and his army, for several of my people were taken by him as slaves to row his ship. When the others saw what happened to them, and how evilly they fared, their courage melted like fat in a cooking fire, and their bravery dwindled as the sun at evening.'

'So you signed the agreement under force and threat?'

'It is to my shame to admit that this is so. I was afraid, tuan, and I was alone.'

'Maybe it is to your good fortune that you were,

because under the law of my country—which, in the lack of any other, obtains in these islands—no agreement signed under threat of force is binding. To be of any value, a treaty must have goodwill on both sides—as the hand extended in friendship does not expect a dagger thrust.

'Without goodwill, your highness, your agreement is worth no more than the parchment itself. But with goodwill and trust and friendship, a contract needs no written words. In London, some years ago a young man, Matthew Clark, who dealt in wines and spirits, became friendly with one of the De Kuyper family of Rotterdam who manufacture Geneva gin and cherry brandy and other drinks. It was agreed that Mr Clark should look after their interests in my country—an agreement between gentlemen, without any official contract, because there was friendship and goodwill on both sides. And this arrangement flourishes to this day. I would like that to be an example to us, your highness.'

'You speak wise words, tuan,' replied the Sultan. 'Let it be as you say. I will give you a treaty, on terms we can discuss before we agree them. And you can speak to your advisers and seek their opinion before you accept my offer. But what of Mr Bonnarjee? I fear him.'

'I will take care of Mr Bonnarjee.'

'And Tu Sung?'

'And Tu Sung.'

Gunn drew from a pocket of his jacket the document he had prepared in Singapore before he left and which he had studied again aboard *Hesperides*.

The Sultan scanned the Chinese version and then handed it back.

'I would suggest that you and your people keep one-third of all profits made from selling your coal,' said Gunn. 'We, for our part, will have much expenditure —to build roads and a wharf, and to carry the coal in our ships. For this we must expect two-thirds of any profit. Do you agree with these proposals?'

'They seem fair,' replied the Sultan. 'Yet I would not have expected anything else after the way you helped my nephew.'

'If you sign,' Gunn explained, 'you and your people, and their sons and their sons after them, will draw money from every piece of coal that your island yields up.'

'That is a valuable prophecy. But will it bring them happiness, tuan?' asked the old man quizzically.

'Nothing can guarantee happiness,' agreed Gunn. 'Is it not written that no man is happy until he is dead, for at best he can be but fortunate? But this agreement will certainly bring them prosperity. And that means they will be able to learn to read and write. Your subjects yet unborn will live to be thankful for this document.'

'You speak truth, tuan.'

'I do,' said Gunn. 'Lies and empty promises have no place with either of us.'

'Then I will sign,' said the Sultan. 'Partly because I believe you, and partly because to sign is to show my gratitude and appreciation for helping my nephew and my brother's widow.'

Gunn turned to the sailor who had accompanied him. The man opened a pipe-clayed leather pouch on his belt and unscrewed an inkhorn. Gunn dipped a quill in the ink and handed this to the Sultan. He made his mark on both copies of the treaty. His son, the young man who had first spoken to Gunn, made his mark as a witness.

'So it is agreed,' said Gunn, and held out his right hand. The Sultan took it. For a moment they stood, hands gripped firmly—and then the air beat suddenly about them as though disturbed by the wings of a gigantic bird.

Gunn heard a crash of huge forest branches, and frightened screams from monkeys. A smoking cannon-ball trundled out across the clearing, scoring a furrow in the dust.

'Is this treachery?' demanded the Sultan, his hand instinctively going to the jewelled dagger he wore concealed in the folds of his shirt.

'Not on my side, your highness,' Gunn assured him grimly.

Twenty Chinese coolies wearing plate-shaped hats were entering the clearing. They carried muskets and cutlasses. Ahead, strode a man in loose clothes, taller than the rest, with a coolie holding an umbrella above his head, partly to shield him from the sun, and partly as a mark of dignity.

'It is Tu Sung,' whispered the Sultan. 'He has heard of our meeting. I feared him when he was here before with his army, and I did not fear without cause. Look!'

The Sultan pointed to three bedraggled creatures who marched behind Tu Sung. Gunn recognized Bonnarjee, and with him were two white men he did not know. All had their hands tied in front of them with rattan ropes, and were led as Gunn had seen Malays lead tame monkeys and baboons through native bazaars.

If they hesitated or faltered, someone would beat them across their buttocks with the flat side of a blade. Gunn drew the sailor from his crew to one side.

'Take these documents and preserve them with your life,' he told him, handing over the two copies of his agreement with the Sultan.

'Then give this message to Mr MacPherson personally. Explain that twenty hostile and armed Chinese are here, led by Tu Sung. Bonnarjee and two Europeans I do not know are their prisoners.

'If they have just landed, as I assume, then their vessel should be anchored near the shore. Possibly only a few Chinese are left aboard with the slaves at the oars. I leave him to handle the situation as he thinks best, but we should prevent these creatures from escaping.'

He turned to the Sultan, and explained in Malay what he was going to do.

'Let your son go with my man, so that he may speak to those of your people who have been taken as slaves aboard Tu Sung's vessel. Maybe he can convince them all that freedom now lies within their grasp.'

The Sultan addressed the prince and the young man immediately stepped forward. He led the sailor across the creaking floor to a side entrance only used by servants. They clambered down the pole, which was screened by a bamboo fence, and melted into the green jungle only feet away. Because of the fence, no one on the ground saw them leave.

Gunn watched them go and then opened the front door of the Sultan's house and stood framed in the doorway, hands on his hips, contemplating the Chinese in the clearing beneath him.

'Who are you, and what do you seek?' he called down in Malay.

Bonnarjee's voice was a cry of astonishment.

'Dr Gunn!'

Gunn saw hope in the faces of the two white men as they looked up at him in surprise.

'We are this creature's prisoners, doctor,' shouted Jerome. 'We are American subjects. I am a newspaper correspondent, and Mr Jones is American Consul in Singapore. I beg of you to help us.'

Tu Sung held up his hand, and the Chinese gripped their prisoners and held them while he crossed the clearing on his own.

From every house, frightened eyes peered out. Somewhere, a child began to cry, and dogs were barking on the edge of the clearing.

'I have heard of you, Dr Gunn,' said Tu Sung. 'I know your reputation as a hard man of business rather than as a physician. I also know that you have defiled many of my countrymen by selling them the mud that brings them brief oblivion, and in so doing you have gravely offended the Son of Heaven, the Emperor I am honoured to serve.

'I give you now the opportunity of surrendering to me. If you decline, I will seize you by force, and at the same time, as evidence of my strength, will put to the sword and flame all these people in their houses.'

'You speak as a barbarian,' replied Gunn. 'As a man who shouts against the wind, which blows his words away. I also know your reputation—as a seller and driver of slaves. I do not like what I know. I cannot treat with a man like you. But I will speak with you to save innocent lives. It is my training to save life, as it is yours to take it.'

Gunn turned to the Sultan.

'I will go down and speak with this Chinese person. Whatever may appear to happen, even though I leave —or am forced to leave—with this creature, do not be concerned. Your treaty will be honoured. But on no account show hostility to these Chinese coolies because their retribution will be terrible. Allow me to deal with them. And have faith that I shall.'

'You, tuan?' replied the Sultan hesitantly. 'On your own?'

Gunn smiled at the Sultan's dubious face and climbed down the pole. As he reached the ground, he raised his pistol above his head slowly, to show he did not mean to fire at anyone in the clearing. He pressed the trigger and threw the weapon from him to prove that he was unarmed. The puzzled Chinese coolies watched the flare explode high up the sky in a blaze of red and green stars, and then drop, trailing a white beard of smoke. Parakeets spread bright wings and monkeys fled from the branches of the nearest trees. Gunn felt the presence of hundreds of hidden eyes watching him, as he walked towards Tu Sung. The villagers' fear and dread of what might be about to happen to them hung like a physical weight in the hot, humid air.

'Now, what is it you seek?' Gunn asked Tu Sung.

'Your removal to my ship while I renegotiate an agreement that Mr Bonnarjee has signed with the Sultan. I do not trust you here.'

'You have arrived too late to negotiate anything,' Gunn told him. 'The Sultan and I have already signed an agreement between us. There is nothing more to add, and no changes will be made. That is the Sultan's wish —and mine.'

'I have a prior agreement,' interrupted Bonnarjee, avarice overcoming his fear.

'So you have, but your document was negotiated under duress and the threat of violence, and is without value. Since you enjoy the privileges of English law, Bonnarjee, you must also abide by it. A contract obtained under force or threat of force is like a book written on water or the wind—useless for anyone to read.'

'They will kill us, doctor,' said Jerome. 'Bonnarjee here says they are only keeping us alive until this Chinaman has his agreement. I beg you, do not frustrate him.'

'The days of man are but as grass which withereth and is cut down,' replied Gunn philosophically. 'Maybe your time—and mine—is come. No doubt you also sailed to seek an agreement?'

Jerome nodded.

'Yes.'

'What does any agreement matter against our lives?' asked Jones nervously. 'Dead men draw no dividends.'

Tu Sung motioned to three coolies to approach Gunn.

'We will take you aboard our vessel,' he said. 'Lest you should still hold illusions about your powers and your importance, while I treat with the Sultan. Your agreement with him will not last beyond your life, even under your convenient laws. And your life has but a brief span to run.'

'What about these Americans?' asked Gunn. 'They have no quarrel with you. They are not my countrymen. Show the strength of which you boast by letting them go free.'

'They will stay until I am ready to deal with them,' replied Tu Sung coldly. 'Then I shall decide. In the meantime, I will keep them with you aboard my ship.'

'You speak like Lei-kung, your god of Thunder, who has a loud voice, but lacks any other powers, like a eunuch who talks of deeds but has no performance.'

Tu Sung crossed over to Gunn and stared up into his face.

'Since you speak of a Chinese god, I will tell you of Shou-hsing, the god of Long Life. When he writes a man's name on his sacred tablet, that man dies and none can save him. And, physician Gunn, he has already engraved your name. You are as the dead already.'

A coolie prodded Gunn in the back with the point of his cutlass. Another dug him in an elbow with a blade. They began to walk slowly across the clearing. As they approached the belt of trees, splendidly coloured birds flew out and screeched and fluttered away. Soon, they reached the beach. The bodies of three of Gunn's sailors lay on the hot white sand. The others, with clothes torn, shirts blood-stained, some with head wounds, were tied by the wrists around the base of two palm trees. They looked up dejectedly as Gunn went past.

'You too, sir?' one called.

'Be of good heart,' Gunn replied. 'We are still alive.'

They said nothing, but looked after him, depressed and immeasurably disappointed that he also was a prisoner.

Two Chinese stood by a native dug-out canoe. Gunn

climbed into it with the Americans. Tu Sung sat behind him. The Chinese paddled swiftly and silently out to the junk. Gunn looked over his shoulder at the green feathery trees that stretched down almost to the edge of the sea. He hoped for some sign of *Hesperides*, or of a longboat pulling out from a sheltered creek, but the whole was deserted. Perhaps the sailor and the Sultan's son had been intercepted on their way? For the first time, he felt uneasy. Had he underestimated his adversary?

Aboard Tu Sung's junk, the slaves sat sullenly at the oars. The wind changed and the stench of their unwashed bodies and the piles of excrement on deck made him choke. Most kept their heads down, not meeting his eyes. But one, younger and cleaner than the rest, looked back at him, and in his eyes Gunn saw a faint gleam, like a spark of flame in a dying fire. Perhaps he was one of the Sultan's men who had only recently been kidnapped? The thought cheered him.

Tu Sung stood near the rattan-roofed shelter in the stern of the vessel and clapped his hands imperiously. He looked towards the bows and clapped again. No one answered, and no Chinese overseer appeared in response to his summons.

'What is the matter?' asked Gunn.

'Nothing, running white dog,' replied Tu Sung. But he was concerned, and fear flecked his eyes. He had left six Chinese in charge of the vessel. Where were they? Why did they not appear? Had they seized the opportunity of his brief absence to swim to the shore and escape—or had some other fate befallen them? He glanced at Gunn, who was looking over Tu Sung's shoulder, into the shelter. Tu Sung turned. Both men saw half a dozen Chinese coolies crouched down on their hands and knees.

'Come out, dogs,' Tu Sung shouted angrily. 'Are you worse than curs that you do not obey your own master?'

Still no one moved. Then the British sailor Gunn had despatched with the Sultan's son stood up behind the coolies, pistol in one hand, cutlass in the other.

'We did not wish to kill the creatures, sir' he explained. 'We simply bound them together by their wrists and ankles, and held them here.'

'I am relieved you have arrived,' replied Gunn. 'I did not see the longboat.'

'I reported to *Hesperides*, sir, and on Mr MacPherson's advice we did not bring the longboat lest it should be seen from the shore. We swam, sir. Four of us. And the Sultan's son.'

'You see,' said Gunn to Tu Sung in Malay, 'you spoke too insolently and too soon.'

Tu Sung cupped his hands around his mouth to shout a warning to the Chinese he had left behind him on the shore, but the wind carried away his words. Gunn struck him in the chest, and as Tu Sung fell, the two Chinese jumped at Gunn. Jones kicked one in the groin. The sailor leaped forward and beat the other man insensible with the butt of his pistol.

'Stand up,' Gunn ordered Tu Sung. He crawled reluctantly to his feet.

'Now order your Chinese ashore to come back to this ship. All of them. At once, or you die.'

For a moment, Tu Sung hesitated. Gunn clenched his fist. Tu Sung swallowed and began to shout. Obediently the Chinese came down the beach, climbed into dug-out canoes, and began to paddle out towards the junk. The sun was very hot now, and the surface of the sea seemed smooth as glass. The prows of the canoes scored wide arrowheads in the water, their paddles glistening as they dipped and rose.

'What are your plans, sir?' asked Jones. 'Do we kill these Chinese when they come aboard?'

Gunn shook his head.

'There has already been too much violence. They will be harmless as a serpent without a head when Tu Sung has been dealt with.'

'And how do you propose to do that, doctor?' asked Jerome.

'By giving him over to his slaves he has ruled so roughly for so long. They will deal adequately with him, I have no fear.'

He turned to Tu Sung.

'When we were on shore,' he said in Malay, 'you told me how Shou-hsing, the Chinese god of Long Life, would write a man's name on his sacred scrolls and then that man was bound to die. So you believed I was bound to die at your hand.

'You did not add that this god can sometimes change his mind. Did you never learn the story of the young man who Shou-hsing decreed would die at the age of nineteen? Then this lad gave him a present of a jar of wine, and the god generously reversed the numbers so that the young man lived to be ninety years and more?'

Tu Sung nodded.

'I have heard that story, too.'

'So maybe the god of Long Life changed his mind

about me. And instead of claiming my life, he is prepared to accept yours instead.'

Gunn beckoned to his sailors.

'Cut loose the slaves,' he ordered. 'Let them go free.'

The Sultan's son now stepped from the back of the rattan shelter, a small dagger in his hand. He and the sailor leaped across the planks and began to hack away the fouled rattan collars around the slaves' necks. One by one, the oarsmen stood up, but so deformed were their legs that some stumbled and fell. Others still remained in the position of servitude, hands gripping the polished handles of their oars, unable to comprehend that at last they were free.

Then gradually, moved by the same common impulse, almost as strong as life itself, fuelled by the fury of weeks, months, years of torture and slavery, they slowly began to move in a human tide towards Tu Sung. He looked about him for any weapon to beat them off, but there was nothing. Behind him stood the Sultan's son and the four sailors from *Hesperides*. He turned desperately to Gunn.

'I beg of you,' he cried. 'Save me! They are not human.'

'It is you and your kind who have made them thus.'

'I beg of you, in the name of the August Personage of Jade who rules the whole world, in whose hands lie all our destinies, do not let me go to meet my ancestors in this debased fashion.'

Gunn said nothing. The slaves crawled on, slithering in their own excrement, hair matted, bodies glazed with the sweat of their efforts at movement. They reached Tu Sung and crouched at his feet like sub-human creatures, unable to stand at their full height on their two feet.

Then the nearest struck up towards Tu Sung's stomach with his clenched fist. Tu Sung staggered at the blow and fell, and in that moment they all leaped on him like a pack of curs tearing a wild pig to pieces.

For a second, Gunn's ears rang with the wild shrieks of Tu Sung's insupportable agony, and then there was silence save for the breathing and grunting of the slaves, and the sudden stench of viscera as they clawed their hated torturer to pieces. Gunn turned away from the unspeakable sight.

At that moment, a boom from a cannon drove flocks of tiny birds out from the trees on the island. They scattered like dark specks of dust against the sky as *Hesperides*, white and gold in the noon sun, sailed out from concealment and towards the junk. A puff of smoke hung like a pale blue beard from her forward brass cannon. The ball crashed into the sea near the junk, making it rock violently. The slaves still scrabbled on the deck, slippery now with blood, and then flung the dismembered body of Tu Sung into the sea.

Jerome turned to Gunn.

'We owe you our lives, sir,' he said simply, his face pale with the horror of his experiences.

'Everyone owes his life to someone,' replied Gunn easily. 'To a physician, a friend, a mother.'

'It would be churlish of us not to admit we hoped to have the advantage of you, sir,' added Jones.

'You hoped to have Mr Bonnarjee's treaty rewritten, as lawyers like to say, in your favour?'

Jerome nodded.

'But Tu Sung and his pirates met you on the high seas?'

'Yes. They would have sailed past us had we not deliberately forced them to stop.'

Gunn smiled wryly.

'How often, gentlemen, do we deliberately alter our destinies by trying to prod them along the road, like a native with a reluctant mule? If you had not interfered with the Chinese, then you would have reached Jade Gate first.'

The two Americans nodded glumly. Relief that had flooded over them at being freed was now being diluted by spasms of regret at so narrowly missing the chance of accumulating a fortune.

'I understand your feelings, gentlemen,' said Gunn, 'but there is room on this island for treaties of many kinds. We only seek coal because of our maritime interests. When we market this coal, these crude natives will have money in abundance to spend on all manner of other goods. Why not enter into another treaty with the Sultan for these, as your fellow-countrymen have done with great advantage in other parts of the East?'

'You have no objections, sir?' asked Jones hopefully.

'None. Indeed, I would be delighted. Then we could work together instead of against each other. Mr Jerome, why not write an article in your newspaper extolling the virtues of trade here and the possibilities of commercial advancement that present themselves? That way you will gain readers, and, even more important, the interest of American merchants.'

'Before I met you, sir,' said Jerome slowly, 'I held a very different opinion of you.'

'People once thought the world was flat—until they sailed round it and discovered otherwise. Who gave you that opinion, sir? A lady?'

Jerome nodded.

'I need not ask her name,' replied Gunn, 'but when next you see her, carry her my felicitations.'

A longboat from *Hesperides* came alongside. Mac-Pherson and Fernandes looked anxiously at Gunn.

'Are you unharmed, doctor?' the Scotsman asked.

Gunn nodded.

'Let us return to the island to give our assurances to the Sultan that all has gone in our favour, and to bid him farewell.'

Gunn and MacPherson jumped into the longboat, ferried the two Americans across to the *Hesperides*, and then were rowed ashore. The Sultan and his family and a crowd of elders had gathered on the beach near the dug-out canoes. Bonnarjee stood in their centre, a little apart from the rest, not quite sure how Gunn would deal with him. Gunn jumped out of the long-boat as it grounded, and walked up the beach towards them. MacPherson followed, also wondering how Bonnarjee would fare and what the doctor might have in mind. Gunn bowed to the Sultan.

'Your enemy and mine has been defeated. The slaves will go free and I hope you may give passage to the Chinese coolies in their vessel when they wish to leave.'

'It shall be done, tuan,' said the Sultan. 'It is rare that promises are honoured so quickly.'

'We shall sail now, your highness,' said Gunn. 'We shall dock in Singapore, and when we return it will be with equipment to begin digging for the coal that will change the face of your island. I have kept my word over the pirates. Believe me, I will keep it over this other matter.'

'I believe you,' said the Sultan.

Gunn turned towards Bonnarjee. There was a kind of dejected dignity about the man. He had gambled twice and lost twice. Now would his life also be forfeit?

'You tried to murder me,' Gunn told him. 'You plotted against me, and I spared your life.'

'Don't give him a second chance, doctor,' said Mac-Pherson. 'He is a member of a powerful family. They will mistake mercy for weakness.'

'I have it in my power now,' Gunn told Bonnarjee, 'to take you prisoner, to put you on trial in Singapore for attempted murder, or to kill you here, as you would have killed me, and MacPherson. But I will do neither of these things.'

'You are wrong, sir,' cried MacPherson earnestly. 'The heat has deranged you.'

Gunn shook his head.

'Look at him, and what do you see.'

MacPherson peered more closely into Bonnarjee's brown face. He saw dark stubble on his chin, fear in the Parsee's eyes, and something else he had not noticed before. Bonnarjee's nose was thicker than he had remembered it, the bridge was smaller, the lobes of his ears were pendulous and puffy as though they had been boxed. On his right temple was a long red rash. The fingers of his right hand were turned in like a claw.

MacPherson turned to Gunn.

'He has some disease, doctor.'

'He has leprosy.'

'You lie,' said Bonnarjee. 'You lie.'

'I am a physician,' replied Gunn. 'I know the signs and symptoms. Why should I do in advance the work of Providence?'

He turned to the Sultan.

'This man will die soon, your highness. He may live for a few weeks or a few months, but he has the disease of the East for which there is no cure. Give him a hut somewhere apart from other people. I will advise his family of his predicament, and no doubt they will send a vessel to bring him back so that he dies with his own race.'

The Sultan nodded his head in acknowledgement. Gunn held out his hand.

'Until we meet again, your highness.'

'May the kind spirits of Sea and Wind guide your vessel for a safe return, tuan.'

Gunn turned and walked down the beach with Mac-Pherson behind him. He led the others down the rope ladder into the longboat, and was ferried across to the *Hesperides*. Fernandes was waiting.

'The tide is on the ebb, sir,' he reported. 'We should pull out into the bay for safety. We can anchor there if you so desire.'

'We are leaving now, captain,' Gunn replied.

Behind them, the Chinese junk wallowed on the turning tide. Coolies in their canoes had put ropes aboard her, and were now drawing her slowly into shore. Gunn leaned over *Hesperides*'s stern, lit a Havana cigar, and watched them.

As the wind filled his ship's sails, Jade Gate faded and dwindled on the horizon. The junk and the canoes shrank to the size of toys, and then vanished in the shimmering distance where sun and sea and sky were indivisible.

Had not Wellington written in a despatch after Waterloo that nothing except a battle lost could be so melancholy as a battle won? And now that Gunn had secured the treaty, now that the future was assured, and coal to fuel all steamships in the eastern seas would bring new wealth to his treasuries and security to his country, he missed the excitement of the endeavour, the thrill of the journey before arrival was certain.

MacPherson stood apart, with Jerome and Jones.

'I have instructed the stewards to prepare two cabins, gentlemen. Fresh linen has been ordered, and baths are now being drawn for you.'

'You are very civil,' said Jones appreciatively.

'As North American consul in Singapore, sir,' MacPherson replied, 'you honour us by being aboard. And as a writing gentleman, who has no doubt already remarked upon the chance that rules all our lives, here is another subject for an article.'

MacPherson pulled out from his jacket pocket a whisky flask as he spoke. The round solid silver stopper was scored and scratched, and the body of the flask was bent, flattened and gouged. How long ago was it that they had jammed this into the capstan cogwheels? It seemed as though that episode had taken place in a different life, a different century.

'On the strength of this metal, gentlemen, on the purity of this silver, our whole enterprise was once suspended. And not only our enterprise, but our lives— Dr Gunn's and mine only weeks ago.

'That will make a fine story for your newspaper, Mr Jerome, and we will have plenty of time to discuss it on the voyage to Singapore.'

The two Americans went below to their cabins, and MacPherson glanced towards Gunn, still leaning on the rail.

The doctor's thoughts were miles away. Jade Gate and the problems they had surmounted belonged to the past, and his philosophy was that the past belonged to itself. The present was what mattered now; the present, and the future.

As a schoolboy, Gunn had learned how Alexander had wept when he believed he had no more worlds to conquer. Even as a boy, this information had puzzled and perplexed Gunn. There were always new worlds to conquer; so far as he was concerned, there always would be.

He thought of Blackman in *Aeneas*, beating back across the southern seas to Colombo. He hoped that Blackman's wife would agree that he should leave the Queen's service and join Mandarin-Gold. The climate would do their son Erasmus more good than all the physicians in foggy London and all the physic in all the chemists' shops.

He wondered about Bridges, his order-book full for new steam-engines to be built in his company's Scottish yard, now steaming contentedly in splendid and sulphurous style towards the Cape. Gunn admired Bridges for his enthusiasm and his tenacity; he looked forward to their next meeting, and to working with him designing steamships for his fleet. For Bridges, as for him, work was always a new world to conquer.

He thought of Patricia Bankhausen, alone in her Singapore room, hopefully watching the harbour mouth each night, wondering when Jerome would return, and with what results. He felt pity for her, because she was a woman of spirit—and without spirit and endeavour where would the savour be in life.

Lastly, he thought of Bonnarjee, cuckolded and alone, on the beach of the Island whose name would be a constant burning reminder of his wife's lust for another man. Alone, with the mark of the dead already branded on his body.

On what trembling flame of chance did all human life and progress depend?

MacPherson was quite right. His whisky flask had saved them, and to think, if MacPherson had been teetotal they would both be dead. *Hesperides* would be their coffin at the bottom of the sea, and Bonnarjee, plump, pomaded and triumphant, would even now be landing in Singapore to lap the fat of all their endeavours.

Chance—or Providence?

MacPherson crossed over to Gunn. The breeze was freshening and beat the flag above their heads like a hammer. Flying fish leapt from the waves, sharp as silver darts, and the huge varnished masts dipped and rose under their billowing white breasts of sail.

The two men stood in silence for a moment, relishing the sun and the saltness of the air, and the very precious feeling of being alive and free. Then MacPherson remembered something.

'Fernandes has advised me, doctor, that Castle is very ill.'

'Then I shall attend to him,' replied Gunn, with resignation rather than enthusiasm.

Curiously, he felt no animosity now for the man who had betrayed them both. Like Bonnarjee, Castle had aimed high but had missed his target. And in failing, what hell on earth had he assured for himself? Gunn might bind up his fearful, physical wound, but who could heal his mental scars?

He had watched Castle being carried aboard from the junk, and had instantly placed a cabin at his disposal —ironically, the one which Castle had occupied on the outward voyage—but somehow he had shrunk from examining the man. Life might be likened to a fierce race for enormous prizes. A few would win and others must lose, but it ill became the winners to appear to gloat over those the fates had defeated.

So now he lingered for a moment, reluctant to leave the sunshine on deck and go down to the fetid stench of an ill, defeated man in a small sea-cabin. Then Gunn made up his mind. He stubbed out his cheroot, threw it over the side, and followed MacPherson smartly down the companionway.

He had been a physician before he had become a merchant. Now was the time when he must be a physician again.